SOMETHING BURIED, SOMETHING BLUE

A Mac 'n' Ivy Mystery

by

Lorena McCourtney

Chapter 1

IVY

We, silver-fox senior Mac MacPherson and me, LOL Ivy Malone, stood on the sidewalk outside the Abner post office, gazing at each other like a couple of lovestruck teenagers. He grinned, leaned over the dog lying between our feet, and kissed me. I kissed him back.

If we were a movie, "The End" would scroll across the screen now. With maybe red, white, and blue fireworks for emphasis. A few movie-goers might even brush away a sentimental tear.

I felt a little sentimental too. Well, maybe more like giddy, with a little amazement thrown in. Mac loved me. I loved him. And finally, after hop-scotching around the decision for much too long, we were actually going to do it. Get married!

Okay, there were some speed-bumps on the road to happy-ever-after. We were in this tiny Nebraska town where neither of us knew anyone, wind whipping Mac's hair into a rock-star tangle and billowing my loose shirt to unlikely Dolly Parton proportions. After we'd parted under strained circumstances a few weeks ago, he'd sold his motorhome to come to me in my house in Missouri. I'd sold my house to go to him in his motorhome in Montana. The stuff of great romance, right? But a little iffy on a practical basis. We were, let's face it, *homeless*. All my possessions, including one-eyed cat Koop, were stuffed in my Camry parked down the street. Mac's old Toyota pickup, also stuffed, had two cardboard boxes tied on top. Both vehicles had a hillbillies-on-the-move look.

So what! This time I stretched up and kissed him, and we stargazed at each other some more. I was finally free of the murderous Braxtons, who, vengeful about my helping convict one of their own, had been trying to make roadkill out of me for several years. They were in jail now, with enough charges and evidence against them on various crimes to guarantee any coupons they'd been saving would expire a number of years before they could use them.

"So, how do we get married in Nebraska?" Mac said. He looked down Abner's wide main street, with Harry's Family Restaurant at this end (*Today's special! Chicken-fried steak!*) and a feed store at the other. Abner was probably not a rival for Reno's enthusiastic attitude toward quick marriages.

I looked at the courthouse next to the post office. "Maybe ask in there?"

Mac nodded. "Okay, let's give it a try." Sometimes Mac wears a beard, sometimes he doesn't. He was in beard mode now. He looked good. Felt good when he kissed me too!

We walked over to the courthouse, stray dog following. He looked downcast when Mac told him he couldn't come inside, but he plopped down beside the double glass doors. Inside, we decided the County Clerk's office would be the appropriate place to begin. Mac opened the door with gold lettering on the window, and we stepped up to the counter.

Mac set his elbows firmly on the counter, which put that blue motorcycle tattoo on his arm on display. "We want to get married," he announced.

I guess I expected an incredulous *you gotta be kidding* look, considering our ages, but the young woman beamed as

4

if she might jump into a cheerleader yell at any moment. "Great! You've come to the right place." Then a sly grin. "You look old enough that you won't need your parents' permission, so—"

She reached under the counter, apparently ready to whip out a marriage license, and Mac took a hasty step backwards.

"I guess we need to ask some questions first," he said.

He asked if we'd need a blood test. *No.* Was there a waiting period? *No.* We just had to show photo ID, fill out the application, give our social security numbers, pay the fee, and we could waltz off to become husband and wife. She shoved the application form she'd snatched from under the counter toward us as eagerly as if she got a commission on all sales.

Okay, we could do all that. I got my glasses out of my purse to read the application. Blessedly, since my cataract surgery last year, I need them only for reading now. So why did I – although not literally feeling as if I'd stepped into a bucket of ice – unexpectedly feel a definite twinkle of cold feet?

"Well, uh, okay," Mac said, although he didn't reach for the application form. "Can someone perform the ceremony now?"

"You mean right *here*, right *now*?" the clerk asked.

Was that what Mac meant? I felt another tremor of lower extremities, as if all the feet cells were rushing into a huddle of apprehension.

"Well, uh, yeah," Mac said. "Right here, right now."

I took a deep breath. Well, sure, why not right here, right now? When I bought a new crock pot not long ago, I asked about the length of the warranty, and the clerk gave me a look that said *at your age, what difference does it make?*

Then another jittery thought occurred to me. Was Mac saying *right here, right now* because he was having jitters of his own? Was he thinking if we didn't do this right here, right now, his cold feet might run him right out of the courthouse?

"A judge or retired judge can do it, but our regulations say that an active court judge can't perform marriage ceremonies between 8:00 and 4:30 on weekdays, and the only retired judge in town died last week. The clerk magistrate is authorized to do it, but she's out sick today." The woman seemed genuinely distressed that she couldn't pull off a ceremony on the spot. She tapped her chin. "You might be able to get the judge to do it after 4:30."

"Oh."

She brightened. "But any pastor, priest, or rabbi can do it." Working toward that commission on the marriage license?

"Could you tell us where to find one?" Mac asked.

Another tap of forefinger on chin. "Well, Pastor Mike at First Baptist is in Omaha at a conference this week. Abner Community Church is presently without a pastor, and looking for a new one. You'd have to go over to Actonville for a Catholic priest. And I'm afraid we have no rabbi in the whole county. You need two witnesses too."

Hey, Lord, what's with the speed bumps here? Maybe you aren't on board with our getting married after all?

It hadn't occurred to me that the Lord might not be gung-ho about this. It seemed to me that, up until now, he'd been working overtime behind the scenes to maneuver us into marriage.

"Well, uh, maybe we, uh, should discuss this a little more," Mac said to the clerk. Mac is not generally an *uh* type person. A definite cold-feet syndrome.

He grabbed my elbow and propelled me back out to

6

the hallway.

"Maybe we shouldn't rush into anything?" I said. "Maybe we should think about this a little more?"

He turned and grabbed both my arms almost fiercely. "Ivy, I love you. I want to get married as soon as we can do it. But . . ."

"But?" I loved him and wanted to get married too. I also figured that, once we were married, I could find out what that blue motorcycle tattoo, which he's always been so reticent to discuss, was all about. But I also felt a *But?* cloud hovering over me.

"But I just don't feel comfortable about . . . this." He made a non-specific wave of hand around the gloomy hallway. Was there a spittoon down there by the second door on the left? Hopefully. Or else that guy in overalls just spat into a dark corner.

"Don't feel comfortable in what way?"

"Don't we need rings for the ceremony? A church and a preacher? Not some judge who'll marry us in a two-minute gap between the last traffic ticket of the day and grabbing his phone to check his Facebook page."

Was this where my shuffle of cold feet was coming from? I considered the possibility and then nodded to myself. Yes, it was, especially the church and preacher part.

I believe the Lord provides for us, that we can always count on him, but that wasn't happening here. The speed bumps on the road to happy-ever-after were looking more like road blocks. Was the Lord trying to tell us something?

Mac's cell phone rang. He dug it out of his pocket and looked at the screen.

"It's Dan," he said.

Dan is Mac's son. He's a high school history teacher and athletic coach. I met him when I made my excursion to

7

Wolf Junction, Montana, with the lame excuse that I had a glove to return to Mac. Who wasn't there because he was headed back to me in Missouri. Which is how we wound up meeting here in Abner, Nebraska. As it turned out, the glove wasn't even Mac's. But the meeting brought us to the love-and-marriage decision.

So doesn't all that sound like the Lord's maneuvering?

But, just like the time, back when I thought I might become a knitting person, I misinterpreted the instructions and wound up with a sock big enough to fit the Jolly Green Giant, maybe I'd misread the Lord's workings. Now Mac looked at the phone as if he might just stuff it back in his pocket.

"Shouldn't Dan be in school today? Maybe something's wrong."

"Yeah, right." Mac pushed the button and without preliminaries asked, "Is something wrong?"

Dan apparently said nothing was wrong and asked where Mac was.

"I'm in a courthouse in Abner, Nebraska, with Ivy. We're here to get married."

There was almost a challenge in his voice. Did he suspect son Dan would be less than enthusiastic about our on-the-run decision to get married? Dan had been friendly enough when I met him briefly in Wolf Junction, but maybe, now that I loomed as a stepmother, he saw me differently. I suddenly saw myself differently too. Marrying Mac, I'd be jumping right into his whole family. Stepmother to all three of his grown children. Step-mother-in-law to their spouses. Step-grandmother to his grandkids.

Then a long, rather one-sided conversation. Mac's end consisted of *uh-huh* and *mmm,* an occasional *yeah* and

8

various *uh's*. Finally he held out the phone to me. "Melanie wants to talk to you."

I hadn't met Dan's wife Melanie when I was in Wolf Junction. All I knew about her was that she was a part-time clown. I'd never known a clown before. Or a potential step-daughter-in-law. Had her husband Dan pawned off on her the job of telling me that no way were they letting dear old Dad marry a homeless Little Old Lady with way too many dead bodies in her recent past?

"Hello," I said warily.

Melanie started talking, rivaling the speed of an announcer rattling off the fine print on a radio advertisement. It took me a full minute to realize she wasn't bombarding me with hostile questions pertinent to evil stepmothers. She was making plans, plans that seemed to expand moment by moment, and this time it was me doing astonished *uh's* and *umm's*.

Feeling a little overwhelmed, as if I'd just been inundated in a warm, fuzzy avalanche, I finally said, "Let me talk to Mac for a minute." I plastered the phone against my midsection. "Dan's at home because they had a water breakdown at school and had to close for the day. They're inviting us to get married in Wolf Junction. At a church. With a pastor performing the ceremony. A reception at the house afterward. We can stay at their place until then. I'll be in the guest room. You can bunk with one of the boys. They want to see if Steve and Tina can come too."

Steve was Mac's other son, Tina his daughter. They both lived way off . . . somewhere. At this befuddled moment I couldn't even think where.

"What do you think?" Mac asked.

Another tangle of fuzz in my head. One part of me clapped enthusiastically. A real family wedding! In a church!

9

Another part dug instant potholes. A lot of fuss. In a strange place. With people I didn't even know. And how long would this delay our actually getting married?

Then a different thought.

The Lord was providing: church, preacher, reception, welcoming family, everything.

Hey, Lord, fast work!

Except— "I have a cat," I said into the phone.

A cat was welcome. They had two.

"And we have a dog," Mac said.

I lowered the phone to my midsection again and turned to look at him. "We have a dog?"

Mac motioned to the shaggy creature peering at us through the glass door. "Look how skinny he is. I think he's homeless, just like us."

Mac knew how to get to me. The *homeless like us* observation did it. And the dog was definitely skinny. "We have a dog too," I said to Melanie.

Melanie was surprised, because Mac hadn't had a dog when he left their place a couple days ago, but she assured me that a dog was also welcome. I had the unexpected feeling they'd welcome a menagerie of lizards, llamas, maybe even a behemoth or two, with open arms. They approved of our getting married, and they wanted to be part of it!

I gave any lingering doubts about homelessness and instant step-familyhood a reckless toss. "We think getting married in Wolf Junction is a wonderful idea," I said to Melanie.

She gave what sounded like a yee-haw yell.

I told her we'd see them in a couple days. Mac gave me a big hug.

Then, holding hands, we went to collect our new dog.

Chapter 2

MAC

On Sunday afternoon, I pulled my old pickup into the driveway right behind Ivy's Camry. My daughter-in-law Melanie and two dogs barreled out to meet us. Dog on the seat beside me pressed his nose against the window when he saw the other dogs. He was shaking a bit. Nerves, I guess. I gave his skinny back a long stroke to calm him.

Melanie wrapped Ivy in a big hug as soon as she stepped out of the car. I could see Melanie was talking a mile a minute, as always. There's never a conversational lag around good-hearted, energetic Melanie. I got out of the pickup, and Dog scrambled out behind me. I think he intended to protect me from the two onrushing dogs.

Melanie rushed over to me with the dogs. Another big hug. "We're so happy you're here! A wedding! That's *wonderful!* I'll do a clown party to entertain the kids at the reception. My friend Tracy can do the wedding cake. White cake? Or Tracy does an awesome carrot cake! How about a barbecue for the reception? A buffalo barbecue!"

"We'll talk about it," I said. As much as I appreciated Melanie's enthusiasm, I didn't want to commit to anything until I knew how Ivy felt about clowns and cakes and buffalos. The dogs circled Dog with tails wagging. "Where are the kids?"

"They're off somewhere with their friends." Melanie gave a they-can-take-care-of-themselves flick of fingers. She's a mother who'd jump in front of a train to save her kids, but she isn't obsessed with keeping them under her thumb every minute. Wolf Junction is like everywhere else, where kids apparently arrive with cell phones permanently implanted in their palms, but they still build the occasional tree fort and play ball in the streets here. There are, however, no outhouses to overturn now, as there were in my younger days in a different small town. Which isn't to say I did any overturning, of course. I guess it isn't saying I didn't, either.

"The water problem at the school still isn't fixed, so the kids will have another day off tomorrow." Melanie gave a little groan as she led us toward the back door of the house. "I love 'em dearly, but it was like a whirlwind and stampede combined all summer, and I was ready for *school*. Right now Dan is over helping a friend who's restoring an old Mustang. He should be home before long. Matt is looking forward to having you as a roommate."

Ivy was following but looking a little dazed, same as she had earlier on the phone with Melanie. Melanie is tall and lanky and raw-boned, with red hair and freckles. She was raised on a Montana ranch and she can barrel race, brand a calf, and tame a bronc as well as any cowhand. She'll never feed you something fancy, but she can make melt-in-your-mouth fried chicken or beef stew to stick to your bones. I'm not sure how she acquired clown talents, but her good friend Bethany calls her the "Town Clown," with a sly grin that suggests something of a double meaning in the phrase. The dogs were now in a three-dog, head-to-tail circle, getting acquainted the way dogs do.

Melanie took us into the kitchen. Along the way we passed the new addition to the house that Dan and I had worked on when I was here earlier, with an office for Dan, a clown room for Melanie, and a big family room. Melanie immediately produced iced tea and three kinds of home-

12

baked cookies, and chattered on while she checked something in the oven. I recognized the scent. Tantalizing, even though I knew what it was. Melanie's homemade dog food.

I was proud of Ivy. She'd gotten over looking dazed and was holding her own with questions and comments about a wedding.

Eleven-year-old Elle was the first of what I sometimes think of as "the mob" to get home. The dogs rushed in with her. She'll be a knockout in a few years, but right now she's a ganglier version of Melanie, long legs, bony elbows and knees, and the same red hair. Somewhat outspoken too. She gave both of us a hug when I introduced Ivy, but it was Dog that really interested her. She plopped down on the floor beside him.

"Where'd you get him?"

I explained about finding him as a stray in Nebraska. "We tried to locate an owner before we left, but everybody said he'd just been hanging around for a while. So we brought him with us."

"I like him!" Which wasn't surprising, of course. Elle likes all creatures, and she isn't discriminatory about how many legs they have, if any. I think she'd like to have an octopus, although such creatures are a little scarce in Montana. "What's his name?"

That stumped me for a minute. We'd just been calling him Dog. "I guess he doesn't have a name."

Elle tilted her head and eyed Dog intently. "He looks like a Bo to me."

Ivy apparently had a sudden inspiration. "BoBandy!"

Elle shot her a surprised glance and then gave an approving thumbs up. "Does he sleep in your bed?"

Good question. We gotten rooms in motels the last couple nights, but pets weren't allowed so Dog slept in my

13

pickup. I'm not sure, but I think Ivy sneaked Koop into her room. Actually, this was something to think about. I know Koop usually sleeps in Ivy's bed, but we'll be married soon. I'm not sure what either Ivy or Koop will think about sharing space with both a new husband and a new dog.

Now all I said was a noncommittal, "We'll see."

Elle jumped up. "C'mon, BoBandy. Let's see if you know how to chase a stick!"

Elle and three dogs all raced outside.

"Do you want to bring your cat in now?" Melanie asked Ivy.

"A little later, I think."

After traveling in her motorhome with Ivy for a couple years, Koop is broad-minded about strange places and other animals, but even he might need a bit of adjustment to this hot-wired clan of people and creatures. Elle has a terrarium in her room. I'm not sure what she keeps in it, but I'm not inclined to stick a bare hand in there.

Melanie didn't waste time before jumping into wedding plans. Dan and Melanie aren't more than Christmas-and-Easter church goers, but she knew Ivy and I (though I'd come a little late to the flock) were committed Christians, so she'd already talked to the pastor. He'd said he'd be happy to do a wedding any time a regular church activity wasn't already scheduled.

"So that's what we need to do first. Pick a date! I know people sometimes plan big weddings six months or a year ahead of time, but I doubt you want to take that long—"

"No!" From both Ivy and me.

"How about three months, then?"

Ivy and I looked at each other. "A month?" Ivy said.

I'd wasted too much time not being married to Ivy already. "Three weeks," I said and mentally added, *And not a*

14

minute longer. Ivy gave me a little smile – it might even be called a smirk – and nodded agreement.

"We may have to improvise a little with such a short time frame," Melanie said, "but we'll make it work."

We decided on a Saturday afternoon, three weeks away. Melanie said she'd check the date with the pastor and then get in touch with Steve and Tina about coming. I wished they could be here, but son Steve is in Florida, daughter Tina now in Tennessee.

"Now, about a wedding dress," Melanie said.

This was where I bowed out. Call me sexist, but I figure the whole "something old, something new, something borrowed, something blue" thing is women's territory.

I went outside, where BoBandy was proving he either already knew about fetching a stick, or he was a fast learner. I grabbed my overnight case and some extra shoes from the pickup. I already knew where Matt's bedroom was, so I headed there, by-passing Ivy and Melanie in the kitchen, although I heard Ivy say firmly, "No, I don't think we need bridesmaids."

Twelve-year-old Matt's bedroom wasn't a mess, and no music was playing, but the room *felt* loud, with posters depicting alien creatures in alien colors decorating the walls, and some superhero in action on his bedspread. Someone had set up a cot for me, khaki blanket soothingly free of depictions of anything either human or alien. I went back out to get Ivy's overnight case for her. Koop was curled in his catbed atop all the other stuff.

Dan's SUV pulled into the driveway while I was setting the suitcase on the ground. Dan isn't quite as much of a hugger as Melanie, but he wrapped me in a hug that would do justice to any affectionate grizzly. "Congratulations, Dad. We're glad you and Ivy finally made the big decision."

15

"Apparently we're going to be your houseguests for the next few weeks, until the wedding."

"Great! We're glad to have you as long as you want to stay. But I've been thinking—"

"One of the first things we have to do is find another motorhome," I interrupted before Dan could come up with some polite way to suggest maybe we should slow down our sudden rush to get married. I keep thinking that sooner or later someone is going to object. "Does Double Wells have any RV dealers?"

"Two, I think. You'll have to go over there anyway, to the courthouse, to get a marriage license. But, like I said, I've been thinking—"

"Or maybe we'll have to go all the way in to Bozeman or Livingston for a good choice on motorhomes?" We needed wedding rings too, not something we were likely to find in Wolf Junction. Although the high school here was larger than I'd expected, with kids coming in on buses from all over this half of the county.

"Hold on a minute here, Dad." Dan's voice got sterner. "Let me tell you what I've been thinking."

So here it comes. But he wasn't changing my mind about a wedding in three weeks. No way.

But he asked an unexpected question. "Are you sure you need another motorhome?"

"Ivy and I talked about it. We figure we'll wander around the country until we find the perfect place to settle down."

Not too big, not too small, we'd decided. Not too hot, not too cold. And definitely no murders in the vicinity. I could keep up with material for my travel magazine articles while we were on the road too.

"Why not settle down right here? That's what I've

16

been thinking. You and Ivy living here. It'd be nice to have some family around again. Great for all of us."

My daughter Tina and her husband used to live here, before a new job took them to Tennessee. Dan and Melanie probably did miss having family around.

"And I know a place that might be just right for you. It's not here in town, and the house is rather small and could use some fixing up and maybe an addition. But you and I could do most of the work. There's an awesome rock fireplace. And about 300 acres—"

I found the concept of all that space mind-boggling. What would we do with 300 acres? We're a little old for chasing each other across meadows in the moonlight. Although . . . why not? I'm up for the chase. I think Ivy is too! And all that space would be a nice change from crowded RV parks.

"It's a beautiful setting," Dan went on. "In its own private little valley. For some reason, there's hardly ever as much snow out there as there is here in town. Kind of its own little banana belt."

"How far out is it?"

"About ten miles."

That sounded like a considerable distance, but it was probably less than a lot of people commute in city areas. Snuggling together in front of a blazing fireplace on cold winter evenings would be great. Maybe we could cut our own firewood. We might get a couple of saddle horses. Raise our own beef and have a big garden. Do blueberries grow in Montana? Ivy loves blueberries. Bring the grandkids out. Have Ivy's niece and family up from Arkansas, and our old friends Magnolia and Geoff from Madison Street back in Missouri.

"How much does he want for it?"

17

"Actually, it isn't up for sale yet," Dan admitted. "But I'm sure it will be soon. The old guy who owns it says he's going to move to some middle-of-nowhere place up in Alaska. Getting too populated around here, he says."

"Doesn't look all that populated to me." In fact, a lot of Montana looked downright empty.

"Well, ol' Dawson, that's his name, Dawson Collier, has had only one neighbor on the road out there for years. Now there are two neighbors. Someone leased the rundown old Rocking R ranch a few months ago. I haven't met him, but Dawson says he's been over a few times. City-slicker type, he says. Can barely tell a cow from a goat. But Dawson isn't in a range war with the guy yet, and he's sure in one with the other new neighbor, some former big-star football player from California. We could just take a look at Dawson's place, you know, see what you think."

"What kind of range war?"

"Some of the California guy's buffalo got loose and wandered out to Dawson's place. One of them was chomping on his roses, and he blasted it in the rump with a shotgun. Then he corralled all the buffalo and charged the guy to get them back. Dawson called it a 'caretaker's fee,' but I heard the Californian was complaining it was ransom, plain and simple. Dawson warned the Californian that if the 'mangy critters,' as he called them, ever came back they were going to wind up in his stew pot. He's very protective about those roses. He won a blue ribbon with them at the county fair last year."

"How old is this Dawson guy?"

"Must be eighty, or close to it. Maybe even older. Hard to tell, when you get that old. He's skinny, but in good shape, except for a limp. Tough as old rawhide. He's pretty much of a hermit, but I think his moving to some isolated

18

snowbank in Alaska at his age is a bad idea. Earlier this year, he had to hire help to get his hay in and fix some fences. But he sounded determined to move up there the last time I talked to him. Said he just had a couple things to take care of, and then he was out of here."

Maybe taking off for Alaska was a bad idea for Dawson Collier and maybe it wasn't. I figure it's never too late to do something you have a real urge to do. And I was starting to get a real urge to own 300 acres.

"What does his family think about this move?"

"No family. I usually go out and see how he's doing once a month or so. Although I disguise it as Melanie made too many peanut-butter cookies or brownies or something, and I just came out to see if he could use them. He'd run me off if he figured I was checking up on his welfare. With school closed down for another day because of the water situation, we could go out there tomorrow morning."

"I'll see what Ivy thinks."

Between Matt and Josh getting home and meeting Ivy, Melanie calling Pastor Tom and getting an okay on the wedding date we wanted, all of us gathering around the table for dinner, then more boys coming over to play pool in the new family room, it was a while before I had a chance to talk to Ivy alone. She was doubtful but not hostile to the idea of 300 acres out in the country, but she and Melanie were planning to meet with both wedding cake and wedding dress people the following morning, and she thought maybe I could join them to offer my opinion.

"I want to wear something you like for the wedding," Ivy said, "so if you came along—?"

Considering what I'd like her to wear was sweet of her, typical Ivy, but I'll be happy to see her say "I do" in anything. Tablecloth, Scarlet O'Hara type window curtains, or

19

burlap bag included. But those next-day plans were the clincher on a different decision for me. I love Ivy. I'm eager to marry her. But, let's face it. I'd rather crawl the ten miles out to Dawson Collier's place than spend a morning talking wedding cakes and dresses.

I kissed her on the cheek. "You just pick whatever you like for a dress, a cake, and whatever else the wedding needs, and I'll like it fine."

***

Except that come morning there was a change in plans. Melanie had a plastic bag of chocolate-chip cookies ready for us to take out to Dawson, but Dan got a call during breakfast. The athletic locker room at the school had been broken into and vandalized during the night. It wasn't a major crime, but it was an unusual and unpleasant incident for close-knit little Wolf Junction. Dan had to meet a sheriff's deputy at the school right away.

He drained his coffee cup and stood up "So we'll make the trip out to Dawson's place this afternoon, okay?

I eyed the bag of cookies. I thought about a morning of wedding dress and cake talk. "How about if I just run on out there by myself?"

"Dawson isn't the friendliest guy in the world," Dan said doubtfully. "He got on his new John Deere tractor and ran off a couple guys handing out religious pamphlets. And he might shoot first and ask questions later if he thought you had any connection with the buffalo guy."

Blasting a buffalo's behind with a shotgun was a little worrisome, but a guy who grows roses can't be too bad, can he? "But he hasn't shot any people, has he?"

"No. Not yet anyway. But his old dog Cooper isn't too friendly either. His teeth are about gone, but I wouldn't put it past him to use what he has left on a stranger."

"Sounds as if it could be an interesting visit," I said. "Maybe you could call Dawson first and let him know I'm coming?"

"He doesn't have a land line, and a cell phone won't work out there. I guess he figures he doesn't want to talk to anyone anyway. But if you lived there, we'd do something about phone and internet service," Dan assured me.

He gave me directions, and Melanie handed me the bag of cookies and a paperback book of science fiction. "Dawson's a real reader. You'll see when you get there. Tell him you're Dan's dad, and he probably won't sic the dog on you."

Ivy walked out to the pickup with me.

"Be careful, okay?" she said. "I don't want to come up short a bridegroom at this wedding."

"I won't stomp around in Dawson's roses," I promised. "We'll drive over to Double Wells and get a marriage license and wedding rings as soon as you have some free time. We can look for a motorhome too."

"If we buy this place, we won't need a motorhome."

"Maybe we'll still want to have one for trips later on. And a honeymoon."

"Can people our age have a honeymoon?"

"You bet we can!"

Chapter 3

MAC

Three mailboxes marked the beginning of the gravel road out to Dawson's place. Dan had said that was as far as mail delivery went. The road was washboard rough and pitted with potholes, but the area scenic. In a sparse, no-nonsense, Montana way. Forested hillsides, some whiteface cattle grazing on dry-looking grass, various odd-shaped rock formations, endless blue sky.

The Californian's new place wasn't far out of town. The house had a rustic-lodge look, logs new and shiny, red metal roof topped with a big buffalo weather vane. Several live buffalo grazed in a pasture in front of the house. Sleek and fat, definitely not "mangy." A sign, in the shape of a life-sized buffalo, had *Buffalo Heaven Ranch, Dev and Barbara Pickett,* blazed across it. A pickup and big livestock trailer, buffalo images decorating both, stood outside a log barn that matched the house.

Several miles farther on, a rundown sign arched over a dirt road identified the Rocking R ranch that Dan had mentioned, house and buildings not visible. I didn't meet any other vehicles. Not exactly over-populated in my view, but maybe over-population, like beauty, is in the eye of the beholder. Electric poles continued on past the Rocking R gate, so Dawson must at least have electricity.

Several miles past the Rocking R, a sign abruptly announced *End of County Road Maintenance.* A metal gate barred the road, the name Collier slashed in red paint on a jagged chunk of board haphazardly wired to the metal, and a *Keep Out, Private Property* sign hung below the name. Off to one side of the gate another sign said *No Trespassing, This means YOU.* Below it an oversized image of the double barrels of a shotgun aimed at the viewer added emphasis.

No question about Dawson's attitude toward visitors. The private road beyond the gate had less gravel and more ruts than the county road, but the gate looked almost new. Maybe added since the unwanted visit from the Californian's buffalo?

The buffalo had wandered a long way to get out here to Dawson's roses. Of course the buffalo hadn't been able to read the warning signs, but I could, and I was thinking now that maybe this wasn't such a great idea after all. Dawson might shoot or run me over with his John Deere before I ever had a chance to tell him I was his friend Dan's father.

Okay, I'd let meeting Dawson wait until this afternoon, with Dan along, and this morning I'd avoid cake and dress discussions by taking a hike up to one of those interesting rock formations.

I started to turn around, but then I noticed the gate wasn't locked. I decided I'd drive just far enough to take a look and see if it was even worthwhile coming out again later.

I got out and opened the gate, drove through, then got out again to close it. This was open range country, where a fence and gate were as important for keeping critters out as keeping them in. I hadn't seen any stray buffalo, but I doubted it would endear me to Dawson if one sneaked in through an open gate behind me. A few hundred yards farther on, where the rough road topped a hill, I stopped short, surprised by the breath-catching view below. I'm not usually a breath-catching guy – though sometimes Ivy does it to me – but this view was definitely a breath-catcher.

An idyllic scene, like looking into a more serene and innocent past. The valley stretched out below, snug in its surrounding of forested hills, a higher plateau bordered by an impressive cliff on the far side. A half dozen black cattle and a brown horse grazed beside a stream meandering through grass greener than any I'd seen along the way. A metal windmill turned lazily beyond a picturesque barn of weathered boards. A border of red blooms – Dawson's prize-winning roses? – edged the steep-roofed house.

I had a pleasing vision of Ivy and me here. Riding our horses through the meadow. Raising tomatoes and squash and beans in the garden area out back. Sitting and rocking together in the front yard when we got old. I had to laugh at that one. To much of the world, we were already old.

So who cares what the world thinks?

I eased down the steep hill, not wanting to disturb ol' Dawson by arriving in a cloud of noise and dust, but too intrigued to turn back now. A pickup was parked in the shade of a cottonwood tree where I hadn't been able to see it from the hill. It was as dusty as my old Toyota, but I was surprised to see that it was also much bigger and newer. A husky green tractor stood on the far side of the pickup, no doubt the John Deere useful for chasing off unwelcome visitors. Both had to be expensive. Made me wonder what Dawson lived on. Peace and serenity aside, this didn't look like a real working ranch capable of producing a living. Actually, by Montana standards, six head of cattle and 300 acres was barely a hobby.

As I got closer, I could see a couple of rifles in a gun rack covering the rear window of the pickup. Good. Maybe that meant Dawson didn't have one in the house with which to run me off. Although, on second thought, I suspected he was the kind of guy who probably had a third-world-sized arsenal inside.

I waited in the pickup for several minutes, thinking he'd come to the door to see who was invading his privacy. Behind a closed screen door, the front door stood partly open.

But no one came to the door, so finally, arming myself with the bag of cookies, I got out of the pickup. A gate in a rough rail fence opened onto a dirt path through a weedy yard to the front door. Apparently Dawson's landscaping interest was limited to his roses, and they were indeed glorious even this late in the summer. But the scent when I reached the front steps was more like roadkill than pleasantly rosy. Maybe something had crawled under the roses and died? Or maybe eccentric hermit Dawson had been cooking that roadkill?

No doorbell beside the door, so I knocked. Not too aggressively, considering Dawson's reputation.

No answer.

Another knock, a bit longer and firmer.

Nothing.

With the pickup here, Dawson must surely be around somewhere. Though he could be out riding the range or rounding up dogies or whatever one did on 300 acres in Montana. It occurred to me that it might be a steep learning curve for Ivy and me out here.

A third knock again brought no results, and I decided something stronger was required. "Hey, Mr. Collier," I called. I also waved a hand under my nose. Maybe I should have brought air freshener rather than cookies and a book. "You in there? This is Dan's father, Mac MacPherson."

I took a hasty step to the side, just in case Dawson responded with a blast of shotgun. But again there was no answer, and I leaned in closer to the screen door, listening.

No sound at all from inside, and this suddenly struck me as . . . well, not necessarily *ominous*, but, as Ivy might say, at least semi-ominous. Where was the old dog Dan had mentioned? Or maybe Dawson and dog were taking a mid-morning nap. I decided I'd just wait until he came home or woke up. Whatever.

I sat on the top step, leaned against the wall, and closed my eyes. Sunshine warmed my face. Lush roses crowded the steps. The windmill beyond the barn creaked gently. Bees buzzed companionably in the roses. Several red chickens pecked in the yard.

It should have felt serene and peaceful. I spent several minutes trying to make it feel that way. But peace and serenity escaped me. My back tensed. My nose twitched. My knees stiffened. My eyes popped open. And what did I see? A couple of birds circling overhead, outspread wings motionless as the birds rode a silent updraft.

Buzzards. Like some meaningful omen in an old western movie.

Good thing I'm not into meaningful omens or I'd have jumped in the pickup and run.

Not quite silent now, I realized. Some faint noise I couldn't identify. Kind of a scratching sound.

I stood up cautiously and peered through the screen. All I could see through the half-open door was part of an old blue sofa and the corner of a fringed rug. And books. It looked as if books lined the entire wall behind the sofa. But books surely didn't smell like what I was smelling.

More scratching sounds.

Dawson sneaking up to ambush me with shotgun or pitchfork or some other sharp farm implement in hand?

Then a scratchy, scuffling noise of something hurtling toward me. Well, maybe not hurtling, I realized as the animal stiffly shouldered its way through the half-open door. Dan had said Dawson's dog was old, but his growl didn't sound totally toothless.

"You must be Cooper, right?" I asked. He was thigh-high big, with a gray muzzle and reddish-brown fur, kind of bear-ish looking. "Anyone besides you in there?"

No friendly wags, but no more growl. Maybe he recognized his name?

With sudden inspiration, I grabbed a cookie out of the bag, removed the chocolate chips – chocolate is supposed to be bad for dogs – and opened the screen door enough to offer the crumbles to him. He eyed me suspiciously, but he was apparently hungry enough to take the cookie.

"Good dog," I said. "Nice Cooper."

I de-chipped another cookie and gave it to him. That brought a smidgen of tail wag.

"How about if we take a look around in there?" I suggested.

I tentatively opened the screen door. When Cooper didn't growl again, I slid around him into the living room. Now I could see the rock fireplace, and even with a utilitarian wood-stove insert, it was indeed magnificent. The colorful rocks embedded in it looked like everything from petrified wood to agates and turquoise. Built-in bookshelves lined both sides of the fireplace, more books on the wall across from the sofa. No television. I'd have to remember to give Dawson that science-fiction book Melanie had sent along for him, though he didn't look short on reading material. A big bucket with a half-dozen guns standing in it stood by the front door. A door to the left led to what I assumed was a bedroom. Steep stairs climbed to the second story.

Beyond the living room, an oversized oak table, which looked like something out of *The Waltons*, almost filled a dining room. No room for eating on it, however, with books scattered across it. I wondered what Dawson intended to do with all the books when he headed off to the wilds of Alaska. Cooper wasn't waving any welcome banners, but he offered no resistance and moved stiffly to follow me when I went on to the kitchen.

The kitchen was minimal, but bachelor-usable. A battered table and chairs Dawson apparently used in preference to the big table in the dining room. An old refrigerator and not one, but two kitchen stoves, one electric, one wood-burning. A chest-style freezer. No microwave or dishwasher. Dishes sloshed in gray water in the sink, and something unidentifiable was congealed in a greasy frying pan on the stove. Dog dishes for water and food on the floor were empty. I opened a few cabinet doors until I found a sack of dog food and filled the dish. Cooper might be short on teeth, but he used the few he had to chow down on the dog food. Hadn't Dawson been feeding him?

An open door led from the kitchen to a covered back porch. Cooper nosed the loose screen door open. A door that lifted up from the porch floor apparently led to a basement below, an old-fashioned structural arrangement I don't remember seeing since I was a kid. The door was open, a hole yawning below.

I hesitated, struck by an odd poke of apprehension. Dog hungry, apparently unfed. No unwelcoming moves from Dawson. Peculiar silence. Smell stronger than ever back here. But I rejected the poke and strode briskly to the door in the floor and looked down the steep steps to the dirt floor of the basement below. Light shone from a bare bulb down there.

I've wondered about what has sometimes seemed a peculiar ability of Ivy's to stumble across a dead body or two.

Now I realized it wasn't all that difficult

Chapter 4

MAC

He lay face down on the floor, arms outflung, one leg tangled in the steps, the other leg and his neck bent at unnatural angles. Broken crockery lay scattered around him, one piece the face of an owl. Creepy. He had to be dead—

No, no, he did *not* have to be dead. Unlike Ivy, the number of dead bodies I've discovered in my life is nada. Zip. Zero. I could count them using *no* fingers of any hand.

I descended the steps carefully. They weren't rickety, but they were open, with boxes piled underneath, but no backing and no railing. The gag-inducing scent thickened the closer I got to the body. I remembered hearing somewhere – from Ivy? – that investigators sometimes used a smear of Vicks up the nose to counteract the smell in situations such as this. I wished I had a bucket of the stuff right now.

The dog followed, his stiff old legs navigating the steps awkwardly. He stuck his nose in the tangle of straggly hair and scruffy gray beard. When there was no response, he looked up at me and whined, as if asking me to do something about this situation.

I already knew there was nothing I could do. Ol' Dawson was never going to make it to the wilds of Alaska. He was what Ivy said was sometimes called a DRT. Dead Right There. I gave Cooper a consoling pat. I felt for a pulse in the body anyway, first in the wrist, then the throat, right beside an odd-shaped birthmark. Nothing. The body felt cold but not stiff, which I knew indicated something about how long he'd been dead. Ivy might know what, but I didn't.

The thought occurred to me that since I'll soon be married to Ivy, maybe I'd better bone up on these pertinent facts about dead bodies. And maybe carry Vicks in my pocket . . .

Hey, no way! Dead bodies are not part of my husband/travel-writer/ grandpa job description.

I reached for my cell phone before remembering Dan had said there was no cell phone service out here. I checked anyway, but he was right. I felt uncomfortable just leaving Dawson lying there on the dirt floor, but I'd have to drive back toward Wolf Junction to get a signal, and I didn't think I should be lugging him around.

"You want to come with me, Cooper?" The dog lay down beside the body, his mournful eyes looking up at me. He wasn't about to move away from Dawson. "Okay, I'll be back soon as I can."

I took a moment to glance around the basement. A big, old-fashioned, wood-burning furnace dominated the room. Several square pipes, in kind of a metal-octopus arrangement, ran from the furnace to send heat to rooms above. Two walls had been updated with concrete blocks, but the other two walls and floor were just hard-packed dirt. Wooden shelves from floor to ceiling lined one wall, the kind of shelves some pioneer wife might have filled with colorful jars of canned fruit and vegetables. But all Dawson had on them was junk in various stages of deterioration. A headless ceramic piggy bank. An assortment of chipped and cracked cups. An empty picture frame with broken glass. Old cans with dried paint around the rims.

Why had he been down here? No need for the wood furnace this time of year. I guessed he used the more efficient fireplace insert upstairs for most of his heat anyway. The

31

steps were a death trap for anyone unsteady or uncoordinated, as Dawson likely was at his age. It was no wonder he'd tangled a foot in the steps and fallen.

Unless he was pushed. . .

I instantly scoffed at that thought. Just because bodies Ivy found had mostly turned out to involve murder didn't mean *this* wasn't an ordinary stumble and fall. No push, no murder. Who'd want to push ol' Dawson anyway? The house didn't look as if it had been ransacked for some secret stash of valuables. Dawson's lifestyle didn't suggest any hidden wealth anyway. Although the pickup and John Deere tractor hadn't come cheap. . . But they hadn't been stolen after he was dead, which meant he hadn't been murdered with intent to steal. But people got murdered for reasons other than making off with their valuables. . .

I rejected that thought without further speculation. There's some old saying that in most situations the simplest explanation is usually the correct one. With more elegant wording, the saying even has a name: Occam's Razor. So, Occam's simple explanation here: old Dawson stumbled and fell. Don't mess with far-out improbabilities.

The old steps were well worn, but I could see fresh scratch marks as I climbed back up to the porch. Apparently Cooper had been down here with Dawson, and it had taken my knock at the door to arouse his protect-the-house instincts and struggle up the steps. His effort was the scratching noise I'd heard. The screen door to the kitchen was loose enough that he could nose it open to meet me at the front door. I took a minute to take the water dish back down to him.

Heading back toward town, I tried the cell phone again at the top of the hill, but no service there either. I didn't take time to close the gate behind me when I drove on. Stray

32

buffalo seemed the least of Dawson's problems at the moment. I pulled to the side of the road several times to try to call, but I was almost to the Buffalo Heaven ranch before the phone showed a signal. I called Dan, figuring he'd know how to handle this.

"Dead?" Dan repeated after I told him the minimal details I knew. He sounded flabbergasted. "I can't believe it. He fell down the basement steps?"

"That's what it looked like."

"Dawson was old, sure, but he was solid steady on his feet. I saw him up on the barn roof a few weeks ago, patching holes. He climbed up and trimmed branches on that cottonwood tree too. I can't believe he'd just stumble and wind up dead." Dan paused. "But I suppose he could have had a heart attack or stroke, something like that. He'd never go to a doctor. Said they were all a bunch of quacks and shysters."

"A heart attack or stroke seems possible," I agreed.

"I liked the old guy. He was a grouch sometimes, but we got along. And his dying is a shame. He was really looking forward to heading for Alaska."

I remembered Dan earlier mentioning that Dawson had said there were things he needed to do before taking off for a new home in the wilds. So now I had to wonder, what "things"? Just mundane details such as giving away his books, selling the pickup or tractor, maybe buying some heavy-duty long underwear? Or did he do something to get himself killed? Or maybe someone killed him to keep him from doing something before he left?

Pushed. . .

Delete that. This was a fall, plain and simple. Hold that thought. As if it were carved in stone by old Occam himself.

"I guess we should get hold of the sheriff's office?" I said to Dan.

"Deputy Cargill is still here checking out the damage to the locker room. I just came upstairs to find some papers. I'm sure he'll want to head out there right away."

"I'm parked alongside the road. I'll wait here for you."

I opened the pickup windows and waited. A couple of does ambled out of the trees, took a wary look at me, and sprinted across the road. The crisp September air smelled dry and dusty, with a hint of pine. Nice Montana silence. Incredible blue sky. I wondered about notifying someone about Dawson's death. Was there anyone to notify? Dan, who was probably as close to Dawson as anyone, had no knowledge of any family. What about burial? Somehow I couldn't see Dawson as the kind of guy who'd make prudent provisions for his future demise. He was intent on Alaska. What would become of old Cooper and the property itself now?

I finally saw a vehicle coming down the road. I assumed it was Dan and the deputy, but as it got closer I saw it was a bright red Subaru. I wasn't surprised when the car stopped. That's what people do here, check to see if you're having trouble and need help. I got out of the pickup, wondering if I should mention Dawson's demise to a neighbor.

The woman driver rolled down her window. Long, dark hair, plentiful bronze-y makeup, lots of rouge. No, it wasn't called rouge now. That was old-fashioned. Maybe flush, then? Or bliss? Something like that. Another of the things Ivy would know that I don't. Not that this had anything to do with dead bodies. Oversized sunglasses, dangly gold hoop earrings, leather vest over a black

34

turtleneck. Forty-something, I figured. My first thought was, *You're not from around here, are you?*

"Hi." She smiled and sounded friendly, but she didn't ask if I needed help. "I think I'm lost."

I didn't offer the not-from-around-here comment. Too much like a hokey line out of an old western movie. I seemed to be hitting all the old-western-movie clichés today. I took a different guess. "If you're trying to find the new California people, you passed their place."

"No, I'm looking for Dawson Collier. I've never been here before so I asked at the gas station in town, and they said to come out this way. But there don't seem to be any road signs."

I was immediately curious about why this stylish, not-from-here woman was looking for old Dawson, but I couldn't instantly think of any polite – or even devious – way to ask. So all I said was, "Dawson's place is a few miles farther out, but——"

"Oh, okay. Thanks."

I put a hand on the window frame to keep her from zooming off. I didn't know if I should tell her about Dawson before the deputy arrived, but I didn't want to let her just find him dead there in the basement. A sudden thought.

"Are you a real estate agent?"

"Why would I be a real estate agent?"

"I'd heard Dawson was going to sell out and head for Alaska."

"He's my stepfather! I've come up from California to see him. But you're telling me something's happened to him?"

No, I hadn't told her that, but maybe it was in my voice. "I've just come from Dawson's place. I'm afraid there's been an . . . accident——"

35

"An accident? What do you mean? Is he hurt? Did you just leave him out there *alone*?"

"Well, not exactly, but—"

I was trying to decide what to say next when another dust cloud billowed behind a vehicle headed this way. A few moments later, a car marked with the county sheriff's department insignia pulled up behind the woman's Subaru. The officer in the driver's seat spoke on the car radio a moment before he and Dan slid out opposite sides of the car.

"Everything okay here?" the deputy asked affably. He was middle-aged, but no middle-aged spread softened his mid-section. Maybe covering the wide open spaces of Montana as an officer of the law keeps a man in shape.

The woman jumped out of the car. Black jeans and boots, high-heeled but not cowboy-style like a lot of women around here wore. "I came here to find my stepfather, and now he tells me there's been an accident!" She pointed an accusing finger at me. "And he just left him out there *alone*—"

"We're on our way out to Dawson's to investigate right now," the deputy said. If he intended to ask the woman any questions, she didn't give him a chance.

Without saying a word, she jumped back in the car and jolted some fifty yards down the road before apparently remembering she was lost. The brake lights flared as she skidded to a stop.

The deputy went back to his car. Dan looked momentarily undecided, but then he gave me a little wave and got back in the deputy's car. The deputy drove past the woman and her Subaru, and she followed. I was a little late to the parade because I had to drive on down to the Californian's driveway to turn around. I got further behind when a herd of some twenty or so cattle wandered across the road in front of me. Not unusual, of course. This was open range country, the delay not nearly as bad, I reminded myself, as a city traffic jam. Although city traffic doesn't tend to leave squishy piles in the roadway. I dodged a couple of them but then gave up and squished right on through them.

The deputy's car and the Subaru were parked in front of the house when I arrived and slid out of my smelly-tired pickup. Beyond the back door to the kitchen, I found the woman on the back porch, at the basement door, where the deputy had apparently told her to stay. She had her arms crossed over her chest, fingers tapping, frown on her face. I peered down the open doorway to the basement. The deputy and Dan were kneeling beside the body. Cooper, familiar with Dan from previous visits, had scrunched up close against Dan's leg.

"He's dead," the woman said. "I can't believe it. If I'd just known earlier— But now he's *dead*."

I got the impression she wasn't so much grieving as irritated with Dawson for dying at an inappropriate or inconvenient time.

"I don't think anyone around here knew he had a stepdaughter." I phrased it as a comment, although it was really a dig for information.

She wasn't offering any. "He fell down the stairs?"

"That's what it looks like."

"I have to make a phone call." She whipped out a cell phone and strode off toward the living room.

I could have told her she'd get no signal here, but I figured she'd find that out for herself soon enough. I like to talk to people and be helpful if I can, but her superior, impatient attitude did not encourage helpfulness. She stomped back a moment later.

"No signal. I'll have to use the land line." She glanced

37

around as if I might be hiding it.

"Dawson didn't have a land line."

Her roll of eyes expressed frustration with everything Montana. No road signs. No cell phone service. No land line. Dead stepfather. And now *me,* just standing there being unhelpful.

"I didn't catch your name," I said.

We both knew she'd never given it. She hesitated, as if trying to decide if her name was any of my business, but she finally said, "Natasha Richardson."

"From?"

"The San Diego area."

"Was Dawson expecting you?"

"No. It had been a long time since we had any contact with him, and I thought it might be better to just . . . surprise him." That seemed doubtful logic to me, but, of course, she couldn't have called him anyway.

"But you did have an address for him?"

"The name of the town." She paused. "Part of it."

And she'd come all the way up from southern California, not having seen stepfather Dawson for years, simply on the basis of part of a town name? I wondered what had brought on what sounded like a sudden urge to connect with him. Of course, it wasn't necessarily anything mysterious. Sometimes at mid-life people become interested in genealogy and long-lost relatives. But, as a step-daughter, she wouldn't have had any genealogical connection with him, and Dawson apparently hadn't felt any urge to keep in touch with a family from his past. So why *was* she here?

"I think he was something of a recluse," I offered.

"I'm sure he'd have been glad to see me."

I guessed we'd never know about that one.

Deputy Cargill and Dan came up the basement steps

to the back porch. Cooper wanted to stay with the body, but Dan boosted him up the stairs. Dan leaned over and reached for the handle to close the basement door but apparently thought better of it and left the door open. Deputy Cargill headed through the house to the front door. We followed him as far as the kitchen.

"He has to call the coroner," Dan said. "The radio in the car works here even if cell phones don't."

"What now?" Natasha's nicely manicured fingers wrapped around her useless cell phone as if she were thinking about throwing it at someone.

"We have to wait and see what the coroner says," Dan said.

That was obviously going to take some time. The woman paced around the kitchen, then extended the pace to the dining and living rooms. She pulled an occasional book off a shelf. Looking for a favorite author? Although, the way she stuck her hand into the deep bookcase and felt around behind the books, it almost seemed as if she was looking for something other than books.

I stepped into the living room with her. "Dawson must have been quite a reader."

"Yes, I believe he was." She withdrew her hand rather hastily from behind the books. "I'm going back to town. I need to call my mother." As something of an afterthought she added, "This is going to come as a terrible shock to her."

She slammed through the screen door, but I didn't hear her car start immediately. I went to the window to look out. The deputy had apparently told her he needed more information before she left, and he had his foot on her car bumper to brace a notebook on his leg. It was several minutes before she got in the car and took off up the hill, the usual dust cloud billowing behind the vehicle. Deputy Cargill came back in the house.

"Quite a surprise," I said. "Ol' Dawson having a stepdaughter no one knew about. A wife or ex-wife too."

"He sure never talked about them," Dan added.

"It's an ex-wife," Deputy Cargill said, information apparently gathered when he talked to the woman out by the car. His affable expression went a little sour. "I have an ex-wife I'd rather not talk about too."

"You think this is what it looks like?" I motioned in the direction of the back porch. "An accidental fall down the steps?"

Deputy Cargill gave me an appraising glance. "You think it's something else?"

"No, no, just—"

"Don't mind Dad." Dan's chuckle sounded forced. I suspected my question had embarrassed him, that it sounded as if I wanted to jump in and play amateur sleuth. "He has a suspicious mind. He and Ivy have been involved in a few murder cases. Accidentally involved," he emphasized.

But I was almost certain some suspicious thought had occurred to Dan too. He'd started to close the basement door, then hadn't. Maybe because it occurred to him there could be fingerprints on the handle?

"We'll see what Sheriff Cunningham thinks," Deputy Cargill said.

"In this county, the sheriff is also the coroner," Dan explained to me. To the deputy, as if to further neutralize my question that suggested maybe Dawson's death wasn't as simple as it looked, he added, "Dad and Ivy are here to get married."

I went along with the detour. "Two weeks from Saturday afternoon, at the Wolf Junction Community Church. Everyone's invited."

So then we settled down to wait for the sheriff/coroner. During which time I tried to get my mind off the trail that, like a bloodhound on a scent, it kept stalking.

With signposts reading *Pushed. Shoved. Tripped.*

Chapter 5

IVY

We got the cake details settled easily with Melanie's friend Tracy. Carrot cake, three tiers, decorated with pink roses and a wedding bells ornament on top. Tracy would also make a punch with sparkling apple and grape juices. In the car, Melanie suggested buffalo barbecue for the reception, and I said great, and she right away called someone and ordered it for delivery the day before the wedding.

We'd already decided we wouldn't do formal invitations. Melanie would just call everyone with a y'all come invitation, and bring all your friends and relatives too. She said this might result in some roughneck, outback type guests, although it was possible such guests would come whether invited or not. I said that was fine. Though I privately hoped they'd leave spurs and firearms at home.

The wedding-dress meeting with someone named Trudy came next. Trudy wasn't quite what I expected, but the discussion went quickly. The dress would be cornflower blue, calf length, draped neckline. Trudy took measurements and said she'd call when she had it ready for a fitting.

Okay, going like a wildfire here. Who needs months to prepare for a wedding?

Of course we weren't done yet, Melanie pointed out. She still had a long list. Shoes. Hair. Flowers. Music. Wedding rings. License. Photographer. She said we also needed to fulfill the traditional details of "something old, something new, something borrowed, something blue."

I figured, taking a broad perspective, we had most of those traditional details already covered. The "something old" was *us*, Mac and me. The dress qualified as both new and blue. I'd think of some little thing to borrow.

In any case, I figured we'd done enough for today. I was anxious to hear what Mac thought of Dawson Collier's 300 acres, perhaps drive back out and take another look at it together. I thought he'd be at the house by the time we got there around noon, but he wasn't. Neither was Dan.

Their absences were nothing to be concerned about, of course. Maybe Dawson was showing Mac around some of the far corners of those acres. Dan was probably still working with the deputy about the vandalism at the school. Melanie, Elle, and I had lunch. I unloaded a few more things from the car. BoBandy followed me back and forth. He was wearing a red bandana around his neck now, courtesy of Elle. He seemed quite proud of it. Koop went outside to explore and took time to put all three of the too-curious dogs in their place.

Unfortunately, after that I had time for wedding jitters to surface.

How many guests would respond to that everyone's-invited type invitation? A horde? A handful? With jitters in full swing, either size group gave me uneasiness. My knowledge of buffalo was limited to movie stampedes, so I had no idea how many guests the buffalo Melanie had ordered would feed. I had one vision of running out of food, with people standing around with empty plates and hungry expressions. Another, more likely vision, of an over-supply of food, Mac and me struggling through leftover buffalo until long after the honeymoon was over. Buffalo pot pie. Buffalo tacos. Buffalo chow mein.

Then there was the fact that the pastor had a memorial service to perform in Double Wells just before the wedding. What if he had car trouble and didn't make it back in time? What if he got his burying and marrying lines mixed up and we wound up with a sendoff into eternity rather than lawfully wedded?

There was also the dress. The worrisome detail was, nice as she was, Trudy wasn't really a dressmaker; she was a *hat* maker. She'd had a hard year, Melanie said, with a divorce ending her five-year marriage, and a fire destroying the home she'd shared with that husband, all of which had temporarily side-lined her business. Doing my wedding dress would help get her going again, maybe open up new opportunities for her. Trudy had, Melanie said, made her own wedding dress some years ago, so she *was* experienced, and she had a reputation and clientele in the hat-making business that extended far beyond Wolf Junction. Clint Eastwood had once bought a hat from her.

I'd been a little startled by the enormous, inflated cowboy hat anchored atop the double-wide mobile that was now both Trudy's home and studio. Inside, Trudy was a big woman, and she seemed even bigger wearing a ten-gallon hat of her own creation. I was a little uneasy that the cornflower blue fabric she'd be using, *swishy* cornflower blue fabric as she emphasized, had originally been purchased to make tablecloths for her own 5th anniversary celebration. A celebration that never happened because the husband ungraciously absconded with another woman just three days before the scheduled event. I discarded the bad-omen aspect of that, but the fact that Trudy had measured not only my body but my head struck me as a bit worrisome. I envisioned a worst-case scenario in which my wedding attire turned out to be a set of strategically placed, swishy cowboy hats. And

44

me without a lot of hand and body coordination to keep them in their strategic places.

Then something more important than details of dress and ceremony suddenly hit my overloaded brain. My old friends from back on Madison Street, Magnolia and Geoff! I needed to call them right away. My niece DeeAnn and her family in Arkansas too. Also my good friend Abilene and her veterinarian husband in Colorado. I doubted any of them could come to the wedding, but I wanted all of them to know our good news.

I tackled that job immediately, though it didn't take long because all I got was the letdown of voice mail on calls to Magnolia and DeeAnn. I connected with Abilene. At an about-to-pop stage of her pregnancy, she and husband Mike couldn't come, but she gave me the warmest of congratulations. While I was making the calls, Melanie was busy getting ready for a clown gig at a birthday party that afternoon, which would mean I'd be here alone at the house.

Okay, I wasn't going to just sit around conjuring up various wedding disasters. I asked Melanie for directions to Dawson Collier's place and headed out.

***

It was a long drive, and I wondered if the road was snow-plowed in winter. If it wasn't, Mac and I might be stranded out here for days at a time.

On second thought, I decided being stranded with Mac might be just fine. I saw a Christmas-card vision of us sitting cozily in front of a blazing fireplace, Koop on my lap, BoBandy snuggled up to Mac. I even managed to tuck a sprig of mistletoe into the scene.

I passed a couple of ranches and a fair number of cattle running loose before coming to the gate that marked the edge of Dawson's property. The signs certainly suggested he wasn't a guy with a big welcome mat at his front door. I uneasily wondered how he'd reacted when Mac showed up uninvited.

Then I topped a hill that looked down on the house and valley, and my worries exploded. Police cars! White van with an ominously official look. And then a couple of uniformed officers came out of the house carrying something on a stretcher. I looked for an ambulance but didn't see one. Which meant that the *something* on the stretcher must be a dead body. My heart gave a big, panicky leap. What if the eccentric Dawson had—

Then I saw Mac's familiar figure and relief whooshed from my tight throat to my tense toes. Whatever had happened here, it hadn't happened to Mac.

I drove somewhat less than cautiously down the steep hill, anxious to get to Mac. He was waiting outside the cluster of vehicles when I drove up. The officers were just closing the rear doors of the van. I saw that Dan was here too, a big, furry dog clinging to his leg.

I slid out of the car, and Mac grabbed and hugged me as if we'd been apart much longer than a morning. Mac is always affectionate, but this was a little unusual even for him. I stepped back and eyed him up and down. He looked fine, but—

"You okay?"

"Yeah. Sure." He didn't quite pull off the nonchalance I thought he was aiming for.

"So what happened here?"

Mac gave me a quick rundown on finding Dawson Collier's body at the foot of the basement steps. He'd driven to where his cell phone worked and called Dan, who'd come out with a deputy from the sheriff's department. The sheriff/coroner was here now, along with several other

46

officers. We both turned to watch as the van carrying the body started up the hill.

"I've never found a dead body before," Mac said.

Obviously a reference to the fact that I had. "It's not something you ever get used to," I said sympathetically.

"I don't intend to have opportunities to get used to it," he muttered.

"Dawson fell down the stairs?"

"Apparently."

"You sound doubtful."

"Well, not exactly *doubtful.* He definitely fell. But Dan says ol' Dawson was pretty sure-footed for his age, and, well.
. ."

"You're suggesting maybe he didn't just stumble and fall?"

Mac's eyes got a squinty look and he stroked his beard with one finger, but he didn't comment.

"No one else was around when you got here?"

"The cattle and a horse out in the field. Couple of vultures in the sky. And old Cooper." He motioned to the dog apparently Velcroed to Dan's leg. Irrelevantly, I wondered how the dog got his name. My cat Koop got his name because he, like a former surgeon general of that name, is fiercely hostile toward smoking. He doesn't make speeches about it, but he's been known to snootily stalk away from the company of a smoker. Sometimes I'd like to do the same.

I looked around at the vehicles and a cluster of officers standing where the van had been. No one seemed to be hurrying to do anything. It didn't look like a crime scene.

"Will there be an autopsy?" I asked.

"I don't know who decides that."

"The coroner, probably. Statistically, I think more people just stumble and fall down stairs than are pushed

47

down them."

If I thought that would brighten Mac's outlook, I was wrong. "Statistics don't matter if you're the one getting pushed," he stated, muttering again. "Or shoved. Or tripped."

"Is there family to notify about his death?"

"It's kind of an odd situation. Dan said Dawson had never mentioned any family, but right away a woman who says she's his stepdaughter turns up. I met her out on the road when she was trying to find his place."

"She came because she knew he was dead?"

"No. At that point no one but me knew he was dead. And Dan and the deputy, of course." Mac paused as if reflecting on the accuracy of that statement. If someone *had* pushed Dawson, that someone probably knew he didn't survive the fall. "She said she'd come up from southern California to see him."

"She'd visited him before?"

"No. She said she'd asked directions to the ranch at the gas station." He paused. "Actually she made kind of a *point* of saying she'd never been here before." Another pause. "Just an unfortunate coincidence in the timing of her visit, I suppose."

"I suppose," I agreed. I looked around but didn't see a stepdaughter-type person among the deputies standing around. "Where is she?"

"She said she had to call her mother, I guess to notify her about Dawson's death, and took off."

"Is she coming back?"

"She didn't say." He turned and looked back at the house. "I guess this changes any possibility of our buying the place."

"Because, with Dawson dead, there will be ownership complications?"

"That too, I suppose. But we already agreed that wherever we decide to settle down, it won't be where a murder was involved. Too bad, because I kind of like the place."

"Is anyone suggesting his death might be murder?"

"Well, no. Not that I know of. And I'm not really *suggesting* it. Just . . . wondering."

"Had the house been broken into?"

"The front door was open, but it didn't look as if it was a forced entry."

"Did Dawson appear to have any wounds inconsistent with a fall?"

"I didn't see a bullet hole in his head or a knife in his back. Other than that, I haven't had enough experience with dead bodies to know what would be inconsistent with a fall." He went silent and then scowled. "Up until a few years ago, it would never even have occurred to me to suspect a fall might *not* be accidental."

Hey, that sounded right on the edge of grumbling or accusing, maybe even snarky. "In your pre-Ivy days, you mean?" I snapped back.

He started to stammer some denial but he broke off, and his half-smile held a twinge of guilt. "Let's just say my level of consciousness has been raised in some areas. Expanded." He paused as if searching for more words. "Widened. Deepened. Matured."

"Nice save," I murmured.

"I wonder, is a stepdaughter considered a relative as far as legal decisions go?" Mac asked. "About the body and everything?"

"I have no idea. I wonder if he had a will? Wills sometimes include instructions about death and burial. And there should certainly be something in it about who inherits the ranch."

"Dan might know if Dawson had a will."

We stood there several more minutes. Two of the sheriff's department vehicles left. Mac identified the two remaining as belonging to the sheriff/coroner and Deputy Cargill, the officer who had been investigating the vandalism at the school. It still didn't appear to be a crime scene investigation.

"I guess there isn't any reason for us to stick around." Mac stuffed his thumbs in his pockets and looked toward his pickup but made no move to go to it.

"Did Dan come out with you?"

"No, he came with Deputy Cargill. I'll go see if he wants to ride back into town with me. Though I may have to stick around until he's ready to go."

"You could come with me and leave your pickup here for Dan to drive."

"Yeah, I could do that."

But I could see Mac was reluctant to leave. Concern for Dan, who'd just lost an old friend? Maybe. Or maybe a different reason. I've been accused of having an oversized, mutant curiosity gene, but Mac isn't short on curiosity, either.

An open door. An un-witnessed fall. At least a fall with no identifiable witnesses. A dead body. Sudden appearance of a heretofore unknown stepdaughter. Definitely a situation to arouse curiosity.

While Mac went to see if Dan wanted to ride back to town with one of us, and with no one standing guard at the door, I slipped into the house to take a look around. The

50

scent, even with the dead body removed, was still strong. Dawson had apparently been dead for several days.

The house was a little old-fashioned but cozy and comfortable looking. More cottage looking than I'd expected of a Montana ranch house. Beautiful fireplace, with what I think is called an insert, so it burned more like a wood stove. A painting hung over the mantel. It showed a wolf howling at a moon, brilliant northern lights in the background. Alaska, I guessed, where Dawson had yearned to go. A real painting, I realized, not a cheap print. In the kitchen, two stoves stood side-by-side. Great! If the electricity went out, there was still a wood stove to cook on. Dawson had been using the electric stove at this time of year, of course. There was still something congealed in grease in a pan on one of the burners. A closed door led to what I assumed was a pantry. A chest-type freezer gone yellowish with age stood in a far corner. I hesitated a moment, then went over to peek inside. That mutant curiosity gene is nosy about everything. Inside, I found packages securely if not exactly neatly wrapped in white freezer paper but without labels about contents. Apparently a take-your-chances system of entrée selection.

I looked out a kitchen window. Peaceful setting, green pasture, meandering creek with some immense old cottonwood trees beside it, grazing cattle and a brown horse, cliff rising to a flat plateau on the far side of the valley. A huge pile of firewood. A garden spot looked as if it might still hold some unharvested vegetables. A dozen or so chickens pecked among the mostly dried-up plants. On the back porch, I looked down the steep basement stairs. Envisioning a dead body at the bottom was disquieting, but, without the ugly scent, this could be a nice, homey place.

Would I have wondered if something other than a natural accident had caused Dawson's fall and death if Mac hadn't brought it up?

Yes, I thought with a certain reluctance, I probably would have. Why? Certainly nothing of the smoking-gun variety here to suggest anything other than a simple stumble and fall. Sheriff and deputies didn't seem excited about it. But, once a curious LOL encounters a few dead bodies that eventually turn out to be murder, maybe her mind just tends to run in that direction. Or at least tiptoe.

But surely Dawson's dead body didn't mean we couldn't buy the ranch, did it? Because this really was a great place, and, most likely, Dawson Collier was simply the victim of a tragic accident. No murder.

That old line, *That's my story and I'm sticking to it*, thrust into my mind.

Chapter 6

IVY

No one was home when I arrived back at the house, but BoBandy wagged up a storm to greet me. Koop, who'd taken over the house as if it belonged to him, opened his one good eye to look at me, then went back to snoozing atop the refrigerator. When Melanie got home from her clown gig at the birthday party, I told her about Mac finding Dawson's body at the bottom of the basement steps.

"Oh, how *awful!* Poor old Dawson. To stumble and fall when you're all alone. To *die* all alone." Softhearted Melanie blinked back tears.

I noted that the thought apparently never occurred to her that the death might be anything other than a natural slip and fall. That was the normal reaction, of course. Although it wasn't as if Mac and I really thought the fall was something other than a natural accident; it was just a moment of *wondering.* Conjecture. Speculation. What–iffing.

"I wonder about Dawson's old dog," Melanie said. "Dawson and old Cooper were both a couple of grumps, but they were inseparable."

"Cooper was there. And Mac said a stepdaughter from California showed up too, though I didn't see her."

Melanie pulled off her blue wig. "A stepdaughter? How interesting! Dawson had never mentioned any family to Dan. It's too bad she didn't get there just a few days earlier, isn't it?"

"Before he fell?"

"Maybe he'd never have fallen if she'd been there. Or even if he did fall, they'd have had a few days together first. It must have been a long time since they'd seen each other. I wonder how old she is?"

"Mac didn't say."

"I wonder if she needs help with funeral arrangements or a place to stay or anything?" Good-hearted Melanie instantly thinking about what she could do to help, even though she'd never met or even heard of this woman before.

"Mac said she took off to find someplace where her cell phone would work so she could call her mother, but I didn't see her on my way back to town."

Melanie clomped off in her floppy clown feet to change out of her polka-dot suit. My cell phone jangled, and I answered a call from my niece, DeeAnn, down in Arkansas. She was delighted with the news of our wedding. She said they'd like to come, though at the moment she didn't know if that would be possible because husband Mike was scheduled to speak at a company conference. Grand-niece Sandy got on the other phone to say, "It's about time!" If it were up to Sandy, Mac and I would have been married long ago, before I had multiple dead bodies in my résumé.

It suddenly occurred to me that both DeeAnn and Sandy might think a wedding gift was called for now. DeeAnn's Christmas and birthday gifts were always appropriate for an LOL, but past gifts from teenage Sandy had included thong panties, toe rings, and stick-on tattoos. Not that I didn't appreciate her imagination and originality, but it made me a little uneasy wondering what she might think appropriate for a wedding.

Hastily I said, "No gifts! We have everything we could

54

possibly need."

Sandy had a quick answer for that. "Then maybe a gift should be something you don't necessarily *need*, but—"

"No gifts," I repeated "Just come if you can."

***

Mac and Dan didn't get home until almost dark. Now we knew what had become of Cooper. He was sitting on the pickup seat between Mac and Dan.

"I couldn't just leave him out there alone," Dan said to Melanie.

"Of course not," Melanie agreed. She didn't ask if Cooper was a temporary or permanent addition to the household. She just set out more dog food. Melanie is very much a "don't sweat the small stuff" person, and one more dog was apparently in the small-stuff category.

Mac said they were so late getting home because the sheriff and Deputy Cargill did, after all, do a more thorough search and investigation of the house, and Dan wanted to stay around until they were finished and be sure everything was locked up.

We talked at dinner about Dawson and the stepdaughter, whom no one had seen after she took off to call her mother. Neither Mac nor I brought up the idea that Dawson's fall might be anything other than accidental, but Elle jumped right in with, "What if he didn't just fall? What if someone pushed him or tripped him or something?"

I looked at her in astonishment. We weren't related by blood, or even by marriage yet, but those suspicious questions sounded almost like a genetic connection.

"Elle, why in the world would you think that?" Melanie sounded shocked.

"He's lived out there alone, like, you know, *forever*. I've seen him on a ladder, fixing the roof. Why would he fall down his basement steps now?" Elle asked. Sounded logical to me.

"Playing Nancy Drew?" Mac inquired.

"Who's Nancy Drew?" Elle asked.

A new generation that doesn't even know Nancy Drew? What's the world coming to? Well, they have the Wimpy Kid and his diaries now. Although I suspected Elle might be into more grown-up reading, maybe Kinsey Millhone in those alphabet-mystery books, or those books with the tough woman medical examiner. And Elle did have a genetic connection to Mac, whose "inner detective" sometimes surfaced. Or maybe Elle just had a mutant sleuth/snoop gene all her own.

A possibility emphasized when she added, "Maybe the stepdaughter had already been there and pushed him, and then she made a big show of just arriving and acting all surprised that he was dead."

Dan and Melanie both looked horrified at that line of thinking, but I was intrigued, especially when Elle added another speculation.

"Or maybe she gave him something to make him really woozy or dizzy, and she didn't have to actually push him down the stairs."

Dan and Melanie exchanged we've-been-letting-her-watch-too-much-TV looks.

But I asked, "Are you thinking of something placed in his food or drink? Or an injection?"

"In something to eat or drink. It'd be pretty hard to give a tough old guy like Dawson an injection. He'd probably whack you with one of his big history books."

"It could be some medicine he was taking," Mac said. "There are certainly medications that have the side-effect of making you dizzy or unsteady and maybe cause a fall.

Although you said Dawson wouldn't go to a doctor, didn't you, Dan? Because he thought they were all incompetents or shysters."

I figured that took care of the legitimate medication possibility for Dawson's fall. But not the possibility someone had given him something to affect his balance. "Why would the stepdaughter want him dead?" I asked Elle.

She gave me a thoughtful look. "I think you'd have to do some digging around in her past to know that. Or maybe Dawson's past."

Hey, I hadn't even thought along these lines, especially the something-in-food-or-drink one. There had been that frying pan on the stove, with something still in it. . . I think I'm going to like being part of this family!

***

Next morning, school was scheduled to open again, and the kids grumbled about that at breakfast. I was still wondering about an autopsy, especially after thinking more about Elle's suggestion that Dawson could have been given some kind of drug. Right after breakfast Dan called Deputy Cargill, but there wasn't much to report. Autopsies were handled by the State Medical Examiner, not locally, but so far the body was still in Double Wells. It didn't sound to me as if an autopsy was likely, and I doubted any thought had been given to testing the leftover food in the pan on the stove or checking for fingerprints on the basement door.

Poor old Cooper kept wandering around as if hoping to find Dawson hidden away somewhere. He didn't seem grumpy here, just a little lost. I hadn't heard any discussion about what would happen to him. I suspected there wouldn't be any discussion. Cooper would simply be absorbed into the family circle.

"A will would help," Dan observed after the call with Deputy Cargill ended.

"Did Dawson ever mention having one?" Mac asked.

"Not to me. And I can't see him confiding in anyone else."

"Did he have a safe deposit box in a bank somewhere, maybe over in Double Wells, where he'd put a will for safe keeping?" I asked. Wolf Junction didn't have a bank.

"I don't think Dawson trusted banks with his money, so I doubt he'd trust a safe deposit box in a bank either." Dan said. "I've always seen him as untalkative, a 'private person' as some people say, but now that a stepdaughter has turned up I'm wondering what other secrets he may have had."

"What did he live on?" Mac asked.

"He got Social Security plus some other pension. I don't know how much or where that pension was from."

"His pickup and that John Deere tractor weren't cheap," Mac commented.

"Right. I wondered about that when he bought them. He said the pension fund had some kind of stock market windfall and gave everyone a big bonus. Happened several times. Except for that he was pretty frugal."

"Suppose we go out to Dawson's place and look for a will or safe deposit box key?" I suggested.

"With school reopening, I can't go right away," Dan said.

"Ivy and I could run out and see if we can find anything," Mac said. He glanced at me. "Although maybe Ivy has more wedding details to work on today?"

Florist was another business that didn't exist in Wolf Junction, so Melanie and I had talked about going over to

58

Double Wells to see one today, but no way was I muddling around in flowers and greenery instead of going out to Dawson's place with Mac. "I can come along."

Dan called Deputy Cargill again, and Cargill, after checking with the sheriff, said their office had no objection to someone trying to locate a will at Dawson's place. The ranch wasn't considered a crime scene, and there wouldn't be an officer stationed there.

"I locked the doors when we left out there, but that won't be a problem," Dan said after he hung up. "I worried about Dawson living out there alone, so I 'borrowed' his key one time and had a copy made so I could get inside in case of an emergency. I never told him, of course."

Now Dan got his keys off a hook by the back door and slid a key off the ring. He handed it to Mac.

"Can I come?" Elle asked Mac eagerly.

Dan and Melanie instantly pounced on that. "No!" they said together.

"I've been out there with Dad before," Elle protested. "Lots of times."

"This is different," Dan growled. Which sounded a lot like the "because I said so" statement common to parents and frustrated children everywhere.

Obviously Dan and Melanie didn't intend to encourage a budding sleuth. The MacPherson kids aren't rebels or whiners, so Elle made do with a put-upon look and flounced off to her room. Where I strongly suspected she intended to get on the internet and search for medications or drugs that could have made Dawson dizzy or unsteady. Maybe a killer had given him an overdose of some otherwise harmless medication, and the wooziness kicked in when he was going down the stairs.

Mac and I headed out the rough road to Dawson's place. I wondered about the buffalo ranch owners when we passed their ranch. Were these the people from whom Melanie had ordered the buffalo for our reception barbecue? There'd apparently been hostile feelings between Dawson and these recent imports from California.

But we were not searching for clues to some nefarious crime, I reminded myself firmly. We were just looking for a will or a safe-deposit box key.

Chapter 7

IVY

A small red car stood in front of Dawson's house. I now noticed that one section of the rail fence was smashed inward. Souvenir of a rose-hungry buffalo? The red chickens were pecking around the yard again. Did they just live off the land? Mac identified the car as the stepdaughter's Subaru. We went through the creaky gate to the front steps. Music blared through the open front door, maybe Taylor Swift, though my identification skill about current stars in the music world is a little shaky.

All the windows on this side of the house were wide open, no doubt an attempt to get rid of the lingering smell. Through the screen door I could see a canister of air freshener on the living room floor and another in the dining room.

Mac knocked, but there was no response. He knocked again.

"This is beginning to feel way too much like yesterday," he muttered.

Could stepdaughter Natasha be dead in there too? A murderous vendetta against the entire family? A hidden killer who'd attacked when the stepdaughter was alone? And maybe the killer was in there waiting to ambush the next people who came along . . . *us*?

"She probably just can't hear us, with the radio on so loud," I said. Hopefully. Although it's a fairly well known fact that the dead don't hear too well. . .

Mac knocked again, this time with his fist, but still no response. He yanked the screen door open, and a crash echoed from somewhere. Another fall? He charged into the kitchen and on through to the back porch, and I followed. I cringed at the string of expletives blasting up from the basement. But I supposed, in a way, the blast was good news. It didn't sound as if it were coming from a dead person. Or from someone waiting to ambush us.

We peered down the basement stairs together. The scent definitely hadn't totally dissipated, but there was a hint of vanilla in it now, probably from the candle burning on the steps. A dark haired woman in jeans and black tank top lay tangled in wooden shelving that had broken loose from a wall. Paint cans had broken open when they crashed, and red, blue, and lime green blobs puddled the dirt floor. A couple more candles that she'd apparently had burning on the basement shelves to help with the scent lay smashed among the other debris, faint wisps of smoke still rising from the wicks.

Mac rushed down the steps to help her. "Are you hurt?" he asked.

She was okay enough to issue another string of ear-blasting expletives. She slapped Mac's hand aside when he tried to help her out from under a broken shelf.

"How'd you get in here?" She glared at us and shoved the plank aside.

"We knocked, but no one answered," Mac said.

"This is what you do, then," she demanded, "if no one answers a knock, you just invade the premises?"

"We heard the crash and came to see what happened," I said.

"I couldn't see what was on the top shelf, so I tried to climb up there. And then the whole stupid wall of shelves collapsed on me." She slung another broken board aside as she crawled out from among more fallen two-by-fours and shelving. The board banged against the big old furnace.

"Climbing shelves can be risky," Mac said. "It's lucky you didn't break something."

Actually, she had broken something. The shelves had a good start on becoming a pile of kindling. But luckily nothing broken on her. Also lucky she hadn't set the shelving and maybe the whole house on fire with the candles. I thought Mac's comments were innocuous enough, but she looked back and forth between us as if trying to decide who to whack first with the chunk of two-by-four in her hand.

"Are you okay?" The radio still blasted so loud up in the kitchen that I was almost shouting.

She swiped a hand across spatters of paint on her face, like a mottling of lime-green freckles. The swipe turned them into moldy looking streaks. "I'm fine."

"I was here yesterday. We met out on the road, remember?" Mac yelled in competition with the radio. "But I don't think I introduced myself. I'm Mac MacPherson and this is my fiancée, Ivy Malone. Ivy, this is Dawson's stepdaughter, Natasha Richardson."

Fiancée. No one had used the word about me before. I liked it! "We're getting married in Wolf Junction in a couple of weeks. Everyone's invited, if you'd like to come." I had to yell the invitation too.

She gave us a look that I interpreted as incredulous that we were getting married at our ages. Or maybe I just thought people were thinking that because sometimes it sneaked into my thoughts too.

"There'll be a buffalo barbecue afterwards," Mac added.

"Thank you, but I'm very busy. I doubt I'll have time." Her cool reaction suggested our wedding ranked right up there with invitation to a naked reality show followed by a cockroach barbecue, and I realized she wasn't incredulous we were getting married, just uninterested.

"Actually, we weren't expecting to find anyone out here today," Mac said. "Did you stay here last night?"

"Dawson was my stepfather. I can stay here if I want." She picked up a dented copper pot, peered inside, and flung it toward a corner. It hit with a hollow *bong*.

We hadn't challenged her right to be here, but she was acting as if we had. Why so defensive? Though I had to wonder why she *was* here. And how did she get in? Dan had said he'd locked the place when they left. Now she didn't exactly push us up the stairs, but I definitely felt herded in that direction. In the kitchen, she turned the radio down.

"I like it up loud when I'm alone. It makes me feel . . . not so alone," she muttered.

I've been known to turn a radio up loud too, for the same reason, and I felt a smidgen of empathy. Maybe she was a bit more uneasy alone out here in her dead stepfather's house than she wanted to admit. Maybe she was also mourning him more than it appeared. At low volume, I didn't find the music soothing, but it was at least tolerable and we didn't have to yell now.

"We didn't mean to intrude," Mac said. "I guess we're just surprised that a young woman unfamiliar with the territory would stay out here all alone."

Maybe it was Mac calling her a "young woman" – which was stretching it a bit considering the gray roots in her dark hair – or maybe she was recovered from the trauma of falling shelves, but her look was now a bit less hostile.

She swiped at a loose strand of hair falling across her face. "I'm sorry. It hasn't been a good morning." She looked at her hand, with scrape marks on the knuckles. Though there was still challenge in her voice when she added, "If you weren't expecting anyone to be here, why are *you* here?"

"We came out to look for Dawson's will. We thought maybe it would say something about his wishes concerning funeral or burial," Mac said. "The sheriff said it was okay to come and look."

"I appreciate your concern, but the sheriff has no right giving anyone permission to snoop around on private property. And there *is* a will. I called my mother yesterday, and she has it. Dawson left everything to her. She has some health problems so I'll be handling everything here for her. Dawson's body will be cremated, and I'll take his ashes back to San Diego."

That certainly sounded as if she had everything under control.

"Is all that okay with the sheriff and coroner's office?" Mac asked. He didn't sound doubtful, but I suspected he was.

"I don't think there's a problem, but my mother is sending a copy of the will. She'll also send along authorization for me to handle everything for her."

A will that benefited Natasha's mother, and, through the mother, no doubt Natasha as well. Was that incentive enough for her to sneak up here, as Elle had suggested, and choreograph a deadly fall for Dawson before anyone even knew she existed? The ranch didn't look all that valuable, but murder has been done for much less.

"Is this a recently written will?" Mac asked.

65

"It's older, but that doesn't change anything." Now Natasha was herding us across the living room. "Thanks for your concern."

I was glad she didn't have one of those electric prods used to move cattle along or we'd definitely have hot spots on the derriere. Mac balked at the front door.

"You plan to stay out here alone?"

"Yes, of course." She apparently had no suspicions about Dawson's death to make her nervous. "There's a lot to do."

Of course she wouldn't be nervous about some lurking killer if *she* were the killer. I studied her more closely. Forty-ish at first glance, but, with a closer look at the lines around her neck and a forehead that looked too flawless to be natural – the wonders of Botox? – fifty-ish seemed more likely. Dark hair tied back in a pony tail. Snappy brown eyes. The skinny-legged jeans and tight tank top showed off well-toned curves and non-saggy arms. That encounter with the fallen shelves would surely have kept me down a lot longer than it had her. She didn't look like a killer, but they don't tend to come with KILLER neatly stenciled across the back of a tank top for identification.

"Did you have a problem getting inside the house?" I asked.

She gave me a sharp look as if suspecting some deeper question lurked in that ambiguous one. Which it did, of course. Had she broken in? She had a quick, mind-your-own-business answer. "No, no problem."

I noted that the painting that had been over the fireplace now leaned against the bookshelves, a lighter oblong on the wall showing where it had been hanging, and the books in the living room were scattered across the floor like garage-sale leftovers. I wanted to ask if she'd been looking

66

for something. I also wondered how long she intended to stay. But her sharp answer about how she'd gotten inside the house told me this was no friendly chat session. I took a roundabout route.

"Again, we want to invite you to our wedding. It's two weeks from this coming Saturday at the Wolf Junction Community Church." Then my sly question disguised as a polite comment. "If you'll be here that long."

She dodged an informative answer. "It all depends."

"Before Dawson passed away, we were thinking about buying the ranch," Mac said. "My son said Dawson was planning to move to Alaska. We might still be interested."

Natasha didn't comment on her stepfather's plans or give us a hard sell on the purchase. "We'll see how things go." She surprised me by adding, "I'm thinking about living here myself." She shoved the screen door open, and I felt her hand on my back.

I resisted the prod. "What about Dawson's dog?" I asked.

"Dog?" Natasha repeated.

"Cooper," Mac said. "He was here yesterday. Big, furry, reddish-brown dog. Quite old. He's at my son's place right now."

Natasha looked startled. "That's his name, *Cooper*?"

I'd wondered about the dog's name too, but I hadn't been astonished by it, as she seemed to be. Now I wondered about that too. Why so amazed at a dog's name?

Then she made a dismissive gesture and added, "I'm really not prepared to cope with a dog."

That didn't earn her any points with me. Shouldn't a caring stepdaughter feel some responsibility, maybe even affection, toward her dead stepfather's old dog, no matter what his name was? And I never felt a dog was something

67

you *coped* with. You just loved and enjoyed a dog. Or a cat. Whatever.

"There are the cattle too. And a horse," Mac said.

"This is ranch country. I can sell them." No sentimental affection for stepfather's horse, either.

We'd just gotten out to the front steps when a big, new looking SUV roared up to the rail fence. The SUV had the name of the buffalo ranch we'd passed on the way out here emblazoned on the door. A big guy in jeans, boots, and tan cowboy hat rivaling the size of the inflatable hat atop Trudy's mobile home stepped out. I remembered Dan saying the guy had once been a big-time football player. The muscles were still there, but they were going a little Pillsbury Doughboy. A hat-band of silver buffalos circled the oversized hat, and a leather holster tooled with an image of a buffalo held a bone-handled gun. The boots had silver-tipped toes, with a buffalo engraved on each one. Wolf Junction was cowboy country, and lot of men wore old jeans, boots, and hats, but this guy looked as if he'd strutted into a wild west store and said, *gimme the works. And make 'em buffalo.*

"Howdy," he said.

Howdy? Had he bought an old movie script too?

"We haven't met, but I just heard about Dawson." He approached with hand stretched out. A gold buffalo decorated his iPad sized belt buckle. "I'm a neighbor, Dev Pickett, Buffalo Heaven Ranch."

Mac stepped out to shake the hand. "Glad to meet you."

Dev Pickett looked me over, apparently decided I was too old to be the stepdaughter he must have heard about, and offered the hand to Natasha.

"I just wanted to tell you how sorry I am about Dawson."

She shook the hand. His oversized ring, which sported a lumpy, 3-D buffalo surrounded by a silver horseshoe, flashed in the sunshine. He wouldn't want to accidentally slap himself on the forehead with that thing on his hand.

"It's come as a terrible shock," Natasha said.

"Yes, a terrible shock," Buffalo Man agreed. Call me a cynic, but I didn't think either of them sounded too sincere. "Ol' Dawson was quite a character. Will the funeral be local? Barb and I want to be there to pay our respects, of course."

Pickett was acting as if he and Dawson were old buddies, and I wondered if Natasha knew about the buffalo/shotgun incident and follow-up hostilities.

"We're not planning anything local, no," Natasha said.

"I'd like to get things settled as soon as possible, of course," Pickett said. "I'm sure you do too, so you won't have to stick around any longer than you have to."

"What things settled?" Natasha asked.

"Dawson and I made a deal on the ranch a couple weeks ago. You didn't know?" He lifted thick, rusty-colored eyebrows. "No, I guess you couldn't know. Dawson was dead when you arrived, wasn't he? But Barb and I have wanted to add this land to ours ever since we bought the home place, and Dawson decided to take our offer."

"It's quite a distance from your ranch," Mac observed.

"Not really. I'm in the process of buying the land between our home place and this one, so it's actually more like next-door."

A Montana land baron in the making? Mac and I hadn't talked any more about our buying Dawson's place, but we hadn't crossed it off as a possibility. Now here was Buffalo Man staking a claim. I looked at Natasha.

She repeated her earlier statement about possibly living here herself, and added, "I'm a writer, and I think this might be an ideal place to work."

"But Dawson and I had a deal!"

"A written deal?" Natasha challenged.

"I gave him a check as earnest money. He said he'd have the papers drawn up."

"Did he cash the check?"

"It's never come through our account," Pickett admitted. "He may not have had time to cash it before he died. But we had a *deal*. You can't just back out of a deal he made."

Natasha gave him a defiant oh-can't-I? look. She turned the look into words. "Without a written agreement, there is no deal." She paused. "Although, if I decide to sell, we might negotiate something later on."

"I offered a good price." Pickett glanced around with a certain disdain. "You're not going to jack me around for some higher price on this rundown old place."

Okay, maybe Dawson's place wasn't as fancy as Pickett's Rancho Rich Dude, but I didn't think it looked all that dilapidated, and Natasha's eyes flashed resentment at the derogatory remark.

"Mac and Ivy here are also interested in buying," she said.

"But—"

"And they talked to me about it first." She folded her arms across her chest and gave him a smug smile. Making me think, *first come, first served.* Or maybe *finders keepers, losers weepers.*

Pickett glared at all three of us as if we were a pack of buffalo rustlers. "My lawyer will be in touch," he snarled as he turned to stalk back to his vehicle. The back of his leather belt had his name engraved in dark lettering. Along with a couple of buffalo, of course.

"There must be a Cowboys-R-Us store for jerks like him," Natasha muttered.

With a special department for guys with a buffalo fixation. The possibilities struck me as mildly alarming. Buffalo tattoos under the cowboy getup. Buffalo brands on the breakfast bacon. Buffalo-imprinted toilet tissue in the bathroom. Buffalo are magnificent creatures, but even magnificence can be over-hyped.

We all watched him storm up the hill as if he were on an SUV invasion of Montana. Did a verbal agreement carry any weight now that Dawson was dead?

"Well, we'll be getting on back to town," Mac said. "If we can help in any way, just let us know."

"I don't need any help, but thank you anyway. Nice meeting you."

The words were polite enough, but she steered us briskly toward the pickup without encouragement to stay longer. Or to return. Whatever she was doing here, she didn't want us around watching. We headed up the hill through the lingering dust of Buffalo Man's exit. I looked back, but I couldn't see through our own dust whether Natasha was watching or had returned to whatever she was doing in the basement.

"So, what do you think?" I asked as we passed through the gate at the top of the hill.

"About Natasha?"

"Natasha, the ranch, Cooper. The will she says her mother has. Buffalo Man's claim that he and Dawson had made a deal on the ranch."

"I suppose, with Dawson planning to take off for Alaska, it's possible they did have a deal. Maybe finishing up a sale was one of the things Dawson planned to do before he left. But I doubt an unsigned agreement with Dawson binds Natasha to anything. Although if he'd cashed the check, I suppose that might raise a legal question. Actually, if Pickett made a good offer, I'm inclined to think she'd be smart to grab the money and run. I can't see her living out here alone."

"Do you wonder how she got in the house?"

"I hadn't, but now that you mention it. . ." He nodded.

"I also noticed she'd cleaned up the kitchen." Which meant that if she'd been at the house earlier and drugged the food that had been in Dawson's frying pan, as Elle had suggested, all evidence was gone now. The other side of that thought, of course, was that if she'd drugged his food she surely wouldn't have left the evidence sitting around in a frying pan. "And she's taken most of the books off the shelves."

"Maybe she's thinking Dawson could have hidden cash in them. Sometimes people do that."

"I wonder if she was looking for a safe behind that painting she took down."

"Could be."

"Does she really think Dawson had some hidden stash of money or valuables?" I asked.

Mac braked for a couple of cattle meandering across the road. Then he surprised me by nodding his head thoughtfully. "I'm beginning to wonder that myself."

"Really? Why?"

"I suppose it's possible his pension fund suddenly came up with big bonuses to pay for that expensive pickup and tractor. Maybe there were more bonuses he'd saved up. But maybe he had some other secret source of funds."

I suspected, if Elle knew anything about pensions, she'd have the same thoughts.

"Natasha didn't exactly encourage us to stick around. She hurried us out as if we had an infectious case of head lice or toe fungus."

Mac nodded again.

"What about this will she says her mother has?" I asked. "Does a will stay in effect even after a long-ago divorce?"

"I don't know. If Dawson never wrote a newer one, I suppose maybe it does."

Was a newer will, or maybe that earnest money check, what Natasha was searching every nook, cranny, and book to find? I also had a sudden suspicion that if she did find either, its chance of survival rivaled that of a snowball in you-know-where.

That evening, Dan talked to Deputy Cargill again. He said that with no sign of forced entry at the house, no suspicious wounds on the body, no motive for anyone to harm Dawson, the sheriff/coroner had concluded Dawson's death was simply an accidental fall. No autopsy.

End of case. Which wasn't really a case to begin with. Probably.

***

Okay, time to concentrate on the wedding.

Melanie and I drove over to Double Wells the next day to see a florist. Flowers for the church. My bridal bouquet. There was no one to give me away, but Dan would be Mac's best man and Melanie my matron of honor, so we

73

needed boutonnieres for Mac and Dan and a corsage for Melanie. I also looked for shoes to go with a swishy blue wedding dress, but nothing really appealed to me. The next day Mac and I went back over to look at motorhomes. That was also unsuccessful, but we did get our marriage license. Hey, that felt good! Made our coming venture into wedded bliss feel . . . well, *real*. Solid.

We didn't have to get blood tests, and I was beginning to wish we didn't have to wait two more weeks for the wedding.

Next day Mac used Dan's computer – Mac's computer was still buried somewhere in the pile of his stuff they'd unloaded into a shed – to look online for motorhomes, but the only interesting ones were on the east coast.

He clicked restlessly to another site. "I'm thinking we shouldn't have set such a far-off date for the wedding," he muttered. "Three weeks is too long."

So, we were in sync on that too. But it wasn't a time-line we could change at this point. "It's less than three weeks now," I pointed out. "Two weeks from Saturday."

"We should have made it no longer than *one* week. At our age, it's not smart to delay things."

On that gloomy note, Mac went back to the internet, this time to see what he could find out about Natasha Richardson. After some confusing trails through information on a deceased actress of the same name, he found a Facebook page with a photo of a younger version of the woman at Dawson's house. The information identified her as an English and writing instructor at a junior college in the San Diego area. She also, as she'd claimed, was a writer. She had a self-published mystery novel available on several e-book sites on the internet, although sales weren't burning up the best seller lists. At her age it seemed likely she'd been married at some time, but Mac couldn't locate anything about marriages or divorces. Neither did he find anything about a criminal record. He grumbled about the inaccuracy of the popular notion that you could find anything on the internet.

I figure finding most anything is probably possible, but only if you were born after the date DNA apparently included a computer gene. Which both Mac and I lacked.

He also checked on Dawson. Surprisingly, that search turned up record of a marriage in Moscow, Idaho, in 1970 between Dawson J. Collier and Lillian M. Richardson. Surprising that the old marriage record was available online, surprising that Natasha was apparently exactly who she said she was, Dawson's stepdaughter. Then I felt a smidgen of guilt. Why wouldn't she be exactly who she said she was? Nothing else on Dawson. He'd managed to keep himself fairly well off the online grid, unlike most people in today's world.

We found several people with the names Lillian Collier and Lillian Richardson, but none of the information seemed to apply to Natasha's mother. Maybe she used a different name now.

I made a suggestion for another internet search. Dev Pickett. That turned up a flurry of information. We found that he'd been out of professional football for a little over five years, the result of a knee injury. But he'd been a highly paid linebacker for an east-coast team, apparently with plenty of money now for buying Montana property. During his playing years, he'd gotten in trouble several times for "unnecessary roughness" that had resulted in injuries to other players. There was speculation that his own injury had been payback on the field from other players.

I was relieved to learn later that day that Melanie had ordered the buffalo for our barbecue from another rancher, not Buffalo Man, who'd no doubt have gleefully supplied us with the toughest parts available. Also, the local photographer Melanie had in mind, although he specialized in rodeo photography, had our wedding date free and could do both a video and still shots of the ceremony and reception. "Although bulls are usually less trouble than brides," he'd told her a bit sourly.

Then Trudy the hatmaker called. She'd just found out the swishy blue material had been ruined with water stains when the local volunteer fire department put out the fire that destroyed her house. Trudy said not to worry, however; she'd come up with something else. The word *improvise* that Melanie had earlier mentioned came to mind, and I found myself a little uneasy about *how* Trudy would improvise. Maybe I'd be juggling cowboy hats after all.

Stop it, I snapped at myself. Enough with what grand-niece Sandy might call imagination on steroids.

But as another day crawled by, my wish that we'd picked a closer date for the wedding grew ever stronger. My impatience had upgraded – downgraded? – into a vague, unfocused apprehension. Unexpectedly, Melanie echoed that feeling.

"I almost wish we'd set the date earlier," she fretted after learning the woman who was supposed to do my hair wouldn't be available because she had to make an unplanned visit to Phoenix to help an ill daughter.

"I know it's awkward having extra people in the house—"

"Oh, no, it isn't that! We love having Mac and you with us. It's just. . ."

"I can do my own hair," I assured her. "I always do."

"It's not the hair either. It's just that sometimes I get this strange feeling that something is about to go wrong, and

76

the wedding will never—" She broke off and gave me a quick, guilty smile. This was so unlike Melanie, who was usually so upbeat. "That's ridiculous, isn't it? Don't pay any attention to me. Dawson's death is getting to me, I guess. I'm sorry. Don't let me upset you." She reached over and squeezed my hand. "Wedding nerves."

Aren't wedding nerves the bride's jurisdiction? But now, with Melanie's out-of-character nerves added to both Mac's and my wish that we'd scheduled the wedding earlier, apprehension suddenly weighed on me like a buffalo sitting on my chest. Not apprehension about marrying Mac. I wanted that. With all my heart. But. . .

"It's going to be a great wedding. You and Mac are going to be very happy together," Melanie assured me. Although, in my gloomy mood, the assurance reminded me of the doctor's glib words when he says, before some dreadful procedure, that you may feel a "minor discomfort."

The Lord is in control, I reminded myself firmly. And I'd trust him, just as I always do.

I didn't know if Mac had a feeling of apprehension or if he was just impatient, but he was definitely restless. He filled time by breaking up an old concrete walkway Dan and Melanie wanted to get rid of, and digging a ditch for an underground electric line to a shed. Wolf Junction didn't have a doctor, but it did have a veterinarian, and Mac took both BoBandy and Cooper in for general checkups and shots.

On Sunday we went to the church in which we would soon be married. Elle was the only member of the family who came with us. I was surprised but pleased when she brought a small, New Testament along. She said she'd gotten it at Vacation Bible School last year. The pastor gave a good message on forgiveness. But afterward Elle had questions that had nothing to do with the message, one of which was, how come such awful things happen to nice people? Didn't God care? Like how come her friend Dakota, who had gone to church with her family all the time, got leukemia, and lost all her hair in medical treatments, and then *died*? Elle, eleven years old, had hit on a question that has troubled both Christians and non-believers ever since God made himself known to man. Bad things happening to good people.

"Oh, hon, I'm so sorry about your friend." I wished I had some pat answer to give her, but I didn't, and I had to admit, "I don't know why things like that happen. I think there are some things we have to wait until we're in eternity to find out. But I think you can be sure Dakota is safe with the Lord now."

Elle nodded.

"God may not change things to how we'd like them in our lives, but he'll always help us through them," I said.

"I guess he helped Dakota. She told me she wasn't afraid to go be with Jesus."

I put my arm around her narrow shoulders and squeezed hard.

"I wish Mom and Dad were more interested in coming to church," Elle said.

"Do they mind if you come?"

"No. It's fine with them. Mom says they're just too busy at this time of their lives."

"Well, there you are then! You come, and maybe sometime they won't be so busy."

The next day, Mac and I were there at the house alone. The kids and Dan were at school, of course, and Melanie went off to help a friend repaint her kitchen cabinets. Mac was out back, ripping out some dead bushes. I was sewing buttons on an old blouse and feeling ever more restless and apprehensive. I'd just decided I needed to take a long walk to exercise away those feelings when a horn honked out in the yard. I figured Mac would see what whoever it was wanted, and just kept looking for my walking shoes, but a few seconds later the horn blasted again.

Now wasn't that a little rude? How come this person didn't just come to the door and knock or ring the bell politely like most people?

I went to a window. A red car stood in the driveway. I'm not great at vehicle identification, but I was fairly certain this was Natasha Richardson's car. The horn blasted again.

I couldn't imagine what she wanted, and I didn't appreciate being summoned like the girlfriend of some teenage guy rudely honking for his date. Especially after she'd given us that electric-prod rush out of Dawson's house. I reluctantly went outside.

Well, okay, to be more accurate, I stomped outside.

Chapter 8

IVY

Mac came around the house from the back yard at the same time, scratch on his cheek.

He didn't look in any better humor than I was. We approached the car together, and Natasha rolled down the car window.

"They told me at the gas station that you were staying at this house."

"I must remember to thank them," Mac muttered.

"Sorry about the horn." Natasha didn't look particularly sorry about the noisy summons, but makeup couldn't conceal a bump and bruise on her cheekbone and a scrape across her nose. Souvenirs of more shelf climbing? "But it's difficult for me to get out of the car."

She opened the car door, exposing one leg of her jeans ripped up the outside seam to make room for a cast running from her knee all the way down to her foot, only her toes sticking out. I also spotted crutches in the back seat of the car. Guilt instantly slapped me for my ungenerous thoughts about her horn technique. It was a wonder she could drive, let alone politely come to the door.

"What happened?" I asked.

"I drove down to the barn to look around. There's no electricity down there, and it was all shadowy and dark inside. I caught my foot on some old machinery and fell. I heard something go *pop* in my leg, and it felt like I'd been hit with a sledgehammer. I couldn't walk—"

"And you couldn't even call anyone for help from out there!"

"I finally managed to drag myself out to the car and get inside. There isn't a doctor in Wolf Junction – information again courtesy of the gas station – so I drove all the way over to the emergency room at the hospital in Double Wells. Broken leg."

"Oh, I'm so sorry!"

"I guess I should be grateful it isn't the compound type of break. The bone didn't come through the skin."

"When did this happen?" I asked.

"The day after you were out at the ranch. They kept me overnight in the hospital and did surgery on it the next morning. They couldn't put the cast on right away, and then I developed a fever and they thought I might have an infection, so I've been in the hospital until they put the cast on this morning."

"You aren't going back out to the house now, are you?" Mac asked. "In your condition, you shouldn't be out there alone."

"I couldn't get out of the car to lock the house before I left the ranch, so I need to get back out there as soon as possible. I've been gone too long already. I think someone was snooping around outside the night before—" She broke off and amended the statement. "But I was probably just imagining noises. The wind in the trees or something. You know, strange environment and all."

"I remember seeing a number of guns out there," Mac said. "Dawson was quite well armed. You know how to shoot a gun?"

"I'm sure I can figure it out if I have to." Natasha gave the gun situation a dismissive, "no problem" flip of hand, but I wasn't so sure. It's a little late to start reading the instruction manual when you're in a high-noon showdown with a bad guy. "The reason I'm here is because I do need help after all."

I started to say *of course we'll help,* but a jab from Mac's elbow stopped me. Okay, maybe we should first know what kind of help Natasha needed. I'm not much of a shelf-climber. Or gunslinger, either.

"I want to hire you. I need you to do something for me." She glanced between us. "Both of you, I guess, since you seem to be welded at the hip."

Mac looked back and forth between his hip and mine. He winked at me. "Not yet, but we soon will be," he agreed.

"You want us to come out to the ranch and take care of you?" I asked.

"I want to hire you to come and find something for me." So, she *had* been looking for something in the basement and under that painting and in the books. Down in the barn too, I suspected.

"You think there may be a will newer than the one your mother has?" I asked.

Natasha's eyes narrowed at that suggestion, but what she said was, "No. It's something I have reason to believe Dawson hid out there."

Mac asked the logical question. "What?"

"I'll tell you *what* after you agree to look for it. And to keep everything confidential. I can get around with crutches with this stupid cast on, but not well enough to do any real searching." Natasha gave the cast a dirty look.

Now I wondered if she'd retracted her original statement about a prowler because she didn't want to scare us away from doing this search for her. Did she think the prowler was looking for the same *something* she wanted us to find? Maybe a prowler with a dangerously unfriendly attitude about sharing? Did this have anything to do with Dawson's fall down the stairs?

"Why us?" I asked.

"I don't know anyone else around here." She sounded grumpy. "And I don't want to just drag someone in off the street to do it."

So, we weren't exactly a top-of-the-list choice. It was just that she had no list to choose from.

"We might be interested in helping you, but we can't agree to do that until we have some idea what we'd be looking for." I heard the stubborn inflection in Mac's voice.

"I don't see why," Natasha snapped. "If you don't want to look for it, you don't need to know what it is."

I could see a certain logic in that, but Mac just folded his arms across his chest. The poster child for *stubborn*.

"I'll make it worth your while." Natasha glanced toward Mac's old Toyota. "I'm thinking Dawson's pickup. It looks as if you could use a newer pickup."

The offer startled me. Those big, four-wheel-drive pickups like Dawson's cost a fortune. What did she think Dawson had stashed out there, anyway? Old outlaw treasure? Gems and jewels? Stocks and bonds? Mac didn't jump on the offer, however. He just stood there still looking stubborn. Doing a great impression of a man-shaped post.

Natasha gave the steering wheel a frustrated thump and then looked at me. "I saw you looking at the painting that came from over the fireplace. You can have that too. I think it might be valuable."

I liked the painting, but I didn't need even that much incentive to go poking around Dawson's place. That mutant curiosity gene was revved up as an old race horse ready to run. And getting *paid* to poke and prowl? Whooee!

But Mac was still just standing there. "That's very generous of you, but what if we don't find anything? What if we spend a lot of time and energy out there looking, and we don't find whatever Dawson had hidden?"

Natasha hesitated a moment, but then she said, "You can have the pickup and painting anyway, just for looking."

"How long would you expect us to search?" I asked.

She hesitated again, but she finally came up with a reasonable sounding time frame. "Until your wedding. And I'll throw in the cattle too."

I momentarily wondered what we'd do with six cattle in a motorhome, but then she made an obvious clarification.

"You know how much meat costs these days."

I thought Mac had asked the payment question on a practical basis. What if we did put in a lot of work looking, and found nothing more than dust balls and mummified leftovers? But now I realized he had something else on his mind. Some suspicion about Natasha's apparent desperation to persuade us to do this?

"Thanks, but I don't think we can do it," Mac said.

I felt a moment of indignation. Hey, who made him king and authorized him to make decisions for me?

"You want *more* than the pickup and the painting and the cattle?" Natasha sounded rather taken aback.

"We want to *know* more," Mac said. "If what you want to find is some illicit stash of cash or valuables—"

Okay, good point, I acknowledged. "Drugs?" I suggested. "Hidden meth lab? Maybe some valuable Native American or archeological artifact?" Hey, I wouldn't mind finding some old bones. Maybe a nice tyrannosaurus rex skeleton?

"Okay, forget it," Natasha snapped. "Just forget it." She slammed the car door, and, even with only one working

84

foot, she blasted the Subaru backward down the driveway like a drag race in reverse.

We stood together watching her. "What was that all about?" I finally asked.

"It sounds as if Dawson may have had more secrets than just an ex-wife and stepdaughter he never mentioned to anyone."

***

Mac went back to his brush cutting, but I didn't take the walk I'd been thinking about earlier. Maybe because my LOL intuition, which occasionally kicks in, told me we hadn't seen the last of Natasha? Sure enough, about an hour later the car horn blasted again. Mac came out from the back yard. I went out the front door. The dogs, four of them now, all joined us.

Natasha rolled down the window. "Okay, I'll tell you what you'd be looking for." She sounded more resentful than conciliatory. "And it's not drugs, but it is strictly confidential. No telling *anyone*."

Mac and I looked at each other. Did we want to agree to that stipulation if this did involve something illicit or illegal, even if it wasn't drugs? Was it something important or valuable enough that Dawson had been killed for it?

Mac simply shook his head and gave the right answer. "If it involves something criminal or injurious to anyone, we can't guarantee to keep it confidential."

"This isn't going to hurt anyone!" She slammed the steering wheel with her palm in frustration, though I noted that she wasn't saying anything about nothing *criminal* involved. Finally she gave an exasperated sigh. "Okay. Have you heard of D.B. Cooper?"

The out-of-nowhere question barreled around in my head. The name sounded vaguely familiar, but I couldn't grab

85

hold of it. I looked at Mac, and I could see he was feeling the same fuzzy familiarity. Of course Dawson's old dog was named Cooper— Then it hit me.

"D.B. Cooper was the man who skyjacked a plane somewhere in the Seattle area years ago. He got a bundle of money—"

"Two hundred thousand," Mac interrupted as his memory also kicked in. "He got the money, the plane took off, and he parachuted out somewhere over Washington, in the dark. And was never seen or heard from again. His real identity has never been established. He came out of nowhere, and, like some of the more melodramatic accounts put it, jumped into legend."

I was remembering more now. There had been reams of nationwide publicity when it happened, and D.B. Cooper had indeed turned into a legend, even becoming something of a cult hero. Most experts believed he'd been killed in the jump, but some people thought he'd made it safely. In fact they'd cheered him on, some of them probably wishing they had the nerve to do something so memorably reckless.

"A few years later several thousand dollars of the money did turn up on a beach along the Columbia River," Natasha said. "The speculation was that he'd landed somewhere up in the mountains, and the money washed down to the river in a creek."

Mac nodded. "I remember. The money was identified from serial numbers on the bills. But nothing else has ever turned up. I think it's supposed to be the only skyjacking in this country that's never been solved."

"And all this," I asked, "matters because—?"

"Because my stepfather was D.B. Cooper," Natasha said. "And I think the rest of that two hundred thousand is hidden somewhere out there on the ranch."

We were all silent for a long moment until Mac finally said, "That's quite a claim. The authorities have been looking for D.B. Cooper and the money for – what? Forty-some years? And never come up with anything."

"It happened the day before Thanksgiving in 1971, but Dawson has outfoxed FBI and police departments and airline officials all these years." Natasha sounded proud of that.

"If the serial numbers are on record, the money can't be spent even if it's found," I pointed out. "Although, if it's taken out of the country, especially to some country that isn't friendly to the U.S., maybe someone could get away with spending it. . ."

I gave myself a mental whack. Great. If she hadn't already thought of this, I'd just outlined a plan for her. We find the money for her, and she takes off for Lower Slobbovia.

"I don't intend to spend the money," Natasha said loftily. "I'll turn it in to the authorities."

I was certainly surprised, and Mac's lifted eyebrows said he was too.

"That's very noble of you," he said finally. "You're willing to compensate us rather generously to find the money just so you can return it to the authorities, all out of the goodness of your heart?" I heard his skepticism.

"So I can return it to the authorities, yes," Natasha agreed. "But not necessarily out of the goodness of my heart," she admitted. "This is *research*. I am, as I mentioned to that faux cowboy with the buffalo fixation, a writer."

"And an English and writing instructor at . . . some junior college." The name escaped me at the moment, but mention of her job brought an unexpected reaction from Natasha.

"I hate that job. Hate it!" she declared with a burst of passion. "You wouldn't *believe* how incompetent some of those students are when they get to college. Sometimes I feel that if I have to cope with one more lazy smart-aleck who gives me a what-difference-does-it-make shrug when I try to explain lie and lay, I'm going to—" She broke off before stating what she might do and took a deep breath. I suspected she took a lot of deep breaths in her classrooms. "I've always wanted to be a writer. I *will* be a writer. I've already done one mystery novel. But I want a bestseller."

Which *Last Train to Topeka* was not. It languished somewhere in the 1,400,000 numbers ranking on Amazon, a universe away from best-seller status.

"But fiction isn't really my thing." Natasha gave a dismissive flip of fingers. "I like solid facts. And with facts, I know I can write a good book. An *awesome* book. That's why I came up here. Research. To get the facts from Dawson."

"So you could write a book revealing D.B. Cooper's real identity?" Mac asked.

"I could tell about his life before the hijacking and why he did it. What became of him afterwards. Not an exposé, but a real in-depth story about D.B. Cooper. Otherwise known as Dawson Collier."

It was mind-boggling to think that D.B. Cooper had been living quietly here in Montana all these years. Unbelievable, actually. But was naming his dog Cooper actually kind of a private joke with himself?

Real excitement had crept into Natasha's voice as she talked about her book, but I wondered what made her think Dawson, if he'd been in hiding all these years, would go along with such a revelation. That point didn't really matter now, of course. Dawson wasn't alive to supply all this information. Although there was another point to consider: if Dawson had given a flat *no* to her bestseller book idea, had she been frustrated or angry enough to shove him down the stairs?

"But with Dawson dead, you really don't have a book," Mac said.

"Nothing better than any of the other books that have been written about D.B. Cooper," Natasha agreed. "But with the money, and serial numbers to prove it *is* the skyjack money, I'll have a story that can't miss even if Dawson is dead. Finding the money will make headlines, and half the publishers in the country will be bidding for a book from me." A fire of excitement burned in her eyes. "It's the break that will put me on the bestseller lists. And making more money than D.B. Cooper ever got out of his skyjacking. It's great movie material."

She might have something there. No wonder she was willing to gamble the pickup, a painting, and six cattle to try to find it. I looked at Mac.

"Does anyone else know about this possible connection between Dawson and D.B. Cooper?" he asked.

"I don't see how they could. I didn't know it myself until a few weeks ago when my mother told me." She paused, frown lines creasing her forehead. "Although I suppose it's remotely possible."

"Why didn't your mother tell you before this?" I asked. "Why did she decide to tell you *now*, after over forty years?"

"She said she didn't want to get Dawson in trouble earlier. And she's been kind of . . . forgetful for quite a while. She only told me now because I was helping her clean out some boxes of old stuff, and we ran across a birthday card he'd once given her, and she got all teary and sentimental. She gets that way every once in a while now, when she does remember something." Natasha did not sound as if she had

89

much sympathy for old sentimentality. "I certainly wish she'd told me earlier."

"So how did you know Dawson was living up here in Montana?"

"He called her a few years ago. He was looking for some old veteran's records he couldn't find. He thought maybe she had them. She didn't, but he gave her an address to send them to if she found them. She lost the actual address, but she remembered it was in Montana and the name of the town had something about a wolf in it. If I couldn't find him in Wolf Junction, I intended to try Wolf Point next."

"Did Dawson have any kind of criminal past before the skyjacking?" I asked.

"Not that I know of." Natasha paused. "Although I suppose he could have had a past he never told my mother about."

"Give us some time to think this over," Mac said.

"It's my story! You can't tell anyone. You promised!"

Not exactly. I recalled Mac saying just a few minutes ago that if anything criminal was involved, we *couldn't* keep it confidential. This did involve a criminal act, although I couldn't see our going to the authorities with a claim that dead Dawson might have been D.B. Cooper. Other people had made similar claims, about people both living and dead. What was the right thing to do here? *Any comments, Lord?*

"Finding the money would be a good thing," Natasha pointed out. "It would solve the mystery of a decades-old crime for the authorities, and the airline, or whoever put up the money, would get most of it back. No one would be hurt, and it would give me the break I need in my career. A win-win situation all around."

True, I agreed, but warily. Was there something I wasn't seeing, or something she wasn't telling us? Maybe something about a sneaky prior trip to the ranch and a shove on the basement stairs?

"We'll think about it and let you know," Mac said.

"When?"

"We'll come out to the ranch later today."

Chapter 9

IVY

What we did as soon as Natasha pulled out of the driveway, of course, was run to Dan's computer and get on the internet. Information about skyjacker D.B. Cooper wasn't difficult to find. It was, in fact, almost in the TMI category. Too Much Information. Information overload.

Natasha had the date right, the day before Thanksgiving in 1971. A man signing his name Dan Cooper bought an airline ticket from Portland, Oregon, to Seattle, Washington. While in the air, he showed a stewardess what appeared to be a bomb in a brief case. He demanded $200,000, parachutes, and refueling for the plane. In Seattle, Cooper's demands were met and the money paid in $20 bills. He released the passengers, no one harmed. The plane took off, Dan Cooper still in possession of his bomb. He told the pilot to head for Mexico City. But somewhere in the dark, still over Washington, though no one knew exactly where or when, he donned two parachutes, and jumped from the lowered stairway, taking briefcase/bomb and money with him.

I mentioned that the payoff seemed rather low for such a high-concept crime, and Mac pointed out $200,000 was a lot more money in 1971 than it was now. Probably so. Although I picked up lost pennies in 1971, and I still do. I put them in a special jar. It's going to take a while to get to $200,000, even if money isn't worth as much as it used to be.

In the nationwide media frenzy that followed, someone mistakenly called the skyjacker D.B. Cooper, and that name stuck. The investigation and search were intensive, but no solid information turned up until 1980. That year, a boy digging a pit for a campfire on a sand bar on the Washington side of the Columbia River found $5,800 in $20 bills. It was identified by the serial numbers as part of the skyjack money.

There was much speculation about how the money had gotten there. Maybe that D.B. Cooper had been killed in a hard landing from the skydive, and the money washed down from wherever he died. That he'd fallen into a tree and dangled there in the parachute until he died. That he'd landed safely but gotten lost trying to find his way out. That he survived the skydive but succumbed to hypothermia afterward. A wilder speculation was that he'd survived and buried the money along the river himself, though why he'd have done that was never made clear.

Since the skyjacking, there'd been books written about D.B. Cooper, a movie and TV shows made, and a website maintained. You could buy D.B. Cooper comic books, baseball caps, and T-shirts (baby-sized through adult). But no solid information had ever turned up. There were festivals and celebrations commemorating the date, with some people speculating that D.B. Cooper might be attending incognito, laughing all the time. It appeared that the FBI now considered the skyjacking a closed case, even though it had never been solved.

One positive result of the skyjacking was that 727s were afterward equipped with a device to prevent the rear stairs from being lowered during flight. It bore Cooper's name.

No actual photos of D.B. Cooper existed, but there

were a couple of sketches plus descriptions from various witnesses. Mac stood and arched his back to stretch while the sketches printed out. We'd been on the internet a long time.

"Certainly nothing here proves or even suggests Dawson was D.B. Cooper," Mac said.

"Nothing proves he wasn't D.B. Cooper."

"True," he agreed.

"I remember reading once that if a person chooses an alias, he's likely to use one with the same initials as his original name."

Mac nodded. "Dawson Collier. Dan Cooper. Both D and C. And with a dog named Cooper."

"So are we going to help Natasha look for the money?" I asked.

"What do you think?"

What I really wanted to do was rush out to the ranch and start searching. Digging in the basement. Crawling through the attic. Checking for loose floorboards. Prowling the barn. Curiosity like a mosquito the size of a 727 was biting me, and I wanted to start right now!

But another thought brought me down to earth. You'd think it would have occurred to a clever skyjacker that the authorities would keep a record of the serial numbers on the money. But, if Dawson was that skyjacker and hadn't realized the serial-numbers glitch in his plan until too late, he may have buried the money anywhere on those 300 acres without any plans ever to dig it up.

"How many square feet in 300 acres?" I asked.

"Why—?" Then Mac caught my thoughts. "Let's see, 43,500 square feet in an acre. . . " He reached for the little pocket calculator on Dan's desk. "A little over 13 million."

Compared to the national debt, 13 million isn't a huge number, but the idea of digging holes over every one of those square feet felt as daunting as emptying the ocean with a teaspoon.

"How about finding out why Natasha thinks Dawson was D.B. Cooper? If there isn't a plausible reason, there isn't much point in chasing around looking for the money." Although I wasn't sure what it would take to convince me it would be wasted time. My mutant curiosity gene was busier than an ant at a picnic.

"Do we have time?" Mac asked. "How are the wedding plans coming?"

I still didn't know if I'd be juggling a handful of cowboy hats as my wedding ensemble, and there were barbecue details to work out. "There are a few things to take care of yet, but everything's under control," I assured him.

**

We left a note for Dan and Melanie and were heading out to the pickup when my cell phone jingled. My old friend Magnolia from back on Madison Street!

"So you're finally getting married! From the very beginning, I knew you were meant for each other. That's why I introduced you."

"You're a great matchmaker," I agreed. Magnolia puts great faith in her vibrations about romantic possibilities, though her vibration meter could sometimes use a little fine tuning. Witness the vegetarian and the meat-market owner she'd introduced who nearly came to blows over a cross-rib roast. "Can you and Geoff come to the wedding?"

"Of course we'll come! We wouldn't miss it."

I gave her the details, though I didn't bother with directions. Geoff could figure out how to get to Wolf Junction; they'd been all over the country in their motorhome, usually looking for some sixth or seventh generation relative Magnolia was tracking down in her indomitable genealogical search. Then she asked a question that hadn't even occurred to me.

"Who's giving you away?"

"Well, um, no one. I'm a little past the 'giving away' age."

"Every bride needs someone to walk her down the aisle," Magnolia declared. Never one to beat around the bush, she added, "I'd be honored to do it."

A long-time old friend giving the bride away? An unusual arrangement. But . . . why not? I felt a pleasant skitter of excitement. "I'd be honored to have you do it."

So a few more words and it was settled. Magnolia said she'd provide her own dress, and they might, since they were going to be in this area anyway, spend a few days looking for some people in a newly discovered Ukrainian line of her genealogy. Magnolia's genealogy has everything from an American Indian to a Hawaiian royalty line.

Afterward, as we were getting into the pickup, I told Mac, and he said, "Magnolia will make an impressive addition to the wedding ceremony."

No doubt an understatement. I'd long ago realized I've aged into invisibility, but Magnolia has never been invisible. She has *presence*. She also has dramatic changes of hair color, insulation pink to fire-engine red to glitter-dusted platinum. Her figure is of the grand old Victorian variety, and she moves with the majesty of a cruise liner. Yes, she'd do a fine job of giving me away. I felt a nice click of things falling into place.

We hadn't intended to take BoBandy with us, but he sneaked around me and jumped in the pickup and we let him come along. There didn't appear to be any activity at the Buffalo Heaven Ranch when we went by, but an old Ford pickup pulled out as we passed the Rocking R driveway. I

96

couldn't see the driver behind the sunglasses and the tipped-down visor of his baseball cap, but he gave us a standard lift of fingers in greeting.

The sunny day had clouded over by the time we reached Dawson's place, and an unexpectedly chilly wind hit us when we got out of the pickup. I didn't see any chickens today. The door and windows on the house were closed now. I hadn't noticed before, when the door was open, but it had a window covered with an old-fashioned lace curtain. Mac knocked.

After several clunks from inside, an edge of the curtain lifted and one dark eye peered out cautiously. Natasha unlocked the door and opened it. She dropped one of the crutches when she stepped back to let us in.

"Stupid crutches," she muttered as Mac picked it up and returned it to her. She was still wearing the ripped jeans. She jerked when the wind tapped branches of a rose bush against a front window.

"Is everything okay?" Mac asked.

"Someone was in the house while I was gone. Someone *searched* the house while I was gone!" She peered behind her as if afraid the intruder might still be lurking back there. She was obviously nervous, and definitely no longer hiding the fact of a prowler. The radio wasn't on today, which I figured was because she wanted to be able to hear every rustle, creak, and footstep. A gun – I wasn't knowledgeable enough to know if it was rifle or shotgun – lay on the floor near the sofa. Her nerves made me wonder if an intruder *could* still be around. And was that gun loaded? I wasn't sure I wanted to be in the same room with a jittery Natasha and a loaded gun.

"You think someone was here looking for the D.B. Cooper money?" I asked.

97

"What else would they be looking for?" Natasha snapped. "A favorite book?" She lifted a crutch and whacked a couple of books across the floor.

"You think someone knows about the money, then?" Mac said.

"I don't see how they could. But . . . maybe. Or maybe it was just kids up to no good. Or maybe that creepy buffalo guy was snooping around." She crutched across the living room and lowered herself to the sofa. She used her hands to lift her cast onto the sofa, then leaned over to move the gun a few inches closer.

Buffalo Man sounded like a definite possibility to me. But, rather than looking for the skyjacking money, he'd probably wanted to find that check he said he'd given Dawson, or something else that might prove they'd had an agreement about his buying the ranch. So, did that mean he was just land hungry, or did he know something about hidden money?

"Was anything stolen or damaged?" Mac asked.

"I don't know." Natasha jerked her shoulders in a frustrated shrug. "I can't get around well enough to look at everything, and I don't know what should be here anyway."

"What makes you think someone was in the house, then?" I asked.

"The basement door was open and the light was on, and I'm sure I didn't leave it that way when I went to the barn."

"I'll go down and have a look around," Mac said. "Anything else?"

"No. It just *feels* as if someone has been in here."

The basement light on was hardly enough to prove someone had searched the house. I've left lights on and forgotten them. I've also looked for my shoes and found them on my feet. But I couldn't disregard *feelings*. Feelings may tell you something that's outside physical proof. Yet even if someone had been prowling around, I still wasn't convinced Natasha hadn't had something to do with Dawson's fall down the steps. If he'd refused to go along with her D.B. Cooper book plan, she'd have been furious with him for sabotaging her writing career.

Mac headed off to check the basement. I started to follow him, then had a different idea. "May I use the bathroom?"

"It's between the bedroom and the kitchen. You have to go through the kitchen to get to it."

She waved me in that direction and I found a cramped bathroom with a dark ceiling. A rust-stained sink, with pipes showing underneath, stood under a medicine cabinet with a wavy mirror. No bathtub, just a metal shower stall. A second door opened to the bedroom on the other side. One step put my hand on the medicine cabinet door. But then I saw myself in the rippled mirror and hesitated. Natasha wanted to hire us to look for the skyjacking money, but we weren't actually *hired* yet, and there was no possibility this cabinet could hold all that money anyway. What I was doing here was snooping, plain and simple. My interest in the medicine cabinet was about Dawson's death and Natasha's possible involvement, not about the skyjacking money. I wanted to know if he'd been taking some drug or medication that in an overdose amount could have made him woozy or unsteady enough to fall down the stairs. But if some such medication *was* in the cabinet, wouldn't that suggest Natasha probably had nothing to do with his death, that it was just an accidental side-effect of medicine he took himself? I'd be doing her a *favor* to look.

The wonders of rationalization. Or maybe it's just that there's something irresistibly tempting about the contents of someone else's medicine cabinet.

I opened the cabinet door.

No tumble of twenty-dollar bills. Nor of medications. What tumbled was a toothbrush. It bounced off the sink . . . hit my hand when I grabbed for it . . . and plummeted directly into the toilet.

I stared at it in dismay. I've heard of people booby-trapping a medicine cabinet with marbles to mortify a snoopy guest. No rolling, ricocheting marbles here, but I was definitely mortified by the pink toothbrush lying at the bottom of the toilet bowl.

Dawson's old toothbrush? Unlikely. Especially not with a tube of whitening toothpaste and a jar of face cream with retinol the only other items in the cabinet. Definitely Natasha's personal belongings.

I couldn't leave the toothbrush there. Neither could I just pluck it out of the water and put it back in the cabinet. I reluctantly dipped my hand into the toilet bowl, fished out the toothbrush, and found a waste basket under the sink. It was pristinely empty. The toothbrush would stand out like false teeth on a tray of hors d'oeuvers

I scrubbed my hands and the toothbrush in soap and water, but I still couldn't bring myself to put it back in the cabinet where Natasha would use it again. I stepped out of the bathroom. I'd just dump the toothbrush in—

And there was Natasha, clomping her way across the kitchen. She eyed toothbrush and me. "You decided to start a search for the money in the bathroom cabinet?" The question was just snarky enough to let me know she knew I'd been snooping in her private things.

At that moment Mac came in from the back porch. If he was puzzled about why I was holding a toothbrush, he prudently chose to ignore it. "With the broken shelves and splattered paint, it's hard to tell if anyone's been down there. But I can tell that no one's been digging to see if the money was buried there."

"I'm still sure someone's been in here." Natasha glanced around the kitchen as if trying to identify something missing.

"We may be interested in helping you find the skyjacking money, but we need to know more about why you think Dawson was D.B. Cooper. Did Dawson tell your mother he was Cooper?"

Bless Mac. We were now far away from the subject of toothbrushes in toilet bowls. I spotted a waste basket by the fireplace in the living room and hastily dumped the toothbrush there. Natasha got herself back to the sofa. Mac found a place to sit on a lumpy blue chair, and I perched on the edge of a well-worn recliner.

"No. It was quite a while before she figured it out."

"How did she do that?"

"My mother and Dawson were married in 1970. I was less than a year old at the time, and all I remember of him is that for my birthday he bought me a doll, a Barbie doll. Exactly what I wanted. I was thrilled, and I remember giving him a big hug. Mom said he was office manager for a construction company, but his big ambition was to start his own construction business in Alaska."

Mac and I exchanged glances. That fit! Dawson was surely too old to start a construction business, but maybe moving to Alaska in his old age would have fulfilled some of that adventurous yearning from his younger years.

"He needed money to start a business, of course. A few days before 'Dan Cooper' bought his plane ticket, Dawson told Mom he was meeting someone in Alaska to form a construction company partnership. Dawson had the construction experience; the other guy had the money. He was gone a week or ten days, and he came home all battered up. He told her he'd fallen in a creek up there and got washed downstream. He said the financing and partnership deal had fallen through, but he still wanted to move up there. Mom wasn't having any part of chasing off to the middle of nowhere."

"So—?"

"So a few months later they split up, he disappeared, and she divorced him."

"If she didn't know then that he was D.B. Cooper, when did she find out?"

"At the actual time of the skyjacking, she wasn't paying much attention to the news. Her sister was dying of cancer, and she and Dawson were arguing about Alaska. It was the next year, after they were already divorced, when there was publicity about the anniversary of the skyjacking, that she first saw those sketches of him. Then she got to thinking back on Dawson needing money, being gone, coming home all battered up, and she figured out there'd never been any partner with money to invest. He planned to get the money from this skyjacking and then pass it off as coming from the so-called 'partner.'"

Mac pulled out the copies of the sketches he'd printed off the internet and held them up. "This him?"

"Yes!"

"You remember him looking like that?"

102

"Well, no. My memories are kind of . . . vague. My mother said the sketches didn't look *exactly* like him, that his face was a little fuller than that, but it was definitely him."

The sketches showed a face wide across the forehead and narrowing down to an angular chin and a thin upper lip. Dark hair, slightly receding. Well-groomed, clean-shaven, wearing a dark suit and narrow black tie. Not handsome, but not bad looking. The description said he was 5'10" to 6' tall, weighed about 170-180 pounds, had an olive complexion, and appeared to be in his early to mid-40s. Nothing about the limp Dan had mentioned that Dawson had.

"Dawson didn't look like that now. The body of the man I saw was in faded overalls. He was bearded, long-haired, and skinny." Mac paused. "Although that doesn't mean anything, of course. No one looks like a picture from over forty years ago."

Isn't that the truth.

We all sat there contemplating the sketches and considering the facts that were known about both D.B. Cooper and Dawson Collier. And whether they fit together.

"Dawson named his dog *Cooper*," Natasha said, as if that were final proof.

"If D.B. Cooper was in his early or mid-40s at the time of the skyjacking, he'd be right at ninety or over now. My son Dan says Dawson was eighty, give or take a few years," Mac said.

"The witnesses could have been wrong about D.B. Cooper's age back then." Natasha sounded impatient that we weren't instantly accepting her claim that D.B. Cooper and Dawson were one and the same. "Or your son might be off on Dawson's age now."

There could be a little discrepancy in the ages, but they didn't positively exclude the possibility that Dawson and

103

D.B. Cooper could be the same person. "Dawson moved to Montana right after he and your mother separated?" I asked.

"Mom didn't know anything about where he was. He just disappeared. All she ever heard of him was like I told you, when he called a few years ago about his veteran's records."

"Dan says Dawson had a limp. Did he have that when he and your mother were married?" Mac asked. "There's no mention of a limp in any of the descriptions of the skyjacker."

"I can ask her. Though she might not remember. Like I said before, her memory is sometimes a little . . . fuzzy these days."

"Maybe he was injured in that parachute jump out of the plane," I suggested. "Witnesses on the plane wouldn't have seen any limp because he didn't have it then. Your mother said he was in bad shape when he returned from what was supposed to be an Alaska trip."

Natasha sat up straighter on the sofa. "Yes! Exactly." She sounded as if this was the clincher. More silence. Natasha finally broke it. "Look, the more I think about it, the less I think I actually want to live here. So I'll sweeten the deal. You look for the money until your wedding. You get the pickup, the painting, and the cattle just for looking. But, you *find* the money, and I'll also sell you the ranch at a bargain price." She paused, and I could see her calculating what would be enough to entice us. "*Half* the market value the county has on it for property tax purposes."

Wow. Mac and I exchanged glances. Half the market value would be a terrific bargain. We could afford to remodel that bathroom so falling items wouldn't plunge directly from medicine cabinet to toilet bowl, maybe add a bathtub. Most people may like showers now, but I do love a good bathtub soak.

"That's very generous," Mac said. "But we haven't totally decided we want to live out here."

"Then buy it from me at half price and sell it to the faux buffalo cowboy for full price," Natasha said impatiently. "Look, I want to show you something—" She grabbed her crutches and started to stand up, but this time something went wrong. Crutches flew. Books scattered and skidded. Natasha crashed to the floor.

Both Mac and I rushed to her. I figured she'd have a fresh supply of expletives for this occasion, but instead she just groaned. We helped her back to the sofa. I doubted she could have made it on her own.

"You can't stay out here alone," I said.

"I can't leave," she said stubbornly. "Someone's looking for the money."

"If this person pushed Dawson down the stairs, he may be willing to do something similar to you," Mac pointed out.

Natasha didn't argue the point. "Are the two of you going to look for the money or not?"

Mac and I exchanged glances. "We'll look for it," he said. "But you still can't stay out here alone."

"Then the two of you stay out here too instead of running back and forth every day. It'll be better for all of us. There's lots of food. And if we have unfriendly prowlers, there are plenty of guns to go around." She nodded toward the gun-loaded bucket near the door. "More upstairs."

I wasn't too sure about the advantage of having all those guns around, but we figured out a short-term living arrangement. Natasha couldn't make it up and down the stairs, so she'd have to stay in the downstairs bedroom

Dawson had used. It was large enough to hold a folding cot we found upstairs, so I'd also sleep there in case Natasha needed help during the night. Mac would use an upstairs bedroom. After he cleared the bed of guns, deer antlers, and books.

One of us had to make a return trip to town for items we needed for staying here. No discussion about who that would be. Me. No way, Mac said, was he leaving two women out here alone. I could have been insulted by what might be considered a sexist attitude, but I figured he was right.

Mac and I made a quick list of what we needed. We decided sleeping bags would be easier than finding bedding for the additional beds. Natasha had an item to add to the list. A toothbrush. She managed to ask for it nicely, although she did sneak in a semi-snarky comment on how glad she was we were staying to do the search because she'd already had an "impressive demonstration" of my searching talents. She also gave me her mother's phone number and asked me to call and tell her she was back out at the ranch and wouldn't be able to call for a while.

I headed for the pickup. "Okay, I'll be back as soon as I can."

Mac walked out with me. "Be careful."

"You think I might be ambushed along the way?"

"No, but I think Natasha was right about someone being in the house. It looked as if some things in the basement had been moved around. And I'm sure there were more guns in that bucket by the door than there are now."

I drove as fast as I dared. Isn't this the place in the spooky movie where the heroine returns to find the people she's left behind gone? Vanished into thin air.

I drove faster than I dared.

106

Chapter 10

MAC

As soon as Ivy was gone, Natasha remembered what she was going to show us just before she fell. She pointed to a stack of books she'd set aside on the dining room table. "They're all about D.B. Cooper."

I flipped through the books, a half-dozen of them.

"You see?" Natasha said. "He was interested in what they were saying about D.B. Cooper, because he *was* D.B. Cooper. He probably got a good laugh about all the misinformation and wild speculation. And I found a twenty-dollar bill in one of them."

The books did indeed suggest Dawson had a keen interest in D.B. Cooper. Although, poking around through more scattered books, it appeared he'd had a fascination with crime in general. There were books on the Unabomber, Charles Ponzi of Ponzi schemes fame, Ted Bundy, and Billy the Kid. But he'd also liked to read about exotic places: Bora Bora, Mykonos, Easter Island, the Galapagos. And cooking books too. It was hard to imagine the skinny, rough-bearded guy I'd seen dead on the basement floor being interested in paella, artichokes, and jam and jelly making, but he had the cookbooks to prove it.

But books on one subject far outnumbered all the others: Alaska. History. Hunting. Fishing. Living off the land. Oil discoveries. Eskimo life. Plants. Dog-sledding. Sad, I thought, that he never got to go and see it all for himself.

"What kind of formal education did Dawson have?" I asked Natasha.

"I have no idea."

"Do you know anything about his past before he married your mother? Occupation, where he lived, criminal record, health?"

"I don't see that any of that matters now that he's dead."

I thought it might indeed matter, but I made some noncommittal mutter and headed upstairs to clear sleeping space in one of the bedrooms. Dawson wasn't necessarily a pack-rat, but he didn't throw much away. Mountains of old cottage cheese and yogurt cartons. Enough extension cords to hogtie a herd of dogies. All those antlers, which I'm sure Ivy would consider "creepy." Although I figured she should be glad he hadn't saved the heads too. A picture of Ronald Reagan. Even a Bible, although, unfortunately, it looked quite unused. He also collected survival-type supplies. The closet held big cans of nitrogen-packed eggs, fruit, vegetables, and pancake mix, plus sacks of wheat and beans. And he apparently didn't intend to head into the meltdown of civilization without a plentiful supply of toilet tissue. I was just stripping the old blankets off the bed when I heard a vehicle outside.

I also heard, "Mac! Someone's here," in a yell from Natasha that was part panic, part command that I take care of the situation. Something told me the lady could easily become a tyrant there on her sofa, but I went downstairs and opened the front door.

I was expecting another unpleasant encounter with Buffalo Man, or maybe his lawyer, but it was the old Ford pickup we'd seen coming out of the Rocking R driveway. A man and woman got out. They were in their late 50s or early

60s, I guessed. I was feeling a little wary of visiting strangers, but I managed a cordial, "Hi."

"I hope we aren't coming at a bad time," the woman said when they reached the gate. She had a friendly smile, loose-flowing gray hair, and feather earrings. I'd seen similar items in a nice display of Native American crafts in the Wolf Junction store. "We heard about Dawson and thought we'd come over and see if there was anything we could do."

"I'm Jack Hawkins." The man motioned to the woman. "My wife Marnie. We're from the Rocking R."

This was the guy Dan had said Dawson called a city slicker who could barely tell a cow from a goat. He was short and wiry, but tough looking, like a hunk of old leather, his hair in a skimpy pony tail. He and the wife looked cowboy enough in their jeans and boots, but they weren't walking advertisements like Buffalo Man. Jack wore a baseball cap instead of a cowboy hat. It had *Go, Falcons!* and a falcon emblem embroidered above the visor.

We all shook hands. "Mac MacPherson. Come on in and I'll introduce you to Dawson's stepdaughter. She had an unfortunate accident and is incapacitated at the moment."

"Did she fall down the stairs like Dawson did?" Marnie looked at her husband. "Didn't you tell me once that those stairs were a disaster just waiting to happen? And now it's happened *twice*."

"Natasha's accident was down in the barn. My fiancée and I are staying here to take care of her." It was a convenient excuse for our presence and also true. I was guessing now that Natasha might take a lot of taking care of. "Although Ivy isn't here right now. She had to run into town to pick up a few things."

"I think everyone was surprised to learn Dawson had a stepdaughter," Marnie Hawkins said. "We all thought he was a lifelong bachelor."

I led them inside and made introductions. We small-talked about Natasha's injury and the weather, and what a shame Dawson's accident was, especially when he was planning a new life in Alaska. Jack said if we needed any help with the cattle or horse, he'd be glad to do whatever he could, and Marnie said if we needed food or supplies, they had plenty to share. Also that they had a land-line phone, and we were welcome to come over and use it anytime we needed a phone.

"There's a cross-country back way that's a lot shorter to our place than going around by the road," Jack added. BoBandy checked them out, and Jack offered him a doggie treat from a supply in his shirt pocket. "I always carry a little something for Otis. He's our big old German Shepherd," Jack explained.

Marnie rolled her eyes. "I should get the princess treatment that dog gets. Would you believe Jack built steps for her when she injured a hind leg and couldn't jump up on our bed?"

"You injure a leg and I'll build steps for you too," Jack assured her.

"You didn't bring Otis with you?" I asked.

"He has a bad hip and has trouble getting in the pickup, so we usually leave him at home. I never brought him over here because Cooper didn't like dog guests any better than Dawson liked people guests."

It was all very pleasant, and they seemed like nice neighbors, but somehow I got the impression they were marking time, circling around the real target of their visit.

110

At a little lull in the conversation, I asked, "Did you know Dawson very well? Maybe you could tell Natasha more about him. Do you know how he got the limp?"

For a moment I thought *limp* hit some kind of hot spot with them, but then Marnie laughed. "Dawson didn't exactly encourage exchanges of personal information. He could be prickly as an old warthog. But he could be good-hearted too. He came with us to look at some cattle one time and kept us from getting ripped off buying a bunch of cows that were almost old enough to vote."

Jack shifted in his seat. "We wonder what's going to happen to the ranch now, with Dawson gone."

Marnie leaned forward, waiting for an answer.

That was it. The real reason they were here.

"We're interested in it ourselves," I said. "And Mr. Pickett from the Buffalo Heaven Ranch says he'd made a deal with Dawson to buy it."

"Dawson sell out to that jerk?" Marnie scoffed. "No way!"

"Pickett says he gave Dawson a check as earnest money to get the deal started."

"I have a hard time believing that. Dawson told me Pickett made an offer on the ranch, but he said he'd told Pickett to get his 'buffalo butt' off the ranch or he'd blast him like he did those mangy animals of his." Jack smiled. "Dawson wasn't one to mince words."

Natasha got right to the point. "Are you also interested in buying the ranch?" she asked the Hawkins couple.

"We're just leasing the Rocking R. We didn't want to buy until we were sure we'd like ranching life. Now we know we do like it, but the old lady who owns the ranch isn't selling. She thinks a grandson will take it over someday."

111

Marnie's eyes did a meaningful roll at the likelihood of that ever happening. "Anyway, yes, we're interested in Dawson's place."

Buffalo Man was interested. Now this Rocking R couple too. It seemed unlikely either of them could know anything about hidden money. If Dawson had been going to confide in anyone about a skyjacking past, it seemed Dan would have been most likely, not these people. But all this interest in an unremarkable old place seemed odd. I tossed out a test question.

"There an old story about outlaw treasure being buried around here someplace," I said.

Natasha gave me a shocked glance, as if I'd just spilled the beans, but I kept my attention on Jack and Marnie.

"Hey, we heard that, didn't we, Jack?" Marnie said. "Some old stagecoach robbery, wasn't it? Maybe old Dawson actually found it and never told anyone!" She peered around as if hoping to spot the money hidden under the sofa.

Yes, the Hawkins couple were definitely interested in "treasure."

Jack laughed. "Maybe we can find it and use it to pay off the mortgage if we buy the place. Because we can't put up cash like Pickett no doubt can. But we're willing to pay more in total than whatever he offered."

Interesting. They were willing to pay more than Pickett without even knowing what he'd offered. Did that suggest they thought there was some hidden value to Dawson's ranch?

"Actually, I'm thinking about living here myself," Natasha said.

If Jack and Marnie were disappointed, they hid it well, although Marnie finally said, "It would a lonely life out here alone."

"Where are you folks from?" I asked.

Jack pointed to his cap. "Atlanta. I think the Falcons may make it to the Superbowl this year."

"What brought you to Montana?"

"Oh, you know, just wanting to get away from city life," Marnie said. "I have a couple of granddaughters who're crazy about horses. They'll be up to visit at Thanksgiving."

Natasha wasn't one to miss an opportunity. "I'll be glad to sell you Dawson's horse. I don't know anything about him, but he's out there in the field."

"Sure, we'll buy him," Marnie said. "He'll be a good horse for Lexi and Jana."

She and Natasha discussed price for a few minutes. I don't know anything about horse prices, so I had no idea who got the best of the deal. Marnie said they'd be back over the next afternoon with a trailer to pick up the horse.

"We can have him in the barn for you," Natasha said. I presumed that meant she was volunteering me as horse-catcher.

Jack laughed. "You may need help," he warned. "Dawson always said ol' Secretariat looked fat and slow. Until you tried to catch him. That's why he'd named him after that race horse."

"Don't forget, we're interested in the ranch too," Marnie said before they headed back out to their pickup. "And we're looking forward to meeting Ivy."

"What did you think of them?" Natasha asked the minute the couple was out the door.

"Nothing in particular. They were considerably friendlier than the Buffalo Man."

"They're snoopy," she declared. "Didn't you see them checking out everything? I thought she was about to get down on her hands and knees and look under the sofa."

113

"They probably want to know all they can about the place. They said they're interested in buying it."

"Isn't everybody?" Natasha muttered. "But I'm not selling until I find the money, and I *will* live here if I have to."

I wished we had a computer out here. I'd like to do some checking on Jack and Marnie   Hawkins. It occurred to me after they were gone that they hadn't really answered my question about why they'd trekked all the way up here to Montana. They could have found a place "away from city life" a lot closer to Georgia than Montana.

***

Ivy got back just after the sun dropped behind the mountains to the west. BoBandy was already here, and Ivy was carrying Koop. She set him down on the floor. Well-traveled Koop wasn't disturbed to be in a strange new place, but Natasha now eyed both animals as if they were invading space creatures. Ivy did not apologize.

"Koop and BoBandy go wherever we go," she said with an air of take-it-or-leave-it. She pulled a small carton out of her purse. "I'll put your new toothbrush in the bathroom."

I wondered why Natasha didn't already have a toothbrush, but it didn't seem important enough to ask.

"Did you call my mother?" Natasha asked.

"Yes. She said she's thinking about coming up here herself. She's worried about you."

Natasha sat up so fast her cast clunked to the floor. "Oh, no!"

"I told her that wouldn't be necessary, that we were staying with you to help out."

"Thank you. Mom's a wonderful person, but. . ." Natasha let the sentence trail off, giving no clue what the "but" was about.

"I asked if she had any photos of Dawson, maybe their wedding or something. She said she didn't think so, but she'd look."

"She doesn't. I already looked."

"What about the will?" I asked. "Did she say if she'd sent it yet?"

"I asked about that too," Ivy said, "But—"

"I'm paying you two to find the skyjacking money, not dig into my personal life," Natasha snapped.

Touchy. It occurred to me that if we were less than trustworthy types, we could find the money, not tell Natasha, and just make off with it. Was she suspicious we might do exactly that?

"I'm fairly certain the skyjacking money isn't in that upstairs bedroom," I said. "I've been thinking Dawson must have had some place he kept important papers, like a will. Everybody has important papers. But there aren't any in that room. All the cans of survival food look like genuine cans, not the fake kind you can hide something in."

Ivy distributed items she'd brought. I carted my sleeping bag and other stuff upstairs. Ivy took her things to the bedroom she'd be sharing with Natasha. I helped her carry bags of groceries in and set them on the kitchen counter. Koop started an inspection of the house. BoBandy, still wearing the bandana around his neck, plopped down on a braided rug in front of the fireplace, acting as much at home as if he'd been doing it all his life. Maybe an omen about his future?

Ivy reported that Melanie had said not to worry about the wedding. She'd take care of remaining details, and they'd be out to see us in a day or two. Then Ivy headed for the kitchen saying something about making spaghetti for dinner. A few minutes later there was a nice scent of frying onions

115

emanating from the kitchen. I went to see if I could do anything to help. Ivy was standing at the pantry door.

"Have you *looked* in here?" she asked.

No, I hadn't, but some shock in her voice made me step up beside her and look now. I don't know what I expected, and I was a little startled, but not actually surprised. This was, after all, Dawson's pantry. The basics were there, in plentiful supply. At least a couple dozen cans of chili. Pork and beans. Canned peaches. Soup. Sugar, flour, cornmeal. A carton of canned tuna. A few delicacies unexpected in a Montana hermit's pantry: Smoked oysters. Pickled artichokes. Sardines in olive oil. He appeared to favor A&W root beer, although there were a couple of cans of Budweiser.

But what took up most of the space wasn't food or drink at all. It was ammunition. Boxes and boxes of it, of various calibers to fit his various guns apparently.

"It looks as if he was expecting an invasion," Ivy said.

Right. Dawson had enough ammunition here to take on a gang of outlaws – or start an uprising of his own. Or maybe he was prepared to protect that skyjacker's loot?

Ivy opened cans of tomato sauce and added mushrooms and hamburger she'd brought from town to the onions in the pan. I started water to boil for the pasta and made a salad. I think Natasha expected dinner served at the sofa, but, without asking what she wanted, I helped her get off the sofa and come to the table. We had a pleasant dinner, and Ivy got Natasha to talk a little about herself. She'd been married and divorced twice, each time taking back her original birth name. Her attitude toward marriage seemed to be "been there, done that," and she didn't have a high opinion of the institution.

After Ivy and I cleaned up the dishes, we tried listening to talk shows on the radio. We heard discussions about Bigfoot being an extra-terrestrial, how the government was putting us all in danger by promoting solar power, and how the nutritionists were leading us astray by encouraging broccoli consumption.

Ivy stood when the next caller came on. Apparently she'd had enough of opinionated callers for one night. "I'm going to see what's in the freezer that I can thaw out for dinner tomorrow night," she said as she headed for the kitchen.

It was still early for bed and I browsed through books for something to read. I'd just picked up a book about treasure in the Superstition Mountains in Arizona when Ivy yelled from the kitchen.

"Hey, I found something in here!"

Chapter 11

IVY

I was standing on a chair so I could reach farther into the freezer, and for a moment I tipped too far forward and was almost *in* the freezer. I was barely clinging to the chair by my tippy-toes, draped over the edge of the freezer with my derriere ignominiously pointed toward the ceiling. I grabbed what I was reaching for in the freezer, and Mac, gentleman that he is, pulled me back to safety without commenting on my undignified position.

"What did you find?"

"I don't know, but it isn't hamburger."

It was a big envelope tightly wrapped in plastic. I climbed down from the chair, unwound the bag and opened the bulky envelope.

"Hey, it's money!" Mac said. "Just what we're looking for!"

"What's going on?" Natasha yelled from the sofa. "What did you find?"

I carried the envelope over to the table and fanned the chilly greenbacks across the worn surface. Fives, tens, twenties. Lots of twenties. Twenties were what had been in the skyjacking payoff!

Big excitement for about sixty seconds until we both realized that, even though this was a nice bundle of money, there wasn't nearly enough for it to be the skyjacking loot. There was, in fact, after Mac counted it, a total of $2,973. Natasha, when we didn't answer her yelled questions, clomped in to look for herself. With a proprietary air, she also whipped the money into a stack and counted it herself.

"Where's the rest of it?" she demanded. She gave us each a suspicious look, as if I might be hiding more bucks in my bra or Mac in his socks. Then she clomped over to peer in the almost full freezer and her accusing tone changed to excited hope. "Maybe he separated it into bundles, and there are more hidden in here!"

She, taller than I am, didn't have to stand on a chair to reach into the freezer. She leaned her crutches against the freezer, bent her body over the edge, and started flinging packages of meat. They clunked against the freezer walls like . . . well, like packages of frozen meat hitting a wall. Mac leaned into the light over the kitchen sink and inspected a twenty dollar bill more closely.

"What are you looking for?" I asked.

"A series date." He pointed to tiny figures on the bill. "To see if it's old enough to be part of the skyjacking money."

Natasha came up out of the freezer, and we almost clunked heads trying to see what he was pointing at. Series 1969.

Natasha snatched the bill. "That date is before the skyjacking!" She grabbed more bills and looked at the dates on them too. "They're all old! This has to be part of the D.B.Cooper money!"

"But that money was all in twenties," I pointed out. "There are lots of fives and tens here. Ones too."

"Maybe—" Natasha searched for some explanation for the wrong-denomination bills but obviously couldn't think of any. Neither could I. For a moment I wondered, if we really found all the loot, if she would actually turn it in to the authorities. I turned my speculation into a blunt question.

"Are you going to turn this money in to the

authorities?" I asked.

Long moment of silence from Natasha. "I think we need . . . more information first."

Did that answer my question about what she'd do if we found all the skyjacking money? Not necessarily. But it made me wonder if she was trying to figure some way to hold onto the money and still write her D.B. Cooper book.

Mac opened his wallet and got out two twenties. We all peered at the dates. Both were series 2009. Not in existence when the skyjacking took place. "Bills wear out," he said. "Banks turn them in and the government replaces them."

I looked in my purse. One twenty, series 2013. Natasha's purse held two twenties, both series 2009.

So, even if the denominations of the bills didn't fit exactly with the skyjacking, the fact that Dawson had all these older bills in his freezer was both puzzling and intriguing.

"But if these, some of them anyway, are from the skyjacking, why were they in the freezer?" Mac sounded as if he were musing out loud. "We know Dawson couldn't have been spending skyjacking money because the serial numbers would lead back to him. So why would he separate these bills from the rest of the skyjacked money?"

Good question.

"But why would he have all these old bills if they aren't skyjacking money?" Natasha argued.

"Mac's son said Dawson was frugal. Maybe he's just held on to them for a long time," I suggested. "Maybe this is his life savings."

"Or maybe he got someone to trade the skyjacked twenties for money that could be spent," Mac suggested.

"Why would anyone do that?"

"He might offer part or all of the money for less than

120

it was worth. He could trade $100,000 of bills that could be identified for, say, $50,000 of bills that could be spent. Someone might figure that was a good investment, or had an idea about how to take them somewhere where they could be spent."

Sometimes Mac has a surprisingly ability to think like a crook.

Natasha muttered something about her leg hurting. She said she was going to take a pain pill and go to bed. I'd seen bottles of two different kinds of pain pills on her nightstand in the bedroom, along with enough vitamins and minerals to supercharge an elephant. She scooped up the stack of bills. Life savings or skyjacked loot, whatever it was, she obviously claimed it as hers now, although this partial discovery I'd made apparently didn't entitle us to even the seat covers off the pickup. She grabbed her crutches and clomped off to the bedroom, money in hand.

She didn't come out again, though I heard her in the bathroom a little later. No doubt trying out her new toothbrush. Mac and I made a more thorough search of the freezer, digging all the way to the bottom. No more stashes of old bills, but there were two frozen quiches among the packages of beef. A Marie Callendor and a Sara Lee. Was Dawson planning a comparison taste test? A complex man, Dawson Collier. Even mysterious. Maybe a little weird too. Because we also found a pair of frozen socks in the freezer.

Mac and I stayed up a while longer. I like to read my Bible in bed at night, just before sleep. It's a soothing end to the day. But no light showed under the bedroom door so in-bed reading was apparently out tonight. I read in the living room for a while, a couple of chapters in Matthew. I always find the last line in Matthew comforting and reassuring. "I am with you always, even to the end of the age." What more reassuring promise can we have than that? Mac was just starting the Old Testament book of Daniel now. When we finished reading, he took both Koop and BoBandy upstairs with him for the night.

I was tired but not particularly sleepy after I tiptoed into the bedroom and slipped into my sleeping bag on the cot. Finding money that might actually be part of the skyjacking was exciting, and I lay there trying to put myself into Dawson's brain. If I were Dawson, where would I put the big share of the money? House, barn, out in the woods somewhere? Maybe under the woodpile. In a cache high in the big cottonwood tree. In a waterproof container in the creek. Although such fanciful thinking wasn't the only source of my wakefulness. There was also the fact that, in spite of Natasha's slender good-looks, she had a snore like a sumo wrestler gargling gravel.

Maybe I do too, for all I know. I guess I'll soon find out. Mac will be close-by to hear me. Hey, that's more exciting than finding skyjacked money!

***

In the morning, both BoBandy and Koop went outside to explore, and I made hotcakes from Dawson's plentiful supply of pancake mix, along with eggs I'd brought from town. I supposed the wandering chickens might be laying eggs, but who knew where they put them?

Afterward we gathered in the living room to discuss plans. Or rather, Natasha, who'd perhaps always wanted to be a CEO with minions to order around, told us how she wanted the search conducted. The basement first. That's where Dawson had died, where she'd started searching before her accident, and the area she still thought most promising. I, following orders, headed down there. Mac had his horse-catching project to take care of first. He said he'd join me in

122

the basement as soon as he had the horse in the barn. Natasha stayed on the sofa flipping through a stack of books she'd had me gather up for her. BoBandy came in with a dirty face and paws. We were finding out that he liked to dig. Hey, maybe he'd dig up the skyjacking loot!

In the basement, I first sprayed vanilla-scented air freshener all around. A faint scent of death still lingered here – or maybe, when you know death happened somewhere, the scent lingers in your head even if it isn't real. When I'd emptied the spray can I sniffed the air again. Vanilla-scented death. Not really an improvement.

Well, get this done as fast as possible.

I pried open cans of old paint in case they were a clever disguise for hidden money. Nope. They were exactly what they looked like: cans of old paint, with a heavy scum on top.

I dug stuff out from under the stairs. I was hoping for a diary or journal describing the skyjacking, with maybe a diagram to the hidden money, but Dawson was apparently not a keeper of journals. Although he did have a box of old calendars. I inspected them for helpful clues, but they had not so much as a scribble on them. I guess he'd kept them for the pictures. Alaska mountains. Birds of Alaska. Alaska natives.

A box held old mayonnaise jars, reasonably clean. Old cottage cheese cartons filled another box. A baseball bat. I took time to take that upstairs and stash it under my cot. Never know when a baseball bat might come in handy. A stack of National Geographic magazines. A couple more boxes of paperback books. I hauled the books upstairs so Natasha could go through them. Mac had said she'd found a twenty-dollar bill in one book, and she was apparently determined to examine each and every book in the house for more hidden money.

I dragged out the two suitcases remaining under the stairs. Although they were surprisingly expensive looking, I didn't hold much hope of finding anything in them. From what we'd learned on the internet, D.B. Cooper's only luggage on the plane had been that bomb-filled briefcase. There had since been speculation that it wasn't even a real bomb, just a bunch of wires rigged to look like one. No briefcase here, with or without a bomb.

The suitcases were filled with old clothes that smelled musty enough to have been in the basement since Custer had his unpleasant encounter with the Indians here in Montana. The clothes were also of a style Dawson surely hadn't needed here on the ranch, and I wondered if they indicated some different life in his past. White shirts, an outdated blue suit, several ties, dressy dark socks, black shoes. No stash of money hidden within the musty folds. But then, down at the bottom, another suit. Black. I felt a skitter of excitement. D.B. Cooper had worn a black suit when he skyjacked the plane! I burrowed among the ties I'd tossed aside. Yes, a black one!

I laid the suit on top a layer of National Geographics, added a white shirt and black tie, and there it was. A perfect D.B. Cooper costume.

I carried everything upstairs to show Natasha. I was just laying my show-and-tell out on the floor when Mac came in. Stomped in, actually. He stood there dripping on the living room floor, looking like something just risen from the Black Lagoon. Not Mac's usual composed, unflappable look.

But, even red-faced, wet from dripping hair to squishy shoes, and with several strands of green slime decorating his beard, I had a moment of admiration. Mac is a very attractive man.

However, I could see figurative if not actual steam

rising from his ears and prudently stayed silent, but Natasha, with a hint of exasperation, asked, "What happened to you?"

"I fell in the creek trying to catch the horse."

"Did you bring him into the barn?"

No concern about Mac's physical state after a dunk in the creek, I noted.

"It's going to take fourteen people and a very large net to catch that horse," Mac grumbled. He scraped a strand of green slime off his beard. He tried to fling it off his fingers, but it hung there like a prop from a low-budget horror film. "The last I saw, he was headed for the hills at the speed of a low-flying jet."

Maybe ranch life wasn't for us. Or maybe we'd do better with one of those tough little all-terrain vehicles than a horse.

Mac shook his pants leg, sending a wet spatter toward my D.B.Cooper floor display. "I'm going to shower and change clothes," he said and stomped up the stairs.

And then stomped right back down again, because the only shower was down here, of course He gave the D.B. Cooper costume another glance as he clomped by. "Needs sunglasses," he muttered.

I went back to the basement and rummaged through the suitcases again. No sunglasses. I fixed lunch while Mac showered. Looking out the window, I spotted Secretariat now grazing peacefully down near the creek with the cattle. He did indeed look fat and lazy. Which probably means only that there is much you can't tell by surface appearance.

Jack and Marnie Hawkins arrived right after we finished lunch. They had a beat-up looking horse trailer behind their pickup. Marnie had brought a homemade cherry pie, and they also had a horse-catching plan, no net required. The green pasture land was divided into smaller sections by

125

barbed wire fences, with wire gates between. The gates were all open now. The horse had raced through the openings when Mac was trying to catch him, but he was back now, grazing peacefully. Jack went out and closed the closest gate, so the horse couldn't go far, then all four of us circled out beyond him, me keeping a careful eye on the creek. Green slime is not my color. The horse did a lot of racing around, even kicking up his heels a few times, but we slowly herded him toward a corner near the barn. When we finally had him surrounded, he stood peacefully while I fed him a carrot and Marnie put a halter on his head. I'm no expert on horse expressions, but I thought his was quite self-satisfied looking, that even though he'd finally been caught, he'd had a romping good time.

The horse loaded into the trailer without a problem, and I followed when Marnie went inside to pay Natasha with cash in hand. Marnie said they'd be back over in a day or two to see if we needed help with anything.

Natasha looked at the cash after the Hawkins couple left. "They seem nice enough," she said. Somewhat grudgingly.

This time it was my turn to be skeptical of the friendly Hawkins couple. Maybe, like Secretariat, they weren't exactly what they appeared to be on the surface?

Yeah, right. On the surface, they were an older, amiable couple wanting a horse for the grandchildren. And underneath they were – what? Shysters buying valuable horses at bargain prices from naïve sellers who didn't know better? Rich aristocrats disguising themselves with an old pickup and battered horse trailer? Scoundrels bringing tainted cherry pies for nefarious purposes?

Mac wanted a piece of pie right away. So did Natasha. So I shrugged and had one too. It was great pie, nothing tainted or nefarious about it. And I figured Secretariat had found himself a good home with nothing to do but haul granddaughters around a couple times a year.

We probably should have whipped right back into search mode, but after the pie it seemed like time for a nap. Mac went upstairs for his, Natasha went to her bedroom, and I settled into the old lounge chair with Koop on my lap. But I didn't nap. In spite of the "niceness" of Jack and Marnie Hawkins, I had a something-isn't-quite-right feeling about them. I tried to pin it down. Suspicious acting? No. Overly pushy about buying Dawson's ranch? No. Shifty eyes? No, they were nice people, open and friendly. *Too* nice? Well, that was a ridiculous complaint about anyone. And Marnie made great pie too.

After naptime, Mac and I went back to the basement. Mac found an ax and whacked the shelving debris into smaller pieces as kindling for building a winter fire in the furnace. We checked every inch of dirt floor and two unfinished walls, but they didn't look as if they'd been touched since the last ice age. Nothing buried there. It was possible, of course, that Dawson had hidden the money in a dirt wall and built the concrete block wall right over it. But if that was the case, we figured the money was destined to remain unfound. We were now done with the basement and could move on to other areas.

In the excitement of finding money in the freezer the night before, I'd forgotten to thaw anything out for dinner today, so I heated a couple cans of the plentiful chili. I also made cornbread. No complaints. After opening several unmarked packages from the freezer, I found steak and put it in the refrigerator to thaw for tomorrow night.

Afterward, when it was fully dark, Mac and I took a walk. A beautiful night. The moon wasn't up yet and stars crowded the dark expanse of sky. Mac and I had talked about this before. *How come so many stars, Lord?* It's one of the questions I intend to ask him when I come into his presence. Along with, did you really have to make mosquitoes? And parsnips were kind of a waste of time too. But butterflies are great!

Clouds covered the western half of the sky now, but starshine in the remaining clear sky turned the creek into a silvery pathway and the hillsides into enchanted forests. The cattle were peaceful lumps bedded down in the pasture. The evening air smelled fresh and clean, with a hint of rain. An owl hooted softly somewhere in the hillside trees. Mac and I held hands as we walked beyond the barn. Romantic, yet—

"Hey, what's that light over there at the bottom of the cliffs?" I asked.

Mac stopped to watch. "Must be a vehicle. It's moving. And the local wildlife doesn't tend to come equipped with headlights."

We stood and watched the light as it moved slowly but steadily along the base of the far cliffs.

"Is that on the ranch?"

"I think Dan said something about the property line being about where the cliffs are, so it could be."

"Maybe it's a back way into the ranch?"

"We'll see if the light comes this direction."

But a moment later the light disappeared. Had the vehicle gone behind brush or trees, or had the headlights been turned off, maybe for a covert trip into Dawson's place? We watched several more minutes, but the light never reappeared.

It was no big deal. There were old, little-used side roads all over the countryside. Tracks left by hunters, campers, fence-fixers. No reason to think someone was sneaking into the ranch. Though odd for a vehicle to be way out there at this time of night, wasn't it?

"Could it be the road into another ranch?" I asked.

"I suppose. But I think we should check it out."

I thought so too.

I woke sometime in the night. A finely-honed sense of something not quite right? Some sixth sense of danger sneaking up on us? An interior vibration of impending doom?

No, I woke because Natasha was in snoring mode again, loud enough to shake the cot I was sleeping on. I finally got up and put a hand on her arm. She immediately woke and said she had to go to the bathroom. So I got her crutches and then helped her back into bed after her journey to the bathroom.

She didn't start snoring again, but by then I was wide awake. I put on a robe and slippers and went out to the living room thinking I'd read for a while. But now I really did have an odd feeling of apprehension. I opened the back door and went out on the porch. Rain was falling now, wind blowing. The door to the basement set into the porch floor squeaked when I stepped on it. It made me think, if that door were open, how easy it would be to accidentally plunge into the open hole in the dark. Could Dawson have done that? It would also be easy for someone to shove someone else down the open hole. No light over by the cliffs now, but they loomed larger, somehow menacing as they merged with the gloom of clouds. The windmill crouched behind the barn as if poised for attack.

A windmill poised for attack? *Oh, c'mon, Ivy.* No, not poised. But it was slightly tilted, not quite straight up and down. Maybe that was why it looked kind of threatening.

A noise.

I stiffened. Not a bird or animal or breeze-in-the-trees

type noise. Something mechanical? Kind of an r-r-r-r-r noise. Maybe the sound of the windmill turning in the wind Maybe a car up on the road? Sound carried a long way in the silence of the night here.

I recognized those thoughts for what they were. Hopeful.

Because the sound didn't come from up on the road. It was much closer. Down toward the barn and windmill. It came again. R-r-r-r-r. But that was no windmill sound.

I stepped off the porch and moved toward the barn—

And then I turned and headed back to the house. The rain was falling more heavily now, but that wasn't the reason I turned back. The reason was purely a sensible one. No way was I going to the barn alone in the middle of the night. Doing that was like the dumb heroine traipsing off to encounter the multi-armed alien or the murderous villain wielding chainsaw or raygun. The TSTL—Too Stupid To Live—woman. No way.

I could wake Mac— No, I didn't want him encountering some intruder brandishing weapons, either.

I was probably imagining noises anyway. Or enlarging some simple night noise to ominous proportions. The night makes noises, you know, noises that aren't present in daylight. Often they aren't identifiable. Though they don't usually sound like a mechanical growl. . .

Never mind.

I went back inside, encountered Koop wandering around, and took him back to the sleeping bag with me. I didn't hear any more noises. I settled down to sleep. I closed my eyes.

They popped open. I forced them shut. Open again. Like a window shade flying upward.

130

I was about as sleepy as a burglar waiting for the right hour to burgle. That curiosity gene shot questions into my brain like some mental machine gun. Was someone down at the barn? Were the lights we'd seen earlier from his vehicle? Why was he here? What was he doing?

Maybe I could go just part way down to the barn. Or maybe a *little* farther, just far enough to peek around the corner of the barn and see. . .

No. Foolish. Dangerous. I'd had the good sense to turn around once; don't mess up now.

But I've done dangerous things before and come out fine, I reasoned. I once spent numerous nights waiting for a very bad guy to show up at a cemetery. And this wasn't necessarily dangerous. Maybe it was more like *opportunity.*

Surely it wouldn't hurt just to sneak down that way. Not to confront an intruder. No way. But if I could just get a peek at him. . .

I was, I realized, fighting a losing battle with the curiosity gene.

I grabbed my jeans from the bottom of the cot, tugged them over my pajamas, and grabbed a jacket. I left Koop snuggled in the sleeping bag and snuck out the back way. Outside, I planned my route. Run to the big cottonwood where Dawson's pickup and tractor were parked, then to the cover of the pump house. On to a bush—okay, it was a little small. It wouldn't conceal anything bigger than a jackrabbit. But, with night and rain, it was surely too dark for anyone to see me.

I made my run to the cottonwood and paused to listen. More noises at the barn?

No, but I could see a faint light now. It bounced and jiggled, shooting beams upward, puzzling me until I realized what it was. Headlights, headed away from the barn, the beam bouncing up and down over the uneven landscape.

I was disappointed. No point in sneaking down to the barn now. No peek at the intruder possible.

Then I had to smile. Also no murderous encounter with a chainsaw/raygun-wielding /multi-armed intruder. The Lord was looking out for me again, saving me from my curiosity.

Thank you, Lord.

***

A drizzle was still falling in the morning. We began the day's search in the second bedroom upstairs. I intended to tell Mac about last night, of course, but I wanted to check it out first to make sure my imagination hadn't done some stereotyped woman-thing and invented scary noises and lights.

In the second bedroom, there was no bed, just more stuff. Didn't Dawson ever throw a magazine away? *Montana Rancher. Alaska Magazine. Country Cooking.* Old blankets. Snowshoes. It seemed as if snowshoes should come in pairs, but there were three of them here. You don't see too many three-legged snowshoers hiking around. Not even a two-legged one carrying a spare. We also found a metal detector leaning against the far wall. I don't know anything about metal detectors, of course, but Mac did.

He picked it up and examined it. "Top of the line model."

Again, Dawson had spent more money than seemed likely for a man living on a pension income.

Mac tinkered with the detector for a minute, adjusted some dials, and then moved the round plate at the bottom across the floor. Where it screeched as if it had just found the Treasure of Sierra Madre.

"Nails in the flooring," Mac explained. "But it might

132

be useful when we're looking outside."

Yeah, right. How long would it take to cover 300 acres with that thing?

Then we found something behind a tall box of plastic milk jugs that eclipsed the metal detector. It was a small door opening into the attic. Nailed shut!

Full-blown excitement hit me. The perfect place to hide a briefcase full of twenty-dollar bills!

Mac went downstairs for a hammer, but even then it took a good ten minutes to pry the door open. Every nail screeched in protest. The door made a sharp *cr-ack*! when a dry old board split. I held my breath as Mac finally inched the door open, the bottom scraping the floor. And then there it was, an opening into a dark space full of—

Insulation. A half dozen big rolls of it, tan backing on pink fiberglass. Exactly the color my friend Magnolia sometimes tints her hair. Apparently Dawson had plans to insulate the attic, but had never gotten around to doing it. Had, in fact, nailed the door shut. Protecting himself from some irresistible urge to insulate?

After that letdown, Mac declared it was time for a break. The drizzle had stopped, so while the coffee perked in an old-fashioned enameled pot on the stove, I took a little walk. BoBandy accompanied me, stopping to dig occasionally. Not by accident, I took my walk around to the back side of the barn. Tire tracks! The rain had washed most of them away, but in low spots some were dug in deeper, as if the vehicle had come close to getting stuck. Maybe the r-r-r-r-r sound I'd heard?

I leaned over and studied the indentations. Some TV sleuth could probably tell you the tracks were made by a Chevy Silverado pickup between 1:00 and 2:00 last night, and the lone occupant was a male weighing 170-180 pounds who

133

smoked Marlboros and had a recent fight with his girlfriend.

Unfortunately, I couldn't tell anything more than that some kind of vehicle had been here and left two sets of tracks, apparently one coming and one going, though I couldn't tell which was which. Both were headed in the direction of the far cliffs. There was one cigarette butt ground into the dirt, brand unidentifiable. Also a few indentations that might have been footprints left by cowboy boots.

So now all we had to do was scour the countryside for a smoker in muddy cowboy boots, driving a mud-spattered vehicle. Which might take in half the county population.

But this proved my imagination hadn't been playing games last night. Someone had been here at the barn, coming in by some route along the cliffs, leaving the same way.

Of course it could have been an innocent visit. Lost tourist. Young lovers. Homeless person looking for a place to spend the night. Another interested buyer doing research on the property.

Yeah, right. And I'm a double for Lady Gaga. You can hardly tell us apart.

This was someone who'd been here *looking* for something.

I headed back to the house to get Mac. BoBandy brought me an old glove he'd dug up.

And hey, you know what? Those chickens are laying eggs, because I found a lovely brown egg hidden in a grassy nest alongside the barn.

Chapter 12

MAC

Ivy came in through the back door carrying an egg as if it were at least as valuable as the skyjacking money. "Look what I found!" That's one of the many things I love about Ivy. She can get excited about something like an egg.

"Where'd that come from?"

"I found it down by the barn. Of course I don't know how long it's been there, but we can test to see if it's still good."

"Something about putting the egg in water to see if it floats. Isn't that how you do it?"

Ivy was already getting a bowl out of the cupboard and filling it with water. She set the egg gently in the bottom of the bowl, and we watched expectantly. This egg shot to the surface as if it might be planning a launch into orbit.

"What does that mean?" I asked.

Ivy poked the egg with a finger. It bounced merrily. "I guess that's a problem with the test. You have to know, if the egg floats, does that mean it's good or bad?"

The usual yell from the living room. "What's going on?"

"We're taking an egg break," Ivy called back. An answer that would have puzzled me if it were yelled at me, but it silenced Natasha, at least temporarily.

"We need the internet," I said. It would take about ten seconds on the internet to find out if a good egg floated or sank.

"But we don't have the internet," Ivy pointed out. "So we'll just have to go low-tech and crack it."

Ivy got a smaller dish and carefully cracked the egg open. The blast of sulphurish smell made us both step back. I haven't smelled a rotten egg in years, but it's a scent you don't forget. The yolk and white were muddled into a murky mess.

Ivy waved a hand in front of her face. "Now we know," she said. "A floating egg is not a good egg."

And what I knew was that if we lived out here, we'd definitely have to get internet service some way. There were all kinds of things I didn't know about ranch living and might need to look up. How to manage a wood-burning furnace. The windmill. Policing chicken activity concerning a proper area in which to lay eggs. But lack of internet service was not an insurmountable problem, of course. There were satellite-based systems.

I played noble guy and gallantly carried the smelly egg outside and disposed of it well away from the house. The hens clucked companionably around me. I suggested they form a committee and decide on an appropriate area for egg laying. Natasha was in the kitchen when I returned, probably suspecting we were concealing more new-found money from her. I almost assured her no money had been hidden inside the rotten egg, but that sounded a little snarky and I managed not to do it.

Natasha went back to her throne . . . pardon, I mean, her sofa . . . and Ivy said she wanted to show me something. She led me outside and down to the back side of the barn. BoBandy bounded ahead. Chickens and Koop trailed behind. The little parade gave me an unexpected Farmer MacPherson feeling. If we lived here, maybe I'd have to get a pair of bib overalls. The drizzle was giving way to a glorious fall day, the only sound the creaking of the old windmill.

Ivy pointed to tire ruts in the soft ground behind the barn, deep enough that they were still visible in spite of the rain. "I thought I heard something here in the middle of the night. Maybe I should have waked you so we could have checked it out then. We might have caught whoever was snooping around."

I wasn't sure creeping up on an intruder in the middle of the night was a great idea. I was especially glad Ivy hadn't taken it upon herself to investigate alone. Ivy isn't a reckless or foolhardy type woman, but she does have that powerful curiosity gene, and anyone sneaking around here in the middle of the night was probably armed. BoBandy nosed around boot prints in the damp dirt, then dug into one energetically. Was he memorizing the scent for future use? Great! Maybe we had ourselves a tracking dog.

Or maybe not. Because what his nose took him to was an oversized black bug. A chicken disposed of the bug. The food chain in action.

"Maybe BoBandy will dig up the money," Ivy suggested. "Do you think the fact that someone was here means that person knows about the skyjacking money?"

"It seems likely whoever it was came with the idea of looking for something."

"Natasha said the house was searched while she was gone. With us here, they couldn't come back and search the barn in daylight, so it looks as if they came back at night to do it."

"I'll go get the pickup and try to follow the tracks," I said. If I did track down a killer, I didn't want Ivy along and in danger. "You can look around in the barn and—"

I should have known that idea would sink like the rotten egg didn't.

"I'll wait here while you get the pickup. Then we can

137

follow the tracks together. Natasha said we were, how did she put it? Welded at the hip, I believe." She gave me her little Ivy smile, and I knew there was no way she was not coming along. Ivy may be disguised as a Little Old Lady, an invisible LOL as she sometimes puts it, but underneath, she has a backbone of steel and she's tough and determined as an armored tank. She was inspecting a cigarette butt when I started back to the house.

At the house I told Natasha we were going to take a drive around the back side of the ranch. She asked for a glass of water. And a fresh box of Kleenex. Also something to put around her shoulders. I finally got past her before she decided she needed a four-course meal and/or her hair done, and headed out the front door to the pickup. Along the way I grabbed one of the guns still left in the bucket and stuffed it behind the seat of the pickup. It was mostly window dressing because I don't know that much about guns. Although I figured it would make for a good bluff. Who wants to tangle with an old geezer brandishing a gun?

At the barn, Ivy slid into the pickup cab, BoBandy right with her. He took what he'd apparently decided was his rightful place in the world, between us on the bench seat. I doubt I could have followed just the vehicle tracks on the much harder ground out here, but this was actually a semi-road. Dawson must have used it when he needed to get to the back side of the ranch. It circled around outside the fenced-in, green pasture land watered by the creek.

We saw no more signs that anyone had been here. No drips of oil on the dirt, nothing caught on the sagebrush alongside the tracks, no cigarette butts tossed away. The semi-road led over rocks, down into gullies, up the other side. We didn't talk much. Couldn't, bouncing along as if we were a couple of balls inside a Bingo machine.

I wanted to go to the cliffs, but we didn't make it that far. The little Toyota pickup is tough and agile, but we came to one steep gully that I knew we'd never make it across, though whatever vehicle had been here earlier had churned deep ruts up the far side. It no doubt had four-wheel-drive, which the Toyota did not. We were about halfway to the cliffs when we had to back up and turn around.

I had mixed feelings about giving up. I wanted to know who'd been snooping around, but I still had to assume that whoever the intruder was, he was armed. And, unlike me, probably knew how to use whatever he was armed with.

But it made an interesting drive on a beautiful fall day. Some trees were turning color on the hillsides, nuggets of gold glowing among the darker evergreens. I took the gun back to the bucket in the house. After lunch we went back down to the barn to start searching inside. It was a larger building than I'd realized, shadowy inside, but with a sweet, summer-sunshine scent from baled hay stacked in the back half. Right by the door we found a sack of chicken feed in a big metal trash can. I tossed feed to the chickens with an old coffee can that was also in the trash can, which was probably what they had in mind when they followed us around.

Also near the door was one of those tough, four-wheeler ATVs, a little worse for wear from Dawson's hard use, but probably expensive when new. Back near the hay was a newer, sleek-looking snowmobile, which I guessed might mean the road wasn't always kept plowed open in winter. But, as with the pickup and tractor, I had to wonder—how was Dawson paying for this expensive stuff? His Social Security couldn't have been much. Dan had said Dawson had never had a job off the ranch and he'd lived here a long time. That other pension must bring in big bucks. Where was it from?

139

"One of those must be what Natasha fell on."

Ivy pointed to a piece of machinery with several rows of sharp metal disks. There was also a flattish, many-toothed piece of machinery, and another with kind of an upright, movable blade with big teeth. More stuff I'd have to learn how to use. Dawson apparently took good care of his machinery, keeping it inside like this. Along a far wall were several individual stalls and a tall stack of old feed sacks. More interesting was a small room built into a back corner of the barn, next to the baled hay. Especially interesting because it was guarded by a padlock of territorial prison size.

I inspected the padlock. Scratches covered the shackle part. Some marks were even deeper than scratches. Cuts? As if someone had tried to cut the lock open? A big enough bolt cutter would do it. So did that mean this intruder intended to return with bigger and better equipment?

"There must be a key to the padlock somewhere," Ivy said.

We went back to the house and looked at what seemed obvious key places. There were several hooks by the back door, but only some old jackets and a holster, no keys, hung there. No keys in the kitchen drawers. I even checked down in the basement, but no keys there, either. It wasn't until the next day, at breakfast, that Ivy thought of something else.

"We were down at the barn yesterday, and there's a locked room in there. We can't find the key," she said to Natasha. "Do you have any idea where it could be?"

"I found a key ring under a jacket by the back door the first night I stayed here. There's a bunch of keys on it. Dawson apparently liked to keep everything locked up tight. I put them in my purse for safe-keeping."

Sometimes big problems have simple solutions.

140

Ivy got Natasha's purse for her, and she handed me a metal ring jangling with keys. I wondered what they were all for. It wouldn't take that many for what I'd seen so far. But maybe Dawson was like me about keys. I have keys on my chain that I have no idea what they might open, but I don't throw them away because. . . Well, you don't throw away a key because you never know what it might unlock someday. Hmm. That sounds like Ivy logic. Which is good enough for me.

We took the keys down to the barn. Ivy bounced on her toes with anticipation as I tried several keys and finally found one that fit into the padlock. I unfastened the padlock and pulled the door open. No ominous Inner Sanctum type squeal to the door, but it still felt kind of ominous because the room beyond was so dark. I felt around for a light switch before remembering Natasha had said there was no electricity here at the barn. But Ivy found a string, pulled it, and a light came on.

"Battery powered," she pointed out.

With a light on, we inspected the room, about 10 x 12. I didn't really expect a container labeled "skyjacking money," but I wouldn't have been surprised by more guns and ammunition, maybe even a stash of dynamite. I suspected Dawson was a man who'd know how to use dynamite. But this was just an ordinary space that I think would be called a tack room. A saddle, engraved and expensive looking but covered with a layer of dust, sat on a wooden stand. Several bridles and halters hung on the wall, plus a set of fancy spurs inlaid with engraved silver. Also a couple of ropes that looked like the lariats cowboys use, plus another that was just old rope. Insecticides, pesticides, and veterinary-type stuff covered a long shelf, and various tools and a couple of stained and battered old jackets hung from

141

nails above the shelf. A keg of horseshoes stood by the door, along with nails and tools I thought were used for horseshoeing. Did Dawson do his own horseshoeing? An impressive skill, but none of this seemed to justify that industrial-strength padlock

We moved things around and searched the floor carefully, looking for a trap door to something hidden underneath, but it was just a floor. The ceiling was also just a ceiling, no hidden door to anywhere. Helpful BoBandy stirred up a few mice and spiders. Koop found himself a comfortable nest in the hay. He can catch mice if he wants to, but he usually doesn't want to.

Outside the room, I tried several keys on the ATV, and one of them worked. I've ridden a four-wheeler a few times, but that was years ago. I sat on the machine for several minutes, figuring out the gears and brake. Hey, I could use this thing! It would be much better for getting around the ranch than the Toyota. Ivy slid onto the seat right behind me.

"I'm not sure it's meant to hold two," I said.

"I guess we'll just have to see, won't we?" she said cheerfully. "This looks like fun."

Ivy is never going to be left behind.

We decided to give up the search for today. Tomorrow we'd give the dirt floor of the barn a thorough inspection to see if anything may have been buried there. And maybe try a ride on the ATV.

Chapter 13

IVY

I cooked the steak and baked potatoes for dinner. Natasha hadn't been totally idle. She'd gone through an impressive number of books today, no twenty-dollar bill in any of them. She'd tossed what she did find tucked into the books on the coffee table, probably items Dawson had used as bookmarks at various times. An electric bill. A recipe for Red Lobster's cheese biscuits. Several business cards, one from someone in the county assessor's office and several from farm equipment and vehicle salesmen. And one from an attorney in Bozeman. Had Natasha noticed that one? I was just about to point it out to her when a vehicle pulled up out front.

"Hey, Dan and Melanie are here," Mac said. "Elle too!"

We went out to meet them at the gate, with hugs all around.

"You guys getting along okay out here?" Dan asked.

We hadn't told them the real purpose of our stay at the ranch. Now a line creased between Mac's eyebrows. I knew he didn't like being less than straightforward with his son, but we had promised to keep our search confidential for now.

"Sure, we're doing fine," Mac finally said. "Enjoying country life."

"Some good news. Deputy Cargill caught the kid who vandalized the lockers at school. The bad news is, it's going to take a bundle of money to repair the lockers."

"More good news, the water system has gone wonky again," Elle said. "No school tomorrow!"

"That is *not* good news," Melanie scolded lightly.

Elle just grinned and raced around back with BoBandy.

"Hey, we found kind of an old road out behind the barn," Mac said to Dan. "Looks like it heads toward the cliffs. You know anything about it?"

"Yeah. Actually it's a back way into the ranch. Comes out over on the highway."

Melanie touched my arm. "Could I talk to you for a minute? I'm afraid I have some other bad news."

We moved over by the rose bushes so we could talk privately while Mac and Dan went on into the house. Koop disappeared under the rose bushes.

"Trudy called yesterday," Melanie said. "She's leaving for Las Vegas today and doesn't know when she'll be back. So she isn't going to be able to make your dress."

I was disappointed, of course, but this wasn't a true disaster. I could go into Double Wells and buy a ready-made wedding gown. "Why's she going to Vegas?"

"Her ex-husband called. He told her he'd made a big mistake and wants to get back together. Which worries me. Ward is kind of—" Melanie hesitated and finally came up with, "flaky."

I was surprised. Melanie tends to see the best in everybody. *Flaky* isn't a strong condemnation, but it's stronger than Melanie usually uses.

"I'm afraid he may have run out of money and just be looking to con some out of Trudy. I kind of suggested that to her, but she insists he's changed."

I didn't know what to say about Trudy or her flaky husband, so I murmured, "I hope it all works out for the

144

best."

"I feel so terrible about this," Melanie said. "Going to Trudy was my idea. I thought she'd make a great dress for you, and it would help her out too. But now—"

"No need to feel bad about it." I patted her arm. "I'll just go over to Double Wells and buy a dress."

"Actually, I've been thinking. . . I still have my mother's wedding dress stored away in the attic. It's out of style, of course, but it's a beautiful old dress. I'd have worn it when Dan and I got married, but I couldn't get into it. Mom was petite, like you, and if you'd like to wear it, I could get it out and—"

"Oh, Melanie, that's so sweet and generous of you, but—"

"It is, well, second-hand, of course. Actually it was second-hand when my mother got it. She couldn't afford a new one." Melanie broke off, eyebrows scrunched into an anxious expression, as if afraid she may have insulted me with the offer.

That wasn't why I'd hesitated at all. "Melanie, the dress isn't 'second-hand.' It's an heirloom! I'd be afraid I'd trip and rip it, or spill barbecue sauce on it, or—"

"Better it has a barbecue stain than it just crumbles and falls apart with old age and disuse," Melanie declared. "My folks had a wonderful marriage," she added, as if that might be a special recommendation for the dress. "I'd really like you to wear it."

I didn't hesitate any further. "I'd love to wear it," I said.

Melanie said she'd get the dress out of the attic, and next time I came to town I could try it on. Then we went inside where Mac and Dan were looking at the guns in the bucket. Dan set one back and pulled out another one. The

145

first thing he did was check to see if it was loaded. It was.

"You know, these guns really shouldn't be left out here loaded like this. It's not a safe way to handle guns—"

"I want them loaded," Natasha snapped.

Dan frowned, but he didn't unload the gun. "I think you'd be better off with this shotgun than the rifle," he said to Mac. "A rifle is better for distance, of course. Dawson could probably pick a tin can off a fencepost at a hundred yards with that rifle. But a shotgun is great for up close. You don't need any aiming expertise. Just point and shoot. This twenty-gauge shouldn't have much of a kick."

Apparently Mac had decided he needed to know how to use some of Dawson's arsenal. I also had to wonder – if Dawson had been carrying a gun that day he fell down the stairs, would he still be alive? Did the fact that he wasn't carrying a gun mean whoever pushed him was someone he wasn't suspicious of? Although, from what Dan had said, Dawson was suspicious of everyone and had somehow just been caught off guard.

I had at some point, I realized, jumped over any moat of doubt about Dawson's death. He hadn't slipped and fallen; he'd been pushed.

I introduced Natasha and Melanie. Natasha had a glowery, scrunched-eyebrow look, as if she suspected we'd told them everything about D.B.Cooper and we were all plotting against her now.

Before Mac and Dan headed out with the shotgun so Dan could give Mac some shooting instructions, Dan told Natasha that Deputy Cargill had earlier said that Dawson's body had been cremated, and she could pick up his ashes any time. Natasha thanked him but gave no indication when she might do that. Mac and Dan clunked around in the pantry for several minutes, apparently loading up on more ammunition.

Melanie wisely didn't question Natasha about her past or her relationship with Dawson, subjects on which Natasha tended to get all prickly. Instead, in her usual friendly, chatty way, she just talked about the wedding. She'd been calling to invite people, and practically everyone said they wouldn't miss it. She'd lined up music for the barbecue reception, plus extra tables, and she'd ordered extra flowers for Magnolia.

Elle came in, apparently sent inside while Dan and Mac target practiced with the gun. She immediately asked about Secretariat, and Natasha said she'd sold the horse to the neighbors at the Rocking R.

Elle looked disappointed. "Dawson sometimes let me ride him when I came out with Dad."

"They bought him for their grandchildren to ride," I explained.

"Oh. That's nice, then. Where do they live? They don't go to school here."

"Somewhere down south. Atlanta, I think. But they're coming to visit over Thanksgiving."

"Atlanta, Georgia?" Elle sounded interested, which surprised me. What did Elle know about Atlanta?

Quite a bit, as it turned out. The grandparents of her friend Dakota, who had died of leukemia, lived near Atlanta, and Dakota's folks had taken her to visit them before she got too ill to go anywhere.

"They went to a place called Six Flags over Georgia, with big roller coasters and water slides, and she said it was awesome. And to an aquarium and a zoo, and she ate boiled peanuts. Boiled peanuts sound yucky, don't you think?" Elle wrinkled her nose. "But she said they were really good." She swallowed, the hurt of loss still there even as she chattered about her friend. Intermittent booms from the shotgun

147

punctuated her words. "I'm glad she got to do all that."

I wanted to ask Elle what she'd found on the internet about drugs that might induce wooziness or lack of balance, but I didn't want to do it in front of Natasha. Natasha had apparently accepted the official determination that Dawson's death was an accident, and I didn't want to disturb her with suspicions of murder. Although I also hadn't completely dismissed her as a suspect, and I didn't want to give her any hint of that. Then Elle gave us a reason to leave the living room.

"Oh, I found some eggs," she said. "They're out on the back porch. But we probably ought to test to see if they're still good before you use them."

"You know how to do that?"

"Sure. You put them in water, and if they stay at the bottom, they're good, but if they float, they're not. Everybody knows that."

"Of course," I murmured. "Everybody knows that."

We left Melanie and Natasha talking about Melanie's plans to entertain the kids at the barbecue with her clown act, and headed for the back porch. More booms blasted from the direction of the barn. I expected to see maybe a couple of eggs, but Elle had gathered a whole bucket of them, at least a couple dozen. Didn't Dawson ever gather the eggs the hens provided for him?

"Where did you find all these?"

"Here and there. A lot of them out by the woodpile." Elle moved over closer to me and lowered her voice. "I was thinking, maybe I could stay out here with you and Grandpa for a couple days. Since school is closed tomorrow anyway."

I hesitated. Having Elle here would be fun, but was her staying here a good idea, with an unknown intruder sneaking in by a back route and snooping around?

148

I dodged a direct answer. "Would your folks let you?"

Without answering that question, Elle, in an even more conspiratorial whisper, added, "Maybe I can help with, you know, whatever it is you're doing here."

I was startled. Eleven years old, and she'd figured out we were doing something here that we weren't telling anyone about? "What do you think we're doing?" I asked cautiously.

"Trying to figure out who pushed Dawson down the stairs." She squinted at me. "And something else too. I haven't figured out what yet, but—"

"We're taking care of Natasha! You can see she can't get around very well with that cast on her leg."

"Okay, you don't have to tell me. But maybe I can help anyway."

Maybe she could. Anyone who could find two dozen eggs might well be able to find a skyjacker's hidden stash. Definitely some budding sleuth talents. But still, was it safe for her here?

"When you looked on the internet, did you find anything about medications or drugs that might have made Dawson woozy enough to lose his balance on the stairs?"

Now she was the one to look startled. "How'd you know I did that?"

I just smiled at her, and after a moment she grinned back. Two sleuths in a pod.

"So, what did you find out?"

"I found out there are all kinds of bad drugs someone might have given him to make him woozy. Or even kill him. But there are good medicines he might have taken himself that could have made him dizzy or woozy too. Especially if he accidentally took . . . or someone gave him . . . too big a dose. Have you found any medicine bottles here?"

"No, nothing." I dropped the subject. I didn't want to

149

encourage her suspicions about Natasha killing Dawson. "Okay, let's test those eggs."

Which we did. About half of the brown eggs lingered at the bottom of the water in the bowl; the others were definitely questionable in their sometimes leisurely, sometimes hurried, trip to float on top. I put the good eggs in the refrigerator and set the bad ones back out on the porch. By the time we finished, Mac and Dan came in the back door.

"It was a short lesson, but he's a fast learner," Dan said.

"If we're attacked by an army of tin cans, I can wipe 'em out," Mac declared.

Good. Everyone needs to be prepared for a tin-can attack.

We all went into the living room, where Natasha was earnestly telling Melanie about her mother's oddities, which had recently included a call to 911 because her Jello wouldn't set up properly. A question that had drawn an unhappy reaction from the 911 people, although a nice woman had also suggested maybe it was the uncooked pineapple she'd put in the Jello that kept it from solidifying.

"I just can't tell what Mom may do these days," Natasha fretted. "She joined a seniors' dance club a while back, and she goes to that at least once a week. Actually, she seems to be quite the belle-of-the-ball there. Oh, and something else she did. She got a tattoo. *Two* tattoos, actually. One on her neck that you can see and a hidden one you can't see."

I could tell Melanie was reluctantly curious about the one you couldn't see, although all she said was, "One of our son's friends got his girlfriend's name tattooed on his shoulder. I think he may regret that someday."

I didn't mention that I'd had a couple of tattoos

150

myself, courtesy of grand-niece Sandy, but they were the temporary type, and I'd long since washed them off. They were fun, but I'd been thankful I could wash them off. I wasn't about to get a permanent one.

Then Natasha leaned over and whispered something in Melanie's ear, and they both laughed.

Melanie has that effect on people. She chatters so enthusiastically that people can't help but chatter back. Apparently I, however, was not going to be privy to where Mom's tattoo was located.

I think Dan was curious too, but all he said was, "Well, we'd better head on home."

"Before you go, I want to know how to shoot one of the guns too," Natasha said.

"Can you go far enough from the house to shoot?" Dan asked doubtfully.

"Just show me here how to do it."

Dan went through the steps of how to load a shotgun, do what he called "racking" it to put the shotgun shell in the barrel . . . an ominous sound . . . and how to use the safety latch. "And then you just point and pull the trigger. But be careful. It may be a little more difficult to accidentally shoot someone with a shotgun than a handgun, but it's certainly happened."

Natasha nodded as if she understood everything. I'd watched, but I didn't feel as confident as she apparently was.

Elle made her move while Dan returned the shotgun to the bucket. "May I stay out here with Grandpa and Ivy for a couple of days?" she asked. I noted the careful, politically correct *May I?* "There's no school tomorrow, and the next day's Saturday."

Dan ruffled her red hair. "I think you'd better come on home with us. Grandpa and Ivy are busy here, and you

151

might get in the way."

"She wouldn't be in the way," Mac said quickly.

Natasha surprised me by saying, "She can sleep upstairs, and Mac can have the sofa." She gave Elle a critical once-over, and I wondered if she was speculating on Elle's ability to search in places no one else could crawl into.

Not going to happen, I vowed. Elle might have budding sleuth talents, but her safety and well-being came first.

"I can sleep on the sofa," Elle said hastily to ward off what she obviously saw as her parents arguing how her staying here would inconvenience Grandpa.

"But you'd need your pajamas and toothbrush and things," Melanie said.

I was just about to say I could follow them back to town so Elle could pick up her things, and then I'd bring her back out here, but Elle had her own agenda.

"I brought my pajamas and toothbrush and everything along," she said. "Everything's out in the car."

Melanie looked surprised, but she had another argument. "But you have homework—"

"Brought it along." Elle made it a reassuring statement, too smart to let it sound like a victorious crow.

Dan and Melanie exchanged glances. Outmaneuvered.

"Well, okay," Dan said. "But you do whatever Grandpa and Ivy say. Don't go chasing off on your own."

"Don't do anything without asking Grandpa or Ivy first," Melanie emphasized.

Elle was already headed for the SUV to get her overnight things and homework. Dan and Melanie left a few minutes later. I told them we'd bring Elle back to town when we came in to church on Sunday.

Elle came back inside, and I suggested she use my sleeping bag on the couch, which would be easier than trying to fit it with sheets and blankets. Then we went off together to find bedding for my cot. Upstairs, she surveyed the bedroom/storage room where I thought I'd seen some extra sheets and blankets. Mac and I had moved things around and stacked boxes, and it looked considerably neater than it had before.

Elle surveyed the rearrangement and the revealed attic door. "You're looking for something, aren't you?"

I figured there was no point in asking how she knew that. I just said, "It's a secret, okay?"

She gave me a thumbs up. "I can keep a secret."

Chapter 14

IVY

Thursday night was fun. We found popcorn in the pantry, popped a big bowl and smothered it with butter, and played a card game Elle called Concentration. Yes, she'd even come prepared with a deck of cards. Surprisingly, Natasha really got into the game and collected those pairs of cards with a vengeance.

After the cards, victorious Natasha went to bed. Mac and I included Elle in our scripture reading and prayer time before bed. Koop settled down with Elle on the sofa for the night, and BoBandy climbed the stairs with Mac.

The last thing Elle said before I headed for my cot was, "I do get to help you look tomorrow, don't I?"

"Look for what?" I asked warily.

She smiled guiltily, as if she'd been hoping to fake me into revealing what we were looking for before I thought better of it. "Whatever you're looking for."

"Well, we'll see."

Elle wrinkled her freckled nose. "That's what Mom says when she's thinking about how to say 'no' about something."

"We'll talk to your Grandpa and see what he thinks."

"Okay. But if he does say I can help, what do I look for?"

A sly and persistent budding sleuth!

"Papers," I improvised. "Maybe a will. Everybody has important papers, but we can't find Dawson's." I figured that would keep her busy without revealing the real goal of our search here. And papers might indeed be helpful, though I didn't think she'd have any better luck finding them than we'd had.

***

Next morning after breakfast, we checked with Mac, and then Elle started looking for papers in all the places we'd already looked: the bookshelves, kitchen drawers, and various cabinets. She even found a drawer built into the dining room table that we'd missed. You'd think a secret drawer would hold exciting secrets, but all this one held was a jumble of rubber bands and old coupons for everything from toilet tissue to organic Dijon mustard. I wasn't surprised by Dawson's interest in Dijon mustard, given what we already knew of his unexpected tastes, but I wouldn't have pegged him as a coupon user. But there it was.

Natasha sat up on the sofa and watched Elle make her search. Finally she whispered to me, "You didn't tell her about the D.B. Cooper money, did you?"

"No, of course not. I just told her Dawson must have important papers somewhere, and we needed to find them."

And that's exactly what Elle did!

I couldn't believe it when she came out of the pantry carrying that cardboard carton of canned tuna, the top open. Because the box didn't hold cans of tuna. It was full of papers.

With what sometimes seemed like extra-sensory perception, Natasha yelled from her sofa, "What did you find?"

I took a quick peek before taking the box in to her. Property tax bills and receipts. House insurance. Title on the pickup. Various newspaper clippings. A deed to something, probably the ranch. Other miscellaneous receipts. Dawson had an odd system for establishing what qualified as important. One neatly handwritten page was a recipe for oysters Rockefeller; another printed page appeared to be a genealogy for Clint Eastwood. No will. Not even a birth certificate. At least he didn't keep old socks in the box.

Natasha hurriedly dug through the box, discarding clippings along the way, but I had the feeling her hurry was due more to trepidation than eagerness, afraid she might find something she didn't want to find. Actually, what I wished for was income tax returns. I was still curious about where Dawson got the money to pay for his pickup and tractor and snowmobile, plus the fairly expensive ATV and metal detector.

Suddenly she stopped digging, frowned up at me, and snapped, "You don't need to sit there watching."

Oh, yes, she was looking for something specific. And she didn't want me to see her find it. Although she also glanced at Elle, the successful finder of eggs and papers, and I had the feeling she was considering telling Elle what the real search here was for, that Elle might be better at it than we were. Elle was busily collecting discarded clippings.

I looked through the clippings as Elle piled them on a bookcase shelf. Maybe she was just being neat picking them up, but I suspected she had an ulterior motive. "Did Dawson live in Denver at some time?" I asked Natasha.

"Not that I know of," she said. "Why?"

"These clippings are all about small crimes in Denver or towns around there." I glanced at one about the burglary of a sporting goods store. "This one was in Colorado Springs."

Was Dawson using these as how-to guides for taking up burglary as a criminal pursuit less dangerous than skyjacking? But the clippings weren't dated, so I couldn't tell

156

if the crimes in them had occurred before or after the D.B. Cooper adventure. Maybe, after seeing these, Dawson had decided skyjacking would be a more profitable enterprise than burglaring? On one a burglar had gotten only $28.42, and in another, a break-in at a convenience store, only slightly more: $57.00 plus several packages of taco chips and a six pack of root beer. Oh, but on one spectacular heist a pair of bold crooks had managed to hijack an armored car and gotten away with close to a million and a half in cash. Although one of them had been gunned down and paid with his life. But it made me wonder: had the high stakes, armored-car hijacking inspired Dawson to go big-time with a skyjacking of his own? Although he hadn't raked in anywhere near what the armored car hijacker had.

"You want those?" Natasha asked Elle as she pounced on more clippings. "You're welcome to them."

"Thanks!"

Why did Elle want the crime clippings? Oh, I knew. Research material for a budding sleuth.

"You seem like a smart girl," Natasha said thoughtfully. "Maybe—"

"Why don't you go find Grandpa? I think he's down at the barn," I said hastily to Elle. I was not going to let Natasha recruit her on a find-the-skyjacker's-loot mission. Considering Natasha's sudden glare at me, I added, "Actually, I'll come with you."

We left Natasha to her perusal of the box and found Mac at the barn. He had the big, truck-sized door open now, so light flooded the interior. I told him how Elle had found the box of Dawson's papers in the pantry.

"Hey, great! Congratulations!"

Elle shrugged modestly and moved on to inspect the various pieces of machinery in the barn. "Are you going to use all this farming stuff if you buy the ranch?"

"We don't even know what most of it is, much less how to use it," Mac admitted.

Elle knowledgeably identified the farm equipment and what it was used for. A disc. A harrow. A hay-mowing machine. Sleuth and farmer combined. A talented young woman! "So did you find anything out here?" she asked.

"What makes you think I was looking for something here?" Mac managed to put a scoff in his voice.

"You dug a hole. So you must have been burying something or looking for something already buried. But I don't think you had anything to bury."

Observant girl. Logical too. Yes, Mac had been digging. A shovel and the metal detector leaned against the tack room, a shallow hole nearby.

"And got a pretty good blister for my troubles," Mac grumbled. He fingered the space between thumb and fingers on his right hand. "The dirt in here is like trying to dig in concrete."

"But you're not going to tell me what you were digging for?" Elle sighed, but she apparently knew the answer to that and didn't wait for one. "Is it okay if I go around back and look for more eggs?"

"Sure. We'll come out in a minute."

I waited until she was out of hearing, BoBandy dashing with her, and then walked over to the hole. "So why did you dig here?"

"The metal detector picked up something. I thought it might be the buckles on a buried brief case. Full of money. Or maybe a big metal can or bucket. Full of money."

"But it wasn't?"

158

"No. It was a can, but it was full of old bottle caps."

"Why would Dawson bury bottle caps?" I asked.

"Beats me. Why did he have frozen socks in his freezer?" Mac responded.

We couldn't, I realized, use logic to help figure out where Dawson may have hidden the money. His thinking processes didn't seem to follow any known logic. I didn't know how to use the metal detector, and Mac gave me a brief lesson in how to do that. I'd just located a big treasure – a quarter! – on the barn floor when Elle returned. She held something between her fingers, arm outstretched, that she apparently found distasteful.

"Dawson didn't smoke. Neither of you smoke. So who left this?" she asked. "It looks fresh."

It wasn't the cigarette butt I'd found earlier. I'd disposed of that one. "Where did you find it?"

"Out by the windmill."

Mac and I exchanged glances. Was it possible the intruder wasn't snooping around in the barn, and it was the windmill that interested him? Why? We followed Elle out to the windmill. The windmill was – guessing – maybe thirty feet tall, the blades creaking gently as they turned in the slight breeze. The metal framework was old and pocked with rust, each leg sitting on a flat rock. One rock had sunk a few inches into the earth, giving the windmill that tilted look. There was a square of thick planks under the windmill, the wood dark and cracked with age, a round hole in the center. Dirt flew as BoBandy energetically dug around one of the rocks.

"It was undoubtedly used to pump water a long time ago. That hole in the boards was probably where the pump was, and there must have been a tank to pump the water into too." Mac stepped up to the square of planks and cautiously tested them with his weight. Solid. "But I don't think the windmill does anything now. It doesn't appear to be connected to anything. The well in use now is up there near the house."

"But there's probably an old well under the windmill?" I asked. Hey, that suggested possibilities!

Elle instantly grabbed the same thought. "Maybe there's something hidden in it!" She dashed over to the windmill and started tugging on the square of boards.

The square was a little off center, as if someone may have moved it recently, but it was too heavy for her to move. Mac hesitated a moment and then started tugging too. I went to the opposite side and pushed. And then stopped pushing when I realized there *was* a hole down there, a big hole, and if I weren't careful I might give a big push and find myself *in* that hole.

It took several more minutes of grunting effort, but finally we had the square of thick boards out from under the windmill. The hole it had been covering was at least five feet across, maybe even a little more, definitely big enough to fall into. Elle, apparently expecting a reprimand if she tried to lean over and peer into it, got down on her belly and wiggled closer. Looked like a good system to me, and I did the same. Who can see a hole and not try to get a closer look into it?

Including BoBandy. He bellied up beside us and peered down with us. I wondered if he was envious of the hole-digging capabilities of whoever had dug this hole. Mac has his macho-male side, and, instead of using the undignified belly-wiggling approach, he braced himself with one hand on the metal framework and leaned over to peer down.

I couldn't tell how far it was to the water . . . maybe fifteen or twenty feet . . . or how deep the murky water was. An elemental scent rose from the hole, as if it held ancient

160

secrets dredged up from some bottomless pit. I shivered with the sudden feeling the murky water might reach up and drag me down. Then I scoffed at that irrational thought. The well wasn't some malevolent entity. It was just a hole with water in it.

Irrational or not, I scooted a few inches back and pulled Elle with me.

"It's an old hand-dug well, maybe from way back in homesteading days, not even lined, as most wells are," Mac said. "Modern ones dug with a well-drilling machine are only six or eight inches across."

"So why did they quit using it?" I asked.

"Probably didn't produce enough water. Dan says the water table around Wolf Junction has been dropping over the years, and many ranchers have had to dig deeper wells. Or sometimes shallow wells become contaminated."

Also, over the years, the sides of the well had sloughed off, leaving rough, vertical ridges and furrows. As if something had clawed at the dirt while being dragged down—

I broke off that melodramatic line of thought.

"It'd be a great place to hide something!" Elle said.

"Under the water?" Mac scoffed.

"Crooks have been known to hide things in the water of a toilet tank," I said. And this old well could hold something much larger than would fit in a toilet tank. Skyjacking treasure. Old artifacts. Dead body. Though I didn't mention that thought aloud. Mac would probably mutter that I'm the only woman he's ever known who would instantly connect an abandoned well with the possibility of a dead body down there somewhere.

Instead I said, "But once you hid something down there, how would you ever get it out?"

161

"Maybe fasten it on a rope or wire when you put it down there, so it could just be pulled up," Elle suggested.

"I don't see any rope or wire," Mac said.

"Maybe somebody already pulled it up and got whatever was down there. I know what we can do! Tie a rope around me and lower me down, and I can look around and see if there's anything down there!"

Yeah, right. That had about as much chance of happening as Mac strapping her to a clump of dynamite and sending her off to look for little green men in space.

"How about you run up to the house instead and get the big flashlight that's behind the seat of my pickup?" Mac said.

"I guess that'll work too," Elle agreed reluctantly. "But if there *is* something down there, someone has to go down and get it. So then you can tie a rope—"

"If something was down there, and it fell off, it would be all the way down at the bottom," Mac pointed out. "You want me to lower you clear down to the bottom? However far that may be?"

"I guess maybe the flashlight is a good idea," Elle conceded.

"So, what do you think?" I asked when Elle loped off toward the pickup.

"I think my granddaughter may grow up to be anything from a center-of-the-earth explorer to a first settler on Mars."

What I'd meant was, what did he think about the possibility of Dawson hiding skyjacking loot at the bottom of an old well? But he might be right about Elle. Although I figured he'd better add CIA or FBI agent, maybe female Sherlock Holmes to the list.

162

She was back shortly, flashlight in hand. But she was not alone. Jack Hawkins was with her.

"Good to see you folks again!" He thrust out a hand for Mac to shake and tossed a doggie treat from his pocket to BoBandy. "Marnie's up at the house with Natasha, but I thought I'd come out and see if I could give you a hand." He spotted the open well under the windmill. "Hey, that looks dangerous."

"We were just checking it out," Mac said. I could see he wasn't eager to use the flashlight to light up the hole now, just in case it would spotlight skyjacker's loot down there under the water.

Jack spotted the flashlight in Elle's hand. "Want me to take a look for you?"

He didn't wait for an answer, just grabbed the flashlight. He, like Mac, steadied himself with a hand on the windmill framework and aimed the flashlight downward. Mac stepped up beside Jack, and Elle and I used the belly-wiggle approach again.

The light didn't reveal much. The beam just reflected off the murky water. As if something down there had the power to deflect it so as not to be seen. . .

Yeah. Right.

"Maybe the guy who left the cigarette butt already got whatever was down there." Elle whispered, the whisper covered by Mac and Jack's conversation about how many shallow wells dug around here in homesteading times had gone dry because of the dropping water table.

"This one ought to be filled in," Jack said. "I'd be glad to help." He reached down to pet BoBandy.

"It can't be too deep since it was hand-dug, but it could be a lifetime job for two guys with shovels," Mac said.

Jack laughed. "Yeah, you're right. Better to hire a guy with a big backhoe. Though I guess that's Natasha's territory, isn't it?"

Mac and Jack shoved the plank covering back over the well, and we all started toward the house. Elle eyed Jack's cap with the Falcon's name and emblem blazed on it.

"Did you live down there in Atlanta?" Elle asked.

"It was a great place, but Montana is home now," Jack said.

"Did you go to the Falcons' games there?" With two older brothers who were into sports, she apparently knew what and who the Falcons were. I was embarrassed. I didn't know if they played football, baseball, or Tiddlywinks.

"Oh yeah," Jack said enthusiastically. "Great games!"

"Did they have guys coming around selling boiled peanuts like they sell popcorn at our games?"

Jack gave her a blank look. "Why would anyone boil peanuts?"

My thought exactly, but apparently people in Georgia thought it was a good idea, and now Elle gave him an odd look. "A friend of mine was down there, and she said everybody just *loved* boiled peanuts."

"Yeah, well . . . everybody to their own taste, I guess." He turned to Mac. "Has Pickett been back with more of his phony claim about making a deal with Dawson on the ranch?"

"Not yet. But I don't think he's given up."

Back at the house, Marnie said she'd brought macaroni and cheese, and the casserole was in the refrigerator. I thanked her. The day had warmed, so I fixed iced tea, and we sat around the living room chatting. Marnie said Secretariat was doing fine at their place, and Elle asked how old the grandkids who were coming to ride the horse were.

"Lexi is ten and Jana is nine. They're really into soccer at school now." Marnie sounded typical grandma, proud of her grandchildren. Hey, I could soon claim grandchildren to be proud of too! "Do the kids here play soccer?"

"Sometimes. Do your grandchildren ever go to Six Flags over Georgia?" Elle asked.

Marnie didn't say anything for a moment, and I had the odd feeling she had no idea what Six Flags over Georgia was. Well, I hadn't known either, until Elle told me. But it was down there near Atlanta, where Jack and Marnie were from.

"Actually, they're more interested in football than flags," Jack said. He tapped his cap with the Falcons name and emblem. He laughed. "I know. Odd for little girls, but—"

"But that's the way they are!" Marnie said. "You know, tomboy types." She also said not to worry about returning the casserole dish, she'd get it next time they were over.

After they left, Elle watched their pickup climb the hill. "For coming from Georgia, they sure don't know much about it."

Interesting observation. They certainly hadn't wanted to talk about boiled peanuts or Six Flags over Georgia. Although I didn't see any way that could be meaningful.

A little dreamily, Elle added, "I'd like to see Georgia and eat boiled peanuts. I'd like to see pyramids and Iceland and Mozambique and Machu Picchu."

"Me too," I said. We probably couldn't make it to the more exotic places on Elle's list, at least not in a motorhome, but Georgia and boiled peanuts were a possibility. Though at the moment we were still motorhome-less.

We had Marnie's good macaroni and cheese for dinner that evening, and then Elle, BoBandy, Mac, and I took a walk along the road toward the cliffs. Koop tagged along too, of course. BoBandy was wearing the new kerchief Elle had tied around his neck. He dug up some small animal bones from under a bush. Elle found several interesting colored rocks. No moving lights showed along the base of the cliffs.

It was a nice walk, but we didn't go far. Mac wanted to be sure we had Elle safely back at the house before dark. I woke once in the night and got up from the cot to stand on the back porch for several minutes, but no odd noises or lights disturbed the peaceful night.

Which meant . . . what? That the intruder had given up on what he was looking for? That he'd found it? Or he was just biding his time before returning?

***

On Sunday morning we had a quick breakfast. While gulping the handful of vitamins and other supplements Natasha always took, she grumbled about our running off. Apparently we were supposed to devote every waking hour to search for the money. I invited her to come to church with us, but she said she was "busy." I left her supplied with water and snacks so she wouldn't have to get off the sofa and go after anything herself. We left early because we had to go by the house so Elle could change clothes before church.

Melanie had the wedding dress spread out on the bed in the guest bedroom for me to try on. It was indeed a lovely heirloom. Long, lacy sleeves, a modest decoration of seed pearls across the satin bodice, a high neckline, and full skirt.

166

As Melanie had said, not the current style that tended toward strapless, but definitely the right style for me.

"Oh, yes. I love it!" I slipped out of my pantsuit and slid the dress over my head. It didn't exactly slither around me, but I managed to squeeze into it. I also had to suck in everything that could be sucked in before Melanie could pull up the zipper. It was the right length, but I was apparently not quite as petite around the middle as Melanie's mother had been. Or as I used to be, given that I'd put on a few pounds lately.

"Can you breathe?" Melanie asked doubtfully. She smoothed the satin that stretched taut across my ribs. "It probably should be altered, but my sewing capability is limited to clown suits. And, with Trudy gone, I don't know who we could get to do it."

I definitely couldn't go in for deep-breathing exercises in the gown, but I thought I could breathe shallowly long enough for the short wedding ceremony. I'd change for the barbecue reception. "I'm fine. It's a beautiful dress, and I very much appreciate your offering it to me."

"You still need shoes. I don't know what became of the shoes Mom wore with it."

"We can run over to Double Wells the day before the wedding for shoes," I assured her.

***

Dan and the boys stayed home, but Melanie and Elle went to church with us. The pastor, who'd be marrying us in less than a week, had an interesting message connecting current Middle East events with Biblical prophecy. We had a quick lunch with Dan and Melanie and the kids, then headed back to the ranch. Mac wanted to do more searching around the barn with the metal detector yet today. We were about a mile past the buffalo ranch when a vehicle roared up behind

167

us. The horn blasted, and we both jumped. It sounded as if we were about to be run over by an 18-wheeler truck.

I turned to look. Not a truck, but a big car, one of those older luxury models, two-tone burgundy and silver. It reminded me a little of the big '75 Thunderbird I used to own. Texas license plates. Two people in the car. The headlights blinked.

"Looks like he wants us to stop," Mac said.

I'd be inclined to step on the gas, but Mac eased over to the side of the road.

Chapter 15

IVY

A man stepped out of the car and headed for the pickup. I blinked, not sure what I was seeing. *Elvis?*

A much older Elvis, of course. Portly . . . well, rotund might be more accurate. A little jowly. But the hair was as dark as ever. Sideburns too. He was wearing a white jumpsuit, hopefully up to the strain of his generous-sized mid-section, with a black scarf tied around his neck.

Mac rolled down the window as the man approached. "Some horn you've got there."

"Gets your attention, don't it? '77 Cadillac, just like one Elvis once owned. Just had 'er restored. Course the horn wasn't part of the original Cadillac equipment. I had that added." He sounded proud of his noisy addition. "Say, we're lookin' for a little ranch that was owned by a guy who died. Guy at the gas station said it was out this way. Lillian's daughter's livin' there now." He thumb-pointed to the woman in the passenger's seat.

So Natasha's mother had decided to come! But . . . with Elvis? I scrunched around to get a better look at her, but all I could tell was that she appeared to be a small woman with big, Dolly Parton blond hair. She saw me looking at her and waved.

"You're looking for Dawson Collier's place, then," Mac said. "We're headed out there now. You can follow us, if you'd like. As you probably already know, Natasha broke her leg. We've been helping her out."

169

"Dwight Dixon here, Elvis tribute artist, been appearing weekends at the '50s Palace over in Bozeman." He gave us a smile with an Elvis curl of lip and thrust a meaty hand, with three gaudy diamond rings, through the window. A gold medallion with an engraving of a guitar dangled from a chunky gold chain around his neck.

Mac managed an awkward handshake through the window and identified the two of us.

We headed for the ranch, Elvis and Dolly following in the Cadillac. Her mother's arrival, with an aging Elvis in tow, was going to be a surprise for Natasha. Not necessarily a pleasant surprise, I suspected.

At the house, we all piled out of the vehicles. Tiny Lillian immediately rushed over and hugged me with unreserved enthusiasm. "You're the lovely woman who called me, aren't you?"

I was a bit embarrassed at myself, but my first thought about Lillian, after noting a discreet blue butterfly on her neck, was, *So where's the hidden tattoo?* Second thought, *Is all that hair really her own?* It engulfed her small face like a lion's mane on a kitten. Dwight retrieved a couple of suitcases from the trunk of the Cadillac. Then a yell – well, more properly a *shriek* – from the door interrupted. The shock of her mother's arrival had been enough to bring Natasha up off the sofa.

"*Mom!* What are you *doing* here?"

"Sweetie, I had to come soon as I heard you got yourself hurt," Lillian said. "I want you to meet my friend Dwight. I met him when I landed at the Bozeman airport and he was kind enough to give me a ride out here."

Natasha had said her mother was the "belle of the ball" at her seniors dance club; apparently she didn't do too badly at airports either. Bozeman was at least a 125 mile drive, a fair distance for giving a new acquaintance a ride.

"I'm pleased to meet you, Mr., uh, Dwight," Natasha said. Apparently uncertain of his status with her mother, she added, "We're a little crowded here now. . ."

"Oh, Dwight isn't staying," Lillian said airily. I thought Dwight looked disappointed, but he took the news with good Elvis gallantry.

"Yeah, gotta be on my way," he said. "I'm moving on to Missoula to appear at the Lucky Queen this coming weekend."

"Thanks for the ride. If you ever get down to San Diego, be sure to look me up." Lillian stretched up and gave him a goodbye kiss on the cheek, and he dutifully returned to the big Cadillac.

I was a little disappointed too. I'd been looking forward to an Elvis performance. But at the car he turned to give us a wave, then lifted his arms over his head and treated us to an Elvis swivel of hips. Lillian and I both clapped.

Mac frowned. I don't think he appreciated the swivel as much as Lillian and I did. He stomped into the house with the suitcases. I thought Natasha would make further inquiries of her mother about Dwight. I was certainly curious about how one acquired an Elvis and his Cadillac at an airport. I even tried to steer the conversation in that direction.

"I guess 'tribute artist' is another term for impersonator? Dwight is an Elvis impersonator?"

Lillian jumped on that indignantly. "Dwight is much more than an *impersonator*. He's studied Elvis for years. He knows every word of his songs, every movement of his body. His complete life story too, lots of things most people don't know. Dwight is an *artiste*."

But Natasha wasn't interested in the tribute *artiste*. She had more important things on her mind.

"Did you bring Dawson's will?" she demanded.

171

"No. I never could find it," Lillian said. "I'm almost sure I saw it a few years ago. I thought I could go right to it. But I'm thinking now, maybe I tossed it."

"Mom, I've *got* to have that will!"

Yes, she did. I don't know much about law, but I'm pretty sure a divorced wife and an ex-stepdaughter without a will had no legal claim to Dawson's ranch. Or to the horse Natasha had sold to the Hawkins couple. The status of our promised pickup, painting, and cattle also struck me as definitely shaky now.

Natasha clomped over to the sofa and collapsed on it, perhaps in shock at this disastrous news. Lillian got all motherly and solicitous and started fussing over her daughter.

"Nat, sweetie, I'm really sorry about the will," Lillian said. "But it's no big deal, is it?"

"It's a *very* big deal, Mom. I may have to go back and help you look for it."

"Actually. . . Well, we can think about that later. First things first." She turned to me. "I appreciate your taking care of my girl, but now that I'm here—"

"Actually, Mac and Ivy have been doing more than taking care of me," Natasha said. "I hired them to look for the D.B. Cooper money."

Lillian looked from Mac and me. "So you know all about my husband being D.B. Cooper and skyjacking that plane?" She didn't wait for an answer. "A wonderful man, Dawson was. Smart and kind and generous. Ambitious too. It's just too bad we never got to go to Alaska and start that construction business together."

No criticism of skyjacking as a way to finance a business enterprise. I had the feeling age and haziness may have upgraded Lillian's memory of Dawson a bit.

"Maybe you could tell us a little more about

172

Dawson," Mac suggested.

"And D.B. Cooper," I added.

"Well, I didn't realize right away that he *was* D.B. Cooper," Lillian said. "But it was so plain later on."

"He had an injury when he came back from that trip when you think he skyjacked the plane as D.B. Cooper?" I asked. "And it left him with a limp?"

"He was all bruised and scratched up after the skyjacking, but the limp happened later."

"What do you mean, 'later'?" Natasha demanded. "He left a few months after the skyjacking, and you never saw him again. But I do remember him as such a nice man," she added. "He gave me a Barbie doll for my birthday."

I did a quick age calculation from what Natasha had told me earlier about her age when her mother and Dawson married and how soon he'd left after D.B. Cooper pulled off his skyjacking. "You remember a birthday from when you were only a couple years old?"

"Oh, she was older than that when he gave her the Barbie doll," Lillian said. "That was, let's see, on your fifth birthday, sweetie. When he came back after he got hurt in the hunting accident up in Alaska."

Natasha looked puzzled. "I don't remember—"

"You mean Dawson actually did go to Alaska?" I asked.

"Oh, my yes. He was doing fine up there, but then he got his leg shot in an awful hunting accident and came back so I could take care of him. That's when he got the limp, in that hunting accident."

"And then after he'd recuperated you separated again?" Mac asked.

"The biggest mistake of my life, letting him go." Lillian touched her heart in mournful regret. "He gave me ten

173

thousand dollars just for taking care of him for those few months."

"Well, none of this matters now," Natasha said impatiently. "What matters is finding the will and the skyjacking money so I can get on with my book."

"I have a thought," I said tentatively.

All three of them looked at me as if expecting some illuminating epiphany about the whereabouts of the money. Unfortunately, I didn't have one.

"What I was thinking— Remember, Natasha, when you were going through the old books and you found all those business cards Dawson had apparently used as bookmarks? There was an attorney's card in there. Maybe you should contact him."

Natasha took a long minute to answer. "I'm not sure seeing the lawyer would be a good idea," she said finally. She also frowned, as if she thought it actually belonged down there in a *bad idea of the century* category. "Besides, aren't there, you know, confidentiality regulations and all that between a lawyer and client?"

"Oh, but I think it's a marvelous idea!" Lillian exclaimed. "You know, now that I think about it, I'm almost sure Dawson took that will with him when he left."

"Mom, you never said that before!"

"He took it with him the first time or second time he left?" Mac asked.

Lillian dismissed that question with a wave of hand. "If he had a premonition about his upcoming death here at the ranch, I'm sure he'd have taken the will to a lawyer to be sure it was properly executed when he was gone. Dawson and I, we had this connection—" She put her hand to her heart again and lifted her eyes heavenward. "No matter how many miles and years separated us, we had this *bond*. He'd want to

174

be sure I benefitted from whatever he'd accumulated in the years of his life."

Dawson had a premonition about his falling – or being pushed – down the stairs? Possible, I suppose. But a mystical connection between Lillian and Dawson? Definite doubts there.

"With Dawson dead now, if the lawyer has the will it will need to be probated. And with Lillian as a beneficiary, he'll surely talk to you," Mac said.

Natasha shifted restlessly on the sofa. I figured she was worrying about the possibility of a new and different will. But finally she said, "Well, I'll think about it."

Which sounded very much like the "We'll see" kind of statement to which Elle objected. The time seemed a little late for any more searching today, so I fixed dinner. Over meat loaf, I fished for more information from Lillian about Dawson aka D.B. Cooper. She happily talked about their going across the border to Tijuana from San Diego for weekends, and Dawson building a bedroom onto her house, but none of it added much to what Natasha had already told us. Dawson had been gone for a week or ten days around the time of the skyjacking, and he'd come home all bruised and battered, as if he'd had a bad landing from a skydive out of a plane.

"Did Dawson have any skydiving experience?" Mac asked.

"He was in the service, so maybe he did. But he never seemed to want to talk about his time in the service, so I don't really know." Lillian gave a vague wave of hand, as if previous skydiving experience was not important. But she was not vague when Mac brought out the sketches of D.B. Cooper he'd printed off the internet. She grabbed the sketches and nodded vigorously. "Oh, yes. I've seen these before. That's my Dawson."

Afterward I told Lillian she could have the cot in the bedroom with Natasha, and I'd take the sofa, and we got everything arranged for the night. Koop settled down with me on the sofa. I disturbed him once in the night to step out on the back porch. I didn't *hear* anything, but I kept having this feeling . . . premonition? . . . that our midnight intruder would be back.

***

In the morning, I got up early. The sofa wasn't as bad as a bed of boulders, but neither was it any cloud of comfort. I had to wonder how Natasha managed on it every day. Koop went outside to do his business in his favorite spot under the rose bushes out front, and a few minutes later Mac and BoBandy came downstairs. I thought Mac and I could have a cozy, twosome breakfast, but about two minutes later Lillian came out of the bedroom by way of the bathroom. She was all bent over and holding her back. Natasha clumped out right behind her mother.

"Oh, that cot *killed* me," Lillian groaned.

"Mom, I'm so sorry!" Natasha said. "You can have the bed tonight and I'll take the cot."

"Or you can have the bed upstairs, and I'll drag the cot out to the back porch and sleep on it there," Mac offered.

I offered the sofa too.

"No, no, I'll be fine. Natasha needs the bed, and I want to be in the room with her in case she needs help," Lillian, newly-minted-martyr, said, although she groaned again. She straightened her back fractionally. "A long, hot soak in the tub, and I'll be good as new."

"There isn't any, uh, tub," Natasha said.

"No *tub*?"

We had breakfast in tub-less silence, and at the end of

176

it, Natasha reached across the table and put her hand on her mother's arm.

"Mom, you know how glad I am that you came all the way up here. I appreciate how you're willing to stay and suffer to be here to take care of me—"

"Of course, sweetie. I don't mind a little discomfort. That's what mothers are for."

"But I'd really feel better if you went on home. You need your own Sleep Number bed and big bathtub. And didn't you say the dance club was electing the queen of the Senior Fall Festival soon?"

"Well, yes, but I can't leave you here like this—"

"Ivy and Mac take good care of me, and I'll be just fine."

I wasn't sure if Natasha was being self-sacrificing in telling Lillian to go home or if she'd just figured out how to get her mother out of the way. Neither was I sure if Lillian was being self-sacrificing in her insistence on staying, or if she was just marking time until she could be persuaded to go. And finally, after Natasha said the way her mother could help most was to go home and look further for that will, Lillian agreed to do it.

I knew Mac wasn't about to go off and leave Natasha and me here alone, so I offered to drive Lillian back to the airport in Bozeman. We were on the road within a half hour. I figured I could be back at the ranch by dinner time.

It was a pleasant trip. We chatted about Dawson and how Lillian had met him when she was waitressing at a café in San Diego, about her seniors dance club and a nice man named Eldon who danced a mean tango, and about Dwight/Elvis. I asked about their meeting at the airport, if he was just returning from a trip somewhere.

"No," she said, "he just likes to hang out at airports."

177

She seemed to consider that a normal thing to do, so I didn't question it. But she had a surprise for me when we were about halfway to Bozeman. She opened her purse and pulled out a card.

"You mentioned that Natasha had come across a lawyer's business card, so I poked around in some things in her nightstand and found it." She held up the card and read from it. "Michael J. Anderson, Attorney-at-Law on Schutzwohl Street in Bozeman. I think we should go see Mr. Anderson. I'd bet my Sleep-Number bed that Dawson's will isn't anywhere in my house. Maybe this lawyer has it."

"We probably can't see him without an appointment."

"I think we should try." She paused and glanced around as if afraid her daughter might be long-distance eavesdropping. She lowered her voice. "Actually, I'm not sure there ever was a will. I think Dawson and I talked about it . . . at least I thought about it . . . but now I'm just not sure we actually did it."

I wasn't overly surprised by that confidential statement or the vagueness of Lillian's memory, which had drifted from originally telling Natasha she had a will to an uncertainty now about whether a will had ever existed. I didn't see any point in questioning this discrepancy and instead asked, "I wonder why Dawson would go to a lawyer way over in Bozeman rather than one closer to home?"

"Knowing Dawson, he wouldn't of wanted anybody close-by knowing he was seeing a lawyer. He was like that. Private." Lillian hesitated and then put it more bluntly. "Secretive."

Which was why he hadn't told her about his being D.B. Cooper?

I doubted we could find Mr. Anderson's office, let

178

alone get in to see him, but I underestimated Lillian. She used her smart phone to get directions to the address, and we drove right to it, a distinguished looking older home converted to an office. She marched up to the front desk and convinced the receptionist we had an important message for Mr. Anderson about one of his clients.

When Mr. Anderson came out, she announced that Dawson was dead, and that turned out to be news that interested the lawyer. He invited us back to his office. He apparently had no problem remembering this particular client, which I suspected may have been because Dawson was probably a unique client. He asked a lot of questions, none of which suggested he knew anything about an earlier will, about Dawson's connection with D.B. Cooper, or that Dawson had once had a wife and stepdaughter.

I stayed quiet and let Lillian do the talking, and finally Mr. Anderson said that yes, there was a will. Dawson had made it out about a year ago. But a few weeks ago, saying he'd soon be leaving for Alaska, he'd decided to dispose of the ranch before he left.

"Dispose of it?" Lillian repeated.

My thought, of course, was Buffalo Man. Dawson *had* made a deal to sell the ranch to him. So Mr. Anderson's next words came as a total surprise.

"Dawson arranged to donate the ranch to a boys' club in Double Wells for use as a retreat or campground, whatever they want to do with it. I had it all set up, and he just had to sign the final papers. I was waiting for him to show up to do that."

No doubt signing the deed was what Dawson had meant when he told Dan he had a couple things to do before leaving for Alaska. Definitely no deal with Buffalo Man. I tossed in a quick comment. "He must have been eager to get

179

back to Alaska, since he'd lived there before."

"He was eager to go. Definitely. But he'd never been there. He mentioned that. But, since he didn't get around to completing the donation to the boys' club, the provisions of the will take over now."

Mr. Anderson was telling us Dawson had never been to Alaska. But he'd come back to Lillian with a bullet wound he said came from a hunting accident in Alaska. Something else was more important than that inconsistency at the moment, however. Lillian seemed too startled by all this to ask the obvious question, so I did it.

"So what does the will say?"

Mr. Anderson left the room for a few minutes and returned with a file of papers. He'd apparently already refreshed his memory on what was in the file. "Dawson left the ranch and everything else to that same boys' club. He named me executor, so I'll obtain a copy of the death certificate and get probate started immediately."

I thought Lillian would be dismayed, maybe bring up that mystical "bond" she claimed she and Dawson had. Or, more likely, make a fiery threat about contesting the will. But, after a moment's reflection she just sat back and smiled. "Well, isn't that just like Dawson? What a wonderful, good-hearted man he was."

Chapter 16

IVY

Not a sentiment shared by Natasha when I got home and gave her the news. It was a worst-case scenario for her, of course. A new will that left her mother, and thus her, nothing.

After leaving the lawyer's office I'd taken Lillian to the Bozeman Yellowstone International Airport several miles west of town. I'd watched her buy a ticket to San Diego, but her flight wasn't leaving until evening so I couldn't wait to see her actually get on the plane. Which concerned me. I wasn't sure she *would* get on the plane if she happened to run into a Johnny Cash or Merle Haggard tribute artist. Or maybe just a senior dancing man. But she thanked me for taking care of her daughter and, in a confidential tone, said, "I'm glad it worked out this way. I was afraid Nat might decide to live up here, and now she'll have to come home." Her final words, with a little smile, were, "But I'm glad I'm not the one who has to tell Nat about this."

Now what Natasha said was, "Oh, that silly old . . . *goat!* Why would he leave everything to a bunch of boys he didn't even know?" She raged on about the unfairness of this, the *betrayal*. That maybe Dawson wasn't in his right mind when he made out the new will. That maybe Dawson had been *unduly influenced* to write it, that maybe there had been foul play involved in his death, so this *so-called* boys' club could grab hold of the ranch.

I was by now fairly well convinced there *was* foul play in Dawson's death, but I doubted the killer was in a conspiracy with some boys' club in Double Wells. I stayed silent, letting Natasha storm on, figuring she'd run out of steam sooner or later. She did, but not before she made one final declaration.

"I don't care who inherits the ranch, I'm not leaving until I find the skyjacking money."

So much for her mother's assumption that Natasha would be coming right home.

Mac came into the house then, carrying the metal detector. He said he'd used it around the windmill and barn but hadn't turned up anything except old nails, scraps of unidentifiable metal, and a metal box with what looked like old cat fur and bones inside, still a little smelly after who knew how many years. Actually, the metal detector didn't get any credit there; BoBandy had found and dug up the box. Another testimony to his sniffing and digging skills. I'd been undecided about the good-guy/bad-guy level of Dawson's character, and now I saw the box as a point in his favor. He'd cared enough for some cat to give it burial in a metal box. Mac said he'd reburied the bones. Point in his favor too.

I repeated to Mac what I'd told Natasha about our visit to the attorney, although at the same time I scolded myself: why hadn't I taken time while I was in Bozeman to buy suitable shoes for the wedding? Why hadn't I asked Lillian where that hidden tattoo was located?

On second thought, however, although I was still sorry about the shoes, I decided details about some things, such as hidden tattoos, are perhaps better left unknown.

Now Natasha repeated her earlier declaration. "I'm not leaving until I have the D.B. Cooper money."

"You realize, of course, that there's no longer any incentive for us to keep searching," Mac pointed out. "Everything, the ranch, the pickup, the painting, and the

182

cattle all belong to this boys' club."

Any thought about the contents of the new will affecting our involvement in the search had, until this moment, apparently escaped Natasha's attention, although her first fiery statement now was, "The boys' club doesn't own the skyjacking money! It didn't really belong to Dawson, so he can't will it away. I can still find it and write my book!" Then the full effect of this changed situation finally got through to her, and her shoulders slumped. "But I can't look for the money myself with this stupid cast on my leg, and now I don't have anything to pay you with for looking." She banged her fist on the cast.

Neither Mac nor I said anything. Was he thinking we should just pick up and leave? I didn't think we *owed* it to Natasha to keep looking, but neither did I want to just walk out on her. There was also still the matter of Dawson's death on the basement stairs. My curiosity about D.B. Cooper and his money was also still alive and well.

I was relieved to hear Mac say, "We can stay a little longer, but we'll have to leave on Friday. The wedding is Saturday and we're not delaying that."

I nodded agreement.

Natasha considered our deadline, then offered a solution. "You can come stay here after the wedding."

Spend our honeymoon with Natasha? Mac and I didn't even have to share a glance before we both said, "No!"

Natasha gave a put-upon sigh. "We just have to find the D.B. Cooper money before Friday, then. No time to waste."

The money had been missing for 40-some years, and we were going to find it by Friday? Maybe we'd also find Jimmy Hoffa's body.

"When I get an advance from a publisher, I'll pay you

183

a share. I already have the first chapter written. It's my memory of Dawson giving me the Barbie doll. There'll be a special acknowledgement of your help in the book, and I'll make sure you get an autographed copy."

Nice of her, but I didn't intend to stand around on one foot waiting for a cash payoff or autographed book. Even so, I didn't mind giving Natasha a few more days. With the new will, there was no possibility of our owning the ranch now, and I doubted we'd ever get to live on one again. And maybe by some miracle we would find the D.B. Cooper money.

"You can't manage alone here after we leave on Friday," Mac pointed out.

I figured Natasha would stick with her determination to stay here no matter how difficult . . . or dangerous . . . it might be, but finally she nodded. "I suppose you're right. If the money hasn't turned up by then, I'll have to give up and go home." Then her voice hardened. "But until then, there's no need to tell anyone about this new development with the ranch ownership. We'll just keep looking."

"We" as in the royal "we," of course. Because it was Mac and me doing the looking.

But someone else, we discovered for certain that night, was also doing some looking.

***

Before that, however, Buffalo Man showed up again. This time Mrs. Buffalo came along. They arrived just after we'd finished dinner. He was in his buffalo-rancher gear, although this time the cowboy hat was black, and the buffalo hatband was changed to a single copper buffalo staring out from the front of the hat. Mrs. Buffalo wore dangly, silver buffalo earrings with a diamond eye on each one, a buffalo belt buckle that matched her husband's, and boots decorated

184

with insets of blue buffalo in each. She also had lush dark hair in a flattering tousle, and a smile that, though I suspected it had the enhancement of an excellent set of caps, appeared friendly.

Buffalo Man had apparently decided to change tactics, because his smile was also friendly when I met them at the doorway. He introduced her as the "Barb" of the sign in front of their ranch. She gave me an enthusiastic hug. I hugged her back, although I was careful not to get within buffalo-charging distance of those formidable earrings.

"May we come in and talk to Natasha?" he asked. "I'm afraid we got off on the wrong foot the other day, and I want to set things right."

Natasha was by now on the sofa again. Buffalo Man repeated his apology to her, adding, "I can't find that Dawson ever cashed our earnest money check on buying the ranch, so it appears we can just start over with a new agreement." He smiled broadly. "Let the bidding begin."

So he was willing to toss more money into the pot. By now, knowing Dawson had arranged to donate the ranch to the boys' club, I was more doubtful than ever that Dawson had ever had any sales agreement with these people. Which meant that Buffalo Man might not be the most honest and trustworthy of neighbors.

"The ranch has been disposed of," Natasha said in a milder tone than I might have expected from her, although it was not without a hint of smug satisfaction. She might not be getting the ranch, but neither was Buffalo Man.

"But we really want to buy it!" Mrs. Buffalo protested.

"The ranch has been disposed of," Natasha repeated.

"Somebody bought it?" Buffalo man asked.

"I'm not at liberty to go into details at this point."

"Why do you folks want it?" I asked. "You must

185

already own several thousand acres here."

Mrs. Buffalo looked puzzled. Apparently she wasn't accustomed to having to justify wanting something; just wanting it was enough. "Our ranch just isn't complete without these acres out here at the end of the road," she finally declared.

Like an outfit incomplete without the right shoes? Or a trip without the right luggage? I looked at Buffalo Man. Was that his reason too? I didn't think now that he knew anything about hidden money on the ranch, but my suspicions of him went viral. Suppose he and Dawson had made a deal on the ranch – his wife *wanted* that ranch – and Dawson abruptly backed out? Would Buffalo Man have been angry enough to shove Dawson down the stairs?

"It's okay." Buffalo Man put an arm around his wife's shoulders and squeezed. "We'll just make the new owners an offer they can't refuse," he soothed.

Apparently that was the Buffalo Couple's solution to any problem: throw more money at it. Not exactly a philosophy I admired, but preferable to physical violence.

Although I definitely wasn't convinced Buffalo Man hadn't already used physical violence in his pursuit of the ranch.

***

MAC

I took the metal detector out again after the Buffalo Couple left. I prowled around the woodpile with it, but all I found was a nest of brown eggs. Which I didn't need the metal detector to find, of course. I managed that by stepping on them. Ugh. Smell strong enough to decimate life on a small planet. Hadn't Dawson ever gathered eggs in a timely manner? I gave up on metal detection and tried to hose the

186

smelly goop off my shoes, but the shoes seemed to have absorbed the scent down to cellular level. I finally gave up and left the shoes on the back porch. Maybe by morning they'd dry out and become suitable for civilized society again.

Ivy and I shared our usual before-bed Bible reading. She'd moved from the sofa back to the cot in Natasha's room. Upstairs, I read some extra chapters in the book of Daniel. It was late, past midnight by then, but I was intrigued by that handwriting on the wall and had to find out what it said.

I heard something as soon as I turned off the light. I opened the window and peered out. BoBandy put his front feet on the sill and sniffed the air with me. No lights, no further sounds, no flicker of movement. But BoBandy gave a growly woof, and I figured his nose and ears told him more than mine did. Something was out there.

I'd been glad Ivy hadn't gone to investigate that night she heard noises around the barn, but I had an investigative advantage she didn't have. I tiptoed down the stairs, BoBandy following, and grabbed a shotgun from the bucket of loaded guns by the front door.

And made enough clatter dragging it out of the bucket to suggest an imminent attack by terrorists and/or aliens. Which awakened Ivy, of course. She cracked the bedroom door open, peered out, then came all the way out when she saw me.

"What are you doing?" she asked.

"What are *you* doing?" I countered. She was in pajamas, but she was not unprepared for battle. Some women hear a noise and hide under the bed; Ivy comes out wielding a baseball bat.

"I didn't know what was going on out here. I figure it's best to be prepared."

Memo to self: after we're married, don't stumble around looking for a midnight snack or you may find yourself under attack by whatever object Ivy has available.

"Where did you get the bat?"

"I found it in the basement earlier. I stashed it under the cot. Just in case I might need it sometime. This seemed it could be the time."

Could she really swing the bat as a weapon? I didn't know, but I figured I'd rather not be on the receiving end to find out. "Okay, stash it under your cot again and go back to bed before Natasha wakes up."

"What about you and that shotgun?"

I managed to look at the shotgun as if wondering how it had gotten into my hand. "I thought I heard something. But I was probably mistaken." I made an elaborate display of returning the gun to the bucket. I still intended to check out the noise I may or may not have heard, but not until Ivy was safely back in bed. I didn't want her wandering around out there in the dark.

Yeah, right. Lots of luck leaving Ivy out of anything.

She gave me a suspicious look and said, "I'll change into different clothes and we'll see what's going on."

She disappeared into the bedroom and returned a few moments later looking unexpectedly stylish in snug jeans and dark sweatshirt, the outfit accessorized with baseball bat.

I grabbed the shotgun again, which this time made no more noise than Koop creeping up on a dustball. We went out the back way, where I stopped long enough to put on my shoes, still squishy from my cleaning efforts. And still smelly. Ivy didn't ask for an explanation. Maybe she recognized that distinctive scent.

We paused on the steps to listen. I didn't hear anything. Ivy shook her head; neither did she. No comment from BoBandy.

"But isn't that a light showing under the barn door?" she whispered.

Maybe. Or maybe it was starlight shining on a strip of metal under the door. Ivy didn't hesitate. She briskly headed for the barn to check it out. I wanted to yank her back but she had that bulldozer-on-the-move determination she sometimes gets. I followed.

Nice night, clear but cold enough to suggest a Montana winter would be coming soon. I felt a smidgen of regret that Ivy and I wouldn't be here on the ranch to share it. But we'd be together somewhere else, and that was all that mattered.

As we got closer, Ivy whispered, "There *is* a light in there."

With no electricity in the barn, that meant someone was in there with a flashlight or lantern. Doing what?

There was no way to sneak up on whoever was in the barn. This was going to be a head-on confrontation. I stepped ahead of Ivy as we approached the door. "I'll open it. Stay off to the left side. I'll step to the right."

"I've seen detective movies too," Ivy muttered. "I know the drill. Keep out of the line of fire."

I yanked the door open and stepped to the side. A light blazed out from the doorway, bright enough to make me blink. Then a figure darkened the oblong of light. His shadow looked big as a Frankenstein monster. I waited a moment, then hefted the shotgun and stepped around the door to face the person. Ivy loyally stepped up beside me.

He was older, not as big as his shadow, but not unintimidating. Tall and skinny, with a scruffy beard and a gray pony tail. Wearing jeans that were too big and cinched at the waist with a rope for a belt, plus a baseball cap on his head. But he looked mean as a junkyard guard dog and tough as rawhide. He also had a weapon. I hesitated for a moment while I identified what it was. Bolt cutters. At least four feet long. Not originally intended to be a weapon, but, with his hands holding the handles spread open, the bolt cutters looked big and powerful enough to whack through iron bars on a jail cell. Call me judgmental, but I suspected this guy had seen the inside of a jail cell or two. He did not look intimidated by an old geezer with a shotgun and an LOL with a baseball bat.

"What d'ya want?" he demanded, as if we, not he, were the intruders here.

In spite of his hostile attitude and the size of the bolt cutters, I determinedly took the offensive. "What are *you* doing sneaking around in here?"

"Lookin' for what I got coming," he shot back. He wrinkled his sharp nose. "And you know what? You stink. Like rotten eggs."

Just what we needed. A combination burglar and scent police.

"Who are you?" Ivy demanded.

"Who're *you?*" He lifted the bolt cutters and eyed her as if thinking about cutting something more vulnerable than bolts. I edged in front of her.

The shift in my view revealed the door to the tack room in the corner of the barn was open, padlock cut. He'd dragged the saddle, expensive spurs, and various tools out to the center of the barn, apparently preliminary to theft. The light came from one of those newer model LED flashlights sitting on the ATV. It put out enough light for examining microbial life.

"We're—" I broke off. Hey, he wasn't entitled to know who we were. We, not he, were the ones who had a right to be here. Although, on second thought, I wouldn't press that point. Considering Dawson's will, neither Natasha nor we had any rights here. But we weren't stealing anything, and he obviously was. Or at least intending to.

"You were here snooping around before. I almost caught you the other night," Ivy said.

"Dawson *owes* me, fair and square."

I didn't see the connection, but I asked, "Owes you what? And why?"

"I worked for him. Cutting wood. Fixing fences. Haying. Rounding up those stupid buffalo. He *owes* me," he repeated.

"You mean he didn't get around to paying you for any of your work before he died?"

"He paid me every week early on, but he never intended to pay me for the last week, the old buzzard. And I know he had plenty of money."

"What makes you think that?"

"He always paid me with cash. But one time I needed money early to go to town and he said he didn't have any on him, and I'd have to come back later to get it."

"So you came back later?" Ivy asked.

"Yeah. Dawson had the money then. But he didn't leave the ranch to get it. I know 'cause I watched with binoculars." He stabbed the bolt cutters in the direction of the cliffs. "And he never left the ranch. He got the money from some stash right here. A *big* stash. Same stash he used when he bought that snowmobile with cash." He jerked his head toward the sleek machine behind him.

"But if he paid you, he didn't owe you," I pointed out.

"He paid me *that* time, but next time he said I'd been goofin' off and he didn't owe me nothing. But I hadn't

191

goofed off. . . 'cept'n maybe a day or two when I needed a beer 'cause it was so hot . . . and he *did* owe me. But then when I come back that time he—" He broke off, shuffled his feet nervously, and his eyes got fidgety. Finally he said, "He was gone somewhere then. So I never did get the money I had comin'."

"And if you found his stash, you were going to take just what you had coming in unpaid wages, of course. Not a cent more."

He ignored my cynical comment. "I know he has a stash here somewhere, but I haven't found it."

"So you're stealing his stuff instead."

"I have to get what I got coming some way. I worked for it." He kicked a stray tool in the direction of the pile. "Dawson ain't going to pay me himself now he's dead. Not that I'll get enough out of this junk to cover what he owes me."

"When did you last see him?"

"A while back."

"Where was he the last time you saw him?" Ivy asked.

"In the kitchen. Doing something with some old jar looked like an owl. *Alive.*"

The owl face I'd seen smashed on the basement floor when I found Dawson's body. "So he wasn't 'gone somewhere' when you were here after all," I pointed out.

"Look, I know what you're thinking. That I pushed him down the stairs. He might of deserved pushin', and I felt like doing it when he wouldn't pay me what he owed me. But I didn't do it! He was already laying there dead at the bottom of the stairs when I got here."

A little change of story here. First, a live Dawson is doing something with an owl jar in the kitchen. Now Dawson is dead at the bottom of the stairs.

192

"So if he was dead why didn't you report it to the authorities?"

"Why should I?" he challenged.

"I think it's time you talked to the sheriff about this," I said. I shifted the shotgun so it was loosely pointed in his direction. "Tell him what—"

Without warning, the guy headed straight for me, using the bolt cutters as a battering ram. He'd have slammed into me dead center, probably making a hole the size of a football in my midsection, but BoBandy grabbed his leg and he went down. Taking me with him. In a domino effect of collapsing seniors, I took Ivy with me when I crashed.

All of us, BoBandy included, tussled in a free-for-all of arms and legs, bolt-cutters and shotgun and baseball bat, on the hard ground. The guy yelped when Bo got him with a nip. Or maybe it was when Ivy punched him in the ribs with the bat. I floundered across his mid-section and yanked the bolt cutters away from him. He scuttled out from under me and jumped to his feet with surprising agility, and ran. I grabbed the shotgun and started after him, but Ivy was struggling to her knees, and I stopped to help her. An engine roared from around behind the barn, and a moment later a pickup with lights off shot toward the cliffs.

We watched and listened for a minute, but there was nothing we could do to stop him. In the light still streaming from the barn door, we checked ourselves for damages. I figured bruises would show up soon enough, but right now we seemed more-or-less okay. Ivy dusted herself off.

"He was right," she said. "You do smell like rotten eggs."

"I'd have wound up in a lot worse shape than smelly, if it weren't for BoBandy." I gave him a good thank-you pet on the head. I felt a little shaky, thinking how close I'd come to getting impaled on the end of those bolt-cutters. This was one mean dude. He was far enough away now that we couldn't even hear the sound of the pickup engine, but a faint trail of red taillights bounced far out on the rough ground.

"Did he cut the padlock because he wanted to get into the tack room to steal stuff, or because he thought Dawson's 'stash' was in there?" Ivy asked.

"Good question." I hefted the heavy tool. "In any case, he seems to have donated a rather good-quality flashlight and the bolt cutters to us. Maybe we can get fingerprints off them."

"He was wearing gloves."

I hadn't noticed that, but observant Ivy had. Had he been wearing gloves because the night was cold? Or because he was experienced at this sort of thing and had thought ahead about fingerprints?

"But he said he worked for Dawson, so maybe Dan will know who he is," Ivy added.

I tossed the bolt cutters into the barn, and we used the flashlight going back to the house. We walked rather slowly. I could already feel my joints stiffening. It was still a nice night. Crisp and cool and starlit. But we'd encountered a guy who'd been willing to do more than just give us a little shove to make his escape. He'd wielded those bolt cutters with murderous intent. Even BoBandy seemed subdued now. He followed behind instead of running off to sniff and dig.

"Do you think he just came back and saw Dawson dead in the basement? Or did he push him down the stairs because he was angry because Dawson wouldn't pay him?" Ivy asked.

Another good question.

I figured we had an answer to another question, however. Dawson did indeed have money hidden around here somewhere. Somehow he'd managed to turn unspendable skyjacking money into spendable cash.

Chapter 17

IVY

Next morning we told Natasha about our encounter with the burglar at the barn and that we thought the information should be turned into the county sheriff. She pointed out that we'd have to make a trip to town to do it, and we had so little time left for searching. Couldn't we do it when we went in for the wedding?

"Was what this guy did even a punishable crime?" she asked.

He'd certainly had criminal intent, even murderous intent, but he hadn't actually managed to steal anything. It would be our word against his that he'd actually attacked us with the bolt cutters. We decided we'd let it go until we went back to town on Friday.

We moved the items the burglar had piled on the barn floor back to the tack room. I was sore all over. Mac didn't mention aches and pains, but he moved as if his joints needed an application of WD-40. We searched more in and around the barn, with and without the metal detector, but turned up nothing.

Dan and Melanie came out late that afternoon, after school was out, to check on us, Elle with them. First thing Mac did was ask Dan what he knew about a guy who'd worked here on the ranch for Dawson.

"We encountered him last night, trying to steal stuff out of the barn. He said Dawson never paid him for some of the work he'd done, and he seemed to think he had a right to help himself to Dawson's belongings to make up for it."

"What did he look like?" Dan asked.

"Tall, skinny, older guy. Gray pony tail and beard. We stopped him before he got away with any of Dawson's stuff. In fact, he ran off and left a flashlight and the bolt cutters he'd used to cut the padlock on the tack room in the barn." Mac didn't say anything about the guy trying to impale him with those bolt cutters. I think he figured if he mentioned the attack that Dan would go into orbit about our being out here in such a dangerous place.

Dan's forehead wrinkled. "I knew Dawson had someone working for him off and on, but I never met the guy. I don't know where Dawson acquired him, but he wasn't a local. Dawson called him Sam or Slim, something like that."

"He seemed convinced Dawson had some big stash of money hidden here somewhere."

Natasha, from her usual position on the sofa, gave Mac an alarmed look, apparently thinking he was about to reveal the D.B. Cooper connection, but Mac didn't offer any further information. I expected Dan to scoff at the idea of a secret stash of money, but he gave an unexpected nod of head.

"I've wondered about that. Dawson did seem to come up with money whenever he decided to buy something. He gave me that story about his pension fund giving big bonuses. I was skeptical, but I figured his finances were none of my business."

"We think the guy has been snooping around here several times. Natasha thought the house had been searched while she was in the hospital. We're wondering if he might even have had something to do with Dawson's fall down the stairs."

"Sheriff Cunningham seems convinced the fall was an accident, but I've wondered about that—" Dan broke off when he realized Elle was listening with interest while she pretended to browse through Dawson's books. He turned to Mac rather hastily, apparently not wanting to encourage Elle in any sleuthing activities. "Hey, why don't you show me these bolt cutters the burglar left behind?"

They headed for the barn. Koop wanted to go outside, and Elle followed him. Melanie said she was going over to Double Wells the next day to do some shopping, and with sudden inspiration I asked if she could pick up shoes for me for the wedding.

"Oh, Ivy, I can't choose your *wedding* shoes," she objected. "They have to be special. You need to try them on, see how you'll feel walking down the aisle in them—"

"Just get something that will look good with the dress. I've never had any problem buying shoes to fit. Usually size six-and-a-half. Heels, but not too high. I don't want to stumble and fall on my face as I'm coming down the aisle."

"Okay, I'll try. How about pale blue? Then you'll also have the 'something blue' every bride needs."

Great! Shoe and blue problems taken care of. Melanie and I discussed a few more wedding details. I could dress at the house, or the church had a small room connected to the women's restroom that other brides had used. I said the room at the church would be great. Then I wouldn't have to worry about smudging or tearing the dress before I even got to the church. The buffalo for the barbecue had already been delivered, and Dan and a friend would get the fire in the barbecue pit going the evening before the wedding so they'd have good coals by morning. Tracy was bringing the cake over Saturday morning. Melanie would get plates and utensils when she went to Double Wells, paper and plastic because it was an outdoor barbecue, but of a wedding-theme variety.

My apprehension of a few days ago was morphing into a heady anticipation, with a nice touch of tingle. Everything was falling so neatly into place. I might be an LOL, but I'd soon be a bride!

Melanie reached over and patted my hand. "It's going to be wonderful having you as part of the family," she said, and her sweet sincerity made me go all teary. The Lord was giving me not only an amazing man but a great family too.

"It's going to be wonderful to be part of the family."

Natasha gave us a *get real* look, but I figured that cynical attitude about marriage and family came from the failed marriages she'd mentioned, one including a mother-in-law who apparently used a broomstick for most of her transportation. Melanie decided to go down to the barn where the men were. Elle came back inside without Koop.

"I think I embarrassed Koop," she said.

"How's that?"

"He crawled in under the rose bushes, and I thought he had some secret hideaway place in there and I wanted to see, so I crawled under there too."

"I'm afraid that's his favorite bathroom area," I said.

"Yeah, that's what I found out. But with me there, he couldn't seem to find just the right place to dig a hole. I wonder, how do cats decide what is the right place?" She scrunched her face thoughtfully, as if this might be a subject worthy of scientific research.

"I don't know what the specific standards are, but Koop is very particular about such things."

"He dug down a little ways and then moved over to another place where he could dig deeper."

"It could be rocky under there. Or maybe just really hard dirt. Like Mac said the floor of the barn was so hard it was like trying to dig in concrete."

"Yeah, I suppose."

Koop meowed at the door, and Elle hurried over to let him in. "I'm sorry, Koop," she apologized. "I didn't mean to invade your privacy."

Koop didn't hold a grudge. When Elle sat down, he jumped into her lap and started purring.

Mac and Dan and Melanie came back from the barn, Dan saying he thought he'd try to find out more about this handyman-turned-burglar and also mention him to Deputy Cargill.

"Oh, hey, I almost forgot something I should tell you," he added. "I saw a notice on the bulletin board at the store about a motorhome, so I called about it. It's several years old, but this elderly woman and her husband used it only one winter in Arizona before he got too sick to travel. He died last fall, and the widow wants to sell."

"Not that we want to encourage you to buy it!" Melanie said. "We'd much rather you'd buy the ranch and settle down here."

"Right," Dan agreed. His smile held a twinge of guilt. "Maybe that was why I was having a hard time remembering to tell you about it."

"The ranch isn't going to be available after all, so we are going to need another motorhome," Mac said.

"Not available? But I thought—" Dan glanced at Natasha as if he thought she might explain the sudden unavailability, but she just folded her arms and studied a greasy stain on her cast.

"So, the important question is, what's the price?" Mac asked. Dan named a figure that struck me as probably fair,

200

but a little steep for us. Mac looked at me. "What do you think? Maybe we'll have time to look at it on Friday?"

"She's planning to take it to some RV consignment outfit in Bozeman," Dan said. "It sounded as if she was just waiting until she could find someone to drive it over there for her."

"Maybe by Friday she'll already have sent it off to Bozeman." I hadn't thought about our homeless state for a while, but the day was looming. "Maybe we should look at it right away."

Mac and I followed Dan and Melanie back to town, and Elle rode with us. Natasha looked a little sour when we left, apparently unhappy that we weren't using every minute we had left on the search.

Dan led us to Mrs. Erickson's place about a mile on the other side of Wolf Junction. I liked the looks of the motorhome the minute we pulled into the driveway. Nice brown and tan color, stylish but not flamboyant. We got out of the pickup and inspected the outside of the motorhome while Dan went to get Mrs. Erickson. She came out carrying a plastic bag of pamphlets and papers.

"I don't know much about how anything works. Gordon took care of all that. But the instruction books on everything are in here, and everything worked the last time we used it." She waved the bag.

The motorhome was thirty-two feet, three years old, low miles on the odometer, with a slide-out that enlarged the living-room area, nicer than the motorhomes both Mac and I had owned before. Mac and Dan did the male kicking-tires thing, and I figured I could kick tires too, so I did. I wonder what that's supposed to tell you? It didn't tell me anything except that it's not smart to kick tires with open-toed sandals, but Dan said, "Plenty of tread left," and Mac nodded. They opened and inspected the engine compartment. I looked too, but all I could tell was that, yep, that's an engine. Mac climbed the metal ladder and said the roof looked practically new. Mrs. Erickson said they'd always kept the motorhome in the oversized garage her husband had especially built for it.

"It's all set up to pull a car behind it." Mrs. Erickson pointed to the trailer hitch. "We had a little Volkswagen that we took with us."

There was a generous storage space underneath the living area, and a generator in a separate compartment. The interior was nicely arranged, with a walk-around, queen-sized bed, and a generously-sized dinette area, all spiffy-clean and barely-used looking. TV, microwave, double sinks, bathroom with a shower and tiny tub, refrigerator with freezer, everything we needed. I saw Elle note that there was another bed over the driver's and passenger's seats up front.

"Plenty of room for you to come visit us," I whispered, and she grinned.

Mrs. Erickson asked if we'd like to take it for a drive, and we discussed a purchase as we drove the loop around by the store. Although there wasn't much to discuss. We both liked the motorhome, but there was the price barrier. Mac is often a sharp bargainer, but after we got back to the house and talked to her a little more, I could see he was reluctant to haggle with her. As a widow, maybe she really needed the money, and she might be able to get the full price in Bozeman.

Mac glanced at me. "Maybe we should think about it a little more."

"I probably shouldn't be telling you this," Mrs. Erickson said, lowering her voice, "but I'd really like to get rid of it without having to bother taking it to Bozeman. I

202

want to go visit my daughter in Illinois. I'll drop the price for a quick cash sale."

"We have cash."

She astonished me, and I think Mac too, by dropping the price a full twelve thousand dollars. Mac looked at me again, and we exchanged nods.

"We'll take it!"

I had money from the down payment on sale of my home back on Madison Street in Missouri, and we each wrote out a check for half the sales price. She signed over the title, and in minutes the motorhome was rolling down the road with Mac at the wheel, me following in the pickup. We were homeless no more!

Yes, everything was falling into place nicely. *Thank you, Lord!*

Chapter 18

IVY

We left the motorhome parked in the field by Dan and Melanie's house, picked up fresh milk and fruit at the store, and I called Lillian to make certain she'd gotten back to San Diego safely. She had, and she also told me about the "lovely" man she'd met on the plane, a retired plumber who now created yard art out of old pieces of pipe. He was eager to show her the Brontosaurus under the palm tree at his house. An admirable talent, no doubt, but, after considering it briefly, I'm glad Mac isn't into making plumbing-parts dinosaurs to decorate our new motorhome. Mac is a very satisfactory man exactly the way he is.

We were back at the ranch before dark. We spent the next day randomly probing some of the 13 million square feet of the property with the metal detector. By evening, I figured we'd covered a couple hundred square feet and dug up one old nail. Next morning over breakfast we discussed where to continue the search in the minimal time we had left. Natasha said she'd had a prophetic dream about finding the stash buried in metal buckets under one of the cottonwoods down by the creek.

Mac expressed reservations about dream prophecies, but after breakfast he followed Natasha's insistence that the dream was a cosmic revelation and headed to the creek with the metal detector and a shovel. I said I'd be along after I cleaned up the bathroom. I wasn't in any hurry. My own dreams do not tend toward prophetic helpfulness. Like the one I had a few nights ago about seeing my old Thunderbird again, but now it had feet rather than wheels. But some dreams in the Bible were undeniably prophetic, so maybe this dream of Natasha's was too. Right now, her leg was hurting, so, after commanding she be wakened as soon as Mac found the metal buckets, she took a pain pill and drifted off to sleep on the sofa.

I started cleaning the bathroom, being very careful with the toothbrushes, but when Koop notified me he wanted to go outside and immediately scooted under the rose bushes, I remembered what Elle had said about his not being able to dig as deep a hole as he wanted under there. I got down on my knees, then my belly, to watch him creep around under the bushes. He did exactly as Elle had said: dug a shallow hole that didn't suit him and then moved on to where he could dig deeper. Had he encountered some sort of barrier under there?

I felt an odd prickle of excitement. It might even qualify as the more elegant *frisson* I've read about in a few books.

Was it possible Dawson had buried his skyjacking loot right out here under his treasured roses? Or maybe a buried stash of money was the real reason the roses were treasured, and why he objected so vigorously to a stray buffalo stomping around in them?

The area was right next to the house, where Dawson could keep an eye on it, but not so accessible that anyone would accidentally stumble onto it or even find it easily in a search. We hadn't. An ideal hiding spot!

Still I hesitated. It was possible the barrier to Koop's digging was just roots or a rock or an old tin can. It was also possible Koop didn't dig deeper in some particular spot simply because he is something of a feline fussbudget about

205

such things. But the big reason I hesitated was definitely the yuck factor. Did Nancy Drew or Miss Marple or Jessica Fletcher ever have to sleuth around in what was basically an outdoor litter box?

Probably not, but curiosity overcame my aversion. Propelling myself with elbows and toes, I wiggled and squirmed under the big rose bushes that may have been growing here since the house was built. Koop gave me a dirty look with his one good eye for invading his privacy, twitched his stubby tail indignantly, and did a cat version of stomping off. "Sorry, Koop," I muttered and dug my elbows in deeper.

I advanced slowly, my curiosity colliding with the unpleasant facts of this location. How come my sleuthing never takes me to movie opening nights, hotel tea-rooms or elegant soirees? A prickly rose branch snagged my hair and punctured my scalp. A thorn stabbed me in the derriere. One elbow plowed into an underground ambush of thorns buried in years past, and the other elbow pushed into a softer, squishy area that I did not care to speculate about.

Shouldn't I be getting hazardous duty pay for this?

Oh, yeah, I remember now. I wasn't getting any pay.

I also had to wonder about this particular area of investigation on a practical basis. Dawson hadn't had to cope with the yuck factor . . . that was Koop's contribution to the area . . . but he'd surely been a considerably larger person than I am, and I was having difficulty enough squirming my LOL body around in here. More thorns. A branch of them gouged my shoulder right through my tee-shirt. Something crawled over my shoe and started marching up my leg. I froze. What kind of creepy-crawly creatures live in Montana? Fleas? Scorpions? Spiders? Maybe even something of the worm or snake variety? My head said *Jump! Run!* But, aware that any movement might annoy or startle whatever it was into biting or stinging or whatever it was inclined to do, I stayed frozen in place.

When I couldn't stand it any longer, I pounded my leg with a fist, then kicked and shook both feet in a great imitation of a horizontal jitterbug. A small army of oversized ants tumbled out. One of them gave me a sting or bite before exiting. I've always heard wild creatures are more afraid of you than you are of them. I don't think this herd got that memo.

Could Dawson actually have crawled around under here? I couldn't discern any trail left in the dirt by someone creeping around.

Although, if Dawson kept a working amount of cash in the freezer, he wouldn't have had to crawl under here often to access a main stash.

I squirmed another few inches, then paused to rest. Belly travel is not an easy mode of locomotion for an LOL. And in addition to creepy-crawly creatures, some kind of flying bugs lived under here. I snorted and coughed when one flew up my nose. I was just about to give up when I spotted something tucked up right next to the foundation of the house. A garden trowel! It was old and rusty, but someone had dug under here at some time. Re-energized, I edged farther under the bushes and grabbed the trowel.

I reversed my wiggle and shoved the trowel into the pot-holed landscape of Koop's territory. It hit with a mysterious crunch of metal on metal. Something *was* down there, not more than an inch below the surface.

I was suddenly excited enough to start scooping and tossing dirt, an LOL digging machine! The dirt was soft here, as if it may have been dug up before. And there it was! I hastily used the side of the trowel to scrape and expose something metal. What was it? I enlarged the spot. Maybe the top of a trunk? It was old and battered, but little patches of rusty green metal remained. I dug around looking for the edges but immediately realized it was too big for me to dig out. What I needed to do was get it *open*.

But if it really was Dawson's hiding place, Mac should be in on the discovery too. Along with the fact that I could use some help here.

I dropped the trowel and scooted out from under the thorny bushes, acquiring a few more scratches and considerably more dirt on elbows and body, especially after my tee-shirt slid up and I was scooching along on my bare belly. I didn't take time to go inside and clean up. I circled the house to keep from waking Natasha and headed for the creek. I could see Mac down there digging under a cottonwood. I gave a yell and big wave to motion him back to the house.

"I have something to show you," I yelled when he got closer.

"I hope it's better than what I found," he grumbled. He held up his find. Perhaps in some future civilization a sardine can will be an exciting archeological find, but right now it didn't measure favorably against the prophesied buckets of money.

Mac tossed the can in a trash barrel by the corner of the house, and I led him around to the rose bushes. "Under there. You have to get down and wiggle on your belly."

"But this is Koop's private area," Mac objected. "I don't want to crawl around where he's been digging."

"Think of all the hardships the oldtimers endured while hunting for lost treasure. Wolves. Outlaws. Landslides. Blizzards. Et cetera."

"It's the etcetera I'm worried about here," Mac muttered.

208

I got down on my belly and started wiggling under the bushes again.

Mac finally flattened himself on the ground with all the enthusiasm of a man diving into a Dumpster and followed me. "This better be good," he said, but when we reached the shallow metallic thing I'd dug out, he did a double-take. "Hey, maybe this is something."

Taking turns digging and scraping with the trowel, we uncovered more of the metal top of whatever it was. I guessed the full length at about 30 inches, width at 15 or 16 inches. Maybe footlocker size? I couldn't tell how deep in the ground it was. We dug around the sides but couldn't get deep enough to pull the thing out of the ground. I got the impression it had been there a long time, as settled in as a boulder moved into place by some ancient glacier. But we did unearth an old-fashioned, round lock on one side. Which was locked, of course. Had Dawson really thought it necessary to lock a footlocker buried here under rose bushes? Apparently he had. Paranoia in full bloom. But then, someone had murdered him. Perhaps he hadn't been paranoid enough.

A little shiver crawled up my back, creepier than unfriendly ants. Maybe our attitude here was also too casual, not nearly paranoid enough. I glanced back through the bushes, checking to see if someone was sneaking up and watching us. Nope, no one except Koop.

I said, "The key might be on that ring Natasha has, where the tack room key was."

Mac had a faster solution. He whacked the old lock with the handle of the trowel several times, and it popped open. Then we had to get the fastener thingies on either side of the lock undone. We could move the lid a little then, but we still had to dig more to pull the top fully open and scrunch it against the underside of the rose bushes. And then we stared in astonishment at what we were seeing.

Money. Money and more money! A trunkful of money!

A messy jumble of various denominations, one-dollar bills right on up to twenties and hundreds. Musty smelling but green and official looking. Mac grabbed a twenty and we both scrutinized the tiny numbers. 1968. A year that predated the skyjacking. We checked dates on a ten and a hundred. All older.

"I guess I never really thought we'd find it," I said.

"Neither did I," Mac echoed

Koop now wandered back under the bushes, peered into the footlocker, and, unimpressed, strolled nonchalantly across the old bills. Given that BoBandy was such an enthusiastic digger, I'd wondered if maybe he'd somehow dig up D.B. Cooper's hidden treasure. Or that budding-sleuth Elle might do it. But it hadn't occurred to me that Koop might be the successful digger. Never underestimate the power of a cat!

It took us several wiggly trips under the roses to stuff the money into plastic bags and carry them inside. I started having an uneasy – prophetic? – feeling that down underneath the money in the footlocker, we'd find something strange. Maybe a message about a curse on anyone who dug up the money. Or mummified body parts. Skeletal bones. Entrance to a zombie tunnel.

We did find several of those little packets of the stuff that absorbs moisture in an enclosed space . . . very prudent of Dawson to make sure his money didn't deteriorate from dampness . . . but everything else was *money*. And when the footlocker was empty, the bottom was simply the bottom of a footlocker. Old and stained, but normal looking. Like something you might find in grandma's attic. No ominous message or zombie tunnel.

More shocking was what we saw when we carried the last bags inside. Natasha was awake and standing at the dining room table. We'd piled the plastic bags there, but she'd opened them and dumped out the contents. Spread out loosely instead of packed into the footlocker, the mountain of green bills looked unreal, like a prop of phony money set up for an advertising display on how many dollars you could save buying x brand of car insurance.

"Why did you do that?" I gasped.

"I just wanted to see it," she said. "All of it."

Feel it too, apparently. She buried her hands in the loose bills and wiggled her fingers, making the pile look as if it were coming alive. Then her excitement burst through.

"We found it!" She threw her hands up, and bills exploded around the room. "I can't believe it. We really found it! It was right under our noses all the time."

I thought about commenting on the *we* of that statement, but I let it go. This was her party. She picked up a double handful of bills and tossed them in the air. She looked as if she'd be dancing around the table if the cast weren't holding her down. Maybe dancing *on* the table. Koop had come inside with us, and he batted at bills as they fluttered to the floor.

"Isn't this awesome? Isn't this incredible? I can't believe it!" More bills in the air. Natasha gave a giddy laugh. "Whee!"

"Who should we notify?" I asked. "The local sheriff's office? Or maybe the FBI?"

Natasha stopped in mid-toss, apparently brought back to earth by my question. She gathered up the edges of the pile in what struck me as an oddly proprietary gesture. She frowned, and in a let's-not-be-hasty tone, said, "I think the first thing we need to do is count the money so—" She paused as if searching for a good reason. "So we can tell them exactly how much is here."

I figured they'd count it for themselves, but I didn't argue. Who can contemplate a pile of long-buried money and not want to count it?

I went to the bathroom to wash off the dirt now itching on my elbows and belly, and when I came out Natasha and Mac were separating the bills into denominations for easier counting. Natasha made round bundles of hundred dollar bills. She started with groups of ten to make bundles of a thousand dollars, then switched to ten-thousand dollar bundles, each tidy roll held together with a rubber band from the drawer. I went with smaller denominations. Mac did twenties and then organized the various bundles into piles. Watching Natasha made me think of that king Midas greedily counting his gold.

And hadn't something really unpleasant happened to that old counting king?

Eventually Mac stopped counting and stacking. He eyed the growing stacks with an odd expression. "There's something peculiar here."

"You're thinking something's wrong just because they aren't all twenties." Natasha sounded ready to challenge this as a nitpicky point of view.

"No. I figure Dawson must have traded the skyjacked bills for money that didn't have incriminating serial numbers, so he could spend it. He found someone who was willing to buy the bills at a discount, apparently a long time ago, because these all seem to be older bills too. The denomination of the bills doesn't bother me."

"So what's peculiar?" Natasha demanded.

Before he could answer, we heard a vehicle outside. I

ran to the window. "It's the Hawkins couple."

"Quick, cover up everything!" Natasha looked around as if a space ship had landed and we were about to be overrun by aliens. "Get the blanket off the sofa!"

"But if you're going to turn it in to the authorities anyway—"

"I don't want them seeing the money. It's none of their business!"

She whipped off the denim shirt she was wearing over a green tee-shirt and draped it over the money. It was like trying to cover an elephant with a bikini. Stray bills fluttered to the floor. Koop pounced on the fresh supply.

"I'll get the blanket," Mac said. He looked mildly alarmed, as if uncertain how far Natasha might go in her frantic attempt to hide the money. A not-unwarranted uncertainty, I agreed, as she yanked at the tee-shirt. "You meet them at the door," he added to me.

"Don't let them in!" Natasha commanded.

I went to the door, opening it only part way, but not letting Jack and Marnie in was easier said than done. Marnie had a pan in a plastic sack under her arm and her hand on the handle of the screen door.

"Ivy, hi!" she said. "What have you been *doing*? You look like you've been dragged through a truckload of dirt."

I'd washed hands and elbows and belly, but I hadn't changed clothes. Now I brushed ineffectually at my dirt-streaked tee-shirt and jeans. "Well, uh, you know ranch life. Always a little dirt involved."

"Where's Mac?" Jack asked. "I've been thinking, since we're going to be neighbors—"

"It looks as if that isn't going to happen," I said quickly. "We've bought a motorhome and we'll be leaving right after the wedding." Brightly, keeping a firm hold on the

213

screen door, I added, "But we can come out to say goodbye before we go. Or you're coming to the wedding, aren't you?"

"Wouldn't miss it! But are you sure you're okay?" Marnie tried to peer around me, and I wondered if she could see Mac and Natasha back there frantically trying to pick up stray bills and conceal a mountain of money. "You don't look well. Did you fall? I know what you need! I made it just for you folks. Cheesecake!"

"Cheesecake sounds wonderful," I said. "But—"

I felt something flutter around my ankles. I looked down. Koop was still batting green bills around, and now I had a hundred dollar bill caught on my foot. Marnie saw it too.

I snapped out of my momentary state of panic. "Silly cat," I scolded. "I must have dropped that." I grabbed the bill as if hundred-dollar bills fluttered around my feet all the time, and stuffed it in a pocket. I opened the screen door a crack and reached for the sack Marnie held. "Thank you so much! I love cheesecake—"

Marnie kept a tight hold on the sack. "I'll just set it in the refrigerator until you're ready to eat a piece." She yanked the screen door with her other hand, and her tug jerked me outside before I could even let go of the handle.

I was still stumbling, trying to catch my balance, when she slipped inside. Jack gave me a somewhat apologetic smile as he followed less aggressively. I turned, wondering how we were going to explain a dining room table covered with money, and then thinking this concealment was unnecessary anyway. In a few days the whole country would know the D.B. Cooper money had been found.

But Jack and Marnie Hawkins weren't going to know it today. The table was empty, not a bill in sight, Natasha's green tee-shirt still modestly in place. I peered around

214

cautiously. Natasha was standing at the table casually poking through the drawer of rubber bands and coupons. Mac was studying some nicks in the table as if they might hold clues to Montana history. Then I spotted the blanket-covered mound in a corner.

"Why don't we have some of that cheesecake right now?" I said brightly to distract them. "It's lunchtime anyway. I'll make sandwiches too."

"Oh, we have cheesecake?" Natasha clapped her hands. "Wonderful!"

I made tuna sandwiches . . . well, I slapped them together . . . and Marnie cut the cheesecake into squares. Then we all sat at the dining room table and oohed and aahed when we got to the cheesecake. Marnie and Jack couldn't know about the blanketed money in the corner, but to me it felt as large and obvious as the "elephant in the room" we've all heard about. It's oddly difficult to carry on a normal conversation with a pile of hidden money just a few feet away. Especially when, out of the corner of my eye, I saw Koop jump on the pile and, as cats do, start kneading the blanket.

Natasha, apparently to keep Jack and Marnie distracted, or maybe just because she was so excited, chattered with uncharacteristic animation about the weather, the way her skin itched under the cast, the eggs we'd found hidden here and there. She wiggled in her chair. She waved her fork to emphasize a point in her conversation. She tried hard not to look at the covered pile of money in the corner, but her eyes kept skittering in that direction. I kept thinking Marnie surely had to notice that. Or the musty scent of the money. Or both.

Mac tried the diversionary tactic of asking if they knew the man who'd worked for Dawson. "My son said his

215

name was Sam or Slim, something like that."

"He came around the other night wanting to collect some money he said Dawson owed him," I added. *Koop, stop it! You're going to paw that blanket right off the money!*

Then I felt annoyed with myself. With all of us. We were acting as if this were some national-security secret that must be concealed at all costs, and it wasn't. In fact, why not just share our find with Jack and Marnie? They'd be astonished and excited to learn the man they'd known as simply an eccentric old grump had a more fascinating past as a skyjacker. Natasha wanted and needed publicity about finding the money to impress a publisher. Why not start right now?

But then a vague wariness kicked in. We didn't really know Jack and Marnie. I'd been a little suspicious of them to begin with. Although it's hard to be suspicious of people who buy a horse for their grandchildren and come bearing gifts of macaroni and cheese, and now marvelous cheesecake. But maybe, if they saw all that money, they'd suddenly turn into Bonnie and Clyde. Who knows what kind of cook Bonnie may have been when she wasn't robbing banks?

"Yeah, I met the guy. Sam Larson, I think his name was," Jack said. "Dawson was letting him camp over by the cliffs, but he told the guy to move on when he fired him."

"That's where he headed when he ran out of the barn. We found him in there loading up everything from the saddle to tools. We'd tried to follow him an earlier time when he was sneaking around here, but my two-wheel drive pickup couldn't make it on an old road going toward the cliff."

"Yeah, there's old roads all over here. There's one goes over to the back side of the buffalo ranch. Another old one over to our place. I've ridden over on it a few times. But I don't know as I'd want to go following that guy anywhere.

216

He struck me as a pretty shady character. I wouldn't want him hanging around our place."

"You said something about buying a motorhome," Marnie broke in. "You've changed your mind about buying the ranch?"

I thought this would be a good time to tell them Dawson had left the ranch to the boys' club in his will, but Natasha just kept chowing down on cheesecake as if this was the last one in existence.

"Yes, our plans have changed," Mac finally said.

"We're still interested in buying the ranch, if you're not," Jack looked inquiringly at Natasha.

I gave Natasha a surreptitious glance of my own. I didn't like playing this game of hiding facts about the future of the ranch, but neither did I feel I had the right to barge in and reveal the contents of Dawson's will myself. Natasha muttered something about her mother's uncertain plans. Which had nothing to do with the ranch situation, of course.

"Will you be living here, then?" Marnie asked Natasha.

"No, I'm going home soon. I've been planning for some time to write another book, and I think I have all the information I need to do it now."

"Really? I didn't know you're a writer. A book about Montana?"

I could see that in spite of Natasha's reluctance to reveal her stepfather's other existence as D.B. Cooper, and her haste to hide the money, she was almost ready to explode with the secret of finding it. Her stepfather really was the infamous skyjacker, and she had his loot to prove it! But she managed to say vaguely, "Montana and Dawson and everything,"

"I always suspected there was more to Dawson than

217

he let on," Marnie said.

Natasha laughed. "Well, read my book and you'll find out."

"But then, if you're not going to live here, and Mac and Ivy aren't buying the ranch, what's going to happen to it?" Marnie persisted.

"It's, umm, being disposed of," Natasha answered.

"But that isn't fair!" Marnie protested. "We really want to buy it."

Jack asked the logical question. "Disposed of how?"

No response from Natasha, so I offered Jack and Marnie a smidgen of encouragement. "Perhaps it will come up for sale later." I figured that was an actual possibility. A boys' club over in Double Wells might well decide the ranch was too far away to maintain.

Marnie suggested a different possibility. "When that Pickett jerk will probably snap it up." She shot Jack an angry glance, as if this was somehow his fault, but he just concentrated on scraping up the last graham-cracker crumbs from his plate.

Finally, after I put the remainder of the cheesecake in the refrigerator and washed the pan, and we struggled through more small-talk, Marnie and Jack meandered out to their pickup, saying they'd see us at the wedding. It was late afternoon by then. Mac and I followed them out, but Natasha, murmuring something about her leg hurting, stayed in the house. I figured she wasn't about to get beyond sniffing distance from the money.

"Well, that went rather well, don't you think?" Natasha said when Jack and Marnie were gone and we came back in the house. "I'm sure they didn't suspect a thing."

Which was when I looked at the blanket-covered pile in the corner again. Koop was sleeping peacefully atop it now, but a half-dozen bills had slithered out from under the edge of the blanket. Hundred dollar bills. Koop had his paw on one. Had Marnie and Jack seen them?

I suddenly felt very edgy with all that money sitting there in the corner of the dining room. What if handyman/burglar Sam chose now to come back with some new and more powerful weapon? "Why don't we just load up all that money and take it into the sheriff's office right now?" I said.

Natasha ignored my suggestion. She turned to Mac instead. "Just before those people got here, you said something about a peculiarity with the money. What was that about?"

"There's too much of it."

"Too much?" She frowned. "What do you mean?"

Mac went to the blanket-covered pile in the corner and jiggled the blanket until Koop gave him an annoyed look and jumped down. The rubber-banded bundles and loose bills spilled across the floor when he pulled the blanket away.

"D.B. Cooper skyjacked $200,000, right?"

Natasha nodded.

"And $5,800 was found on a beach along the Columbia River."

"So?"

"So, even if Dawson had stuffed every dollar of the skyjacked money in that footlocker, there should be no more than $194,200."

Natasha frowned, but she couldn't argue with Mac's math. So all she said was another, "So?"

"But what we've already bundled up amounts to over $400,000. And there's still a lot left to count."

Chapter 19

IVY

A startling fact. I asked the question this time. "What does that mean?"

"It means there's way too much money here for it to be the skyjacking money," Mac said. "And if Dawson sold the money with incriminating serial numbers to someone else, he'd almost certainly have had to do it at a discount for anyone to be willing to take the risk. But even if he somehow got full value for it, there's still way too much here."

I calculated what we knew about Dawson's spending. "We know he spent money on his pickup and tractor and several other fairly expensive things," I said. "He also gave Lillian $10,000 at some point." And if he had all this money back then, no wonder he could afford to be so generous to her.

"That was several years after the skyjacking," Natasha scoffed.

"He also must have used a fair amount to buy this ranch. Actually, considering what he's spent, it seems like there shouldn't be *any* skyjacking money left."

"He could have had other money," Natasha argued. "From . . . savings. Or selling other property. Or something. Maybe he invested the skyjacking money in the stock market and turned it into a fortune! People do that, you know. Or maybe he made a fortune up in Alaska!"

"He told the lawyer who wrote the will that he'd never been to Alaska," Mac pointed out.

220

"He told my mother he had been! That's where he got his leg hurt in the hunting accident."

"Let's take the money to the sheriff's department and let them figure it out," I suggested again.

"No!" Natasha was even more adamant this time. "If it started out as skyjacking money, and Dawson somehow turned it into a lot more, it still shouldn't belong to that boys' club. Here's what we do," she added with a decisive slap of palm on table. "We split the money. I take half, you and Mac take the other half. And we'll just never mention it to anyone. A win-win situation."

"How generous of you," Mac said.

Natasha was too engrossed in her plans to hear the sarcasm in Mac's words, but I certainly heard it. In her scheme, she alone got half, the two of us got the other half. Which really didn't matter, of course. No way were we going along with this plan. But I asked a different question. "But how would that help you write a best-seller if it's never identified as the skyjacking money?"

"If Dawson invested the skyjacking money and earned more with it, these bills aren't going to have the skyjacking serial numbers to identify them anyway. So I'm not going to be able to prove anything."

"So what you want to do now is just grab the money and run?" I said.

"If that's the way you want to put it," Natasha snapped.

"I suppose part of it could still be original skyjacking money," Mac mused. "They're all older bills."

"Are they?"

Natasha pawed through the pile of money, holding up bills to inspect dates, then flinging them aside. Koop, bored

221

by now with fluttering bills, let them fall around him. Finally she held up one victoriously.

"Here! Here's one with a Series 1973 date. That's after the skyjacking."

"So now you're trying to prove this *isn't* skyjacking money?" Mac asked.

Natasha slumped to a chair, elbows on the dining room table, and plowed her fingers through her hair. "No. Maybe. Oh, I don't know! None of it makes sense. How could he have so much money?" She seemed lost in frustration for a minute, then abruptly straightened her shoulders. "What we need to do is get the money counted. See how much there really is. Then we can decide what to do."

I couldn't see that knowing exactly how much money had been hidden under the roses could change what was surely a legal and moral responsibility to turn it in, but if it would help Natasha accept that, we could count. So count we did, though the more we counted, the more nervous I got. So much money! Once I thought I saw a flicker of movement at the dining room window. I also thought I heard a noise outside, as if someone had stumbled into the trash can back of the house.

Was someone out there watching us count? Maybe Sam, the handyman/burglar?

Or was a paranoid gene kicking in here?

I went over to the dining room window and pulled the curtains. They were lightweight, but better than nothing. We'd never pulled them before. Way out here in the middle of nowhere, it hadn't seemed necessary.

"Good idea," Natasha said approvingly when I returned to the table.

By the time the money was all neatly rolled into bundles, there was $974,861 on the dining room table. Give or take a few bills that may have fluttered into spots where we hadn't found them yet. I thought Koop might be curled up and sleeping on a couple of them. I hadn't heard any more noises or seen any movement outside. Which had probably only been my jittery imagination anyway.

Probably. Although the paranoia gene hadn't lost interest yet.

It was past time for dinner, but when I mentioned eating, Natasha looked at me as if I'd suggested we take time out for a square dance. Who could be interested in food *now*?

Without consulting us, Natasha spread the blanket beside the table and scooped all the money onto it. She muttered something about not leaving it out here where anyone who wandered in might see it, then struggled to carry the bundle into the bedroom. Wrestling with her crutches and the awkward blanket-sack of money, she wound up trailing bundled bills like green crumbs behind her as she struggled across the room.

I was trying to decide whether the right thing here would be to help her or *not* to help her put the money in the bedroom. Apparently Mac was having the same problem, but finally we both gathered up fallen bundles and added them to the pile she dumped on the bed.

We'd no more done that than we heard a vehicle outside.

"I don't want anyone in here." Natasha sounded panicky. "And I need a gun! Bring me a gun!" She pointed an imperious finger toward the bucket by the front door.

Both Mac and I just stood there, stubbornly unmoving. With sudden determination and surprising speed, she crutched out to the living room, grabbed a shotgun, and triumphantly managed to get back to the bedroom with it.

She lay down on the bed, curled herself and the shotgun around the bed-ful of money, and glared at us while someone knocked on the door. "Get rid of whoever it is," she demanded.

It was a strange scene. Her dark hair flowed across the pillow. Her finger curled around the trigger. The name of a grocery store blazed across one of the plastic bags. It all looked arranged, as if she were posing for one of those artsy black-and-white photos that sometimes show up in fashion magazines. Psychotic Woman with Shotgun and Money. With the grocery store's name artfully tucked in, like brand names sometimes show up in movies.

Suddenly she sat up, gun in hand. "I mean it. Get rid of whoever it is. Because I'm going to be watching you. And if either of you says anything about the money or tries to pull anything funny, I—I'll shoot."

"Shoot one of *us*?" I was flabbergasted. "You wouldn't do that!"

"Try me and see."

"You couldn't get away with it!"

"Maybe not. But someone will be dead."

It could be an empty threat. It was hard to think of Natasha as willing to shoot one or maybe both of us. She wasn't someone I'd ever thought of as becoming a BFF, but neither had I seen her turning into Psycho Killer ready to blast us full of shotgun steel.

Money changes people, I guess. When the skyjacking money was still a theoretical possibility, Natasha planned to turn it in to the authorities if we found it. Now that a much larger amount of money was right here in all its greenback glory, she had a different perspective. I suddenly remembered

224

that I'd originally suspected she may have pushed old Dawson down the stairs herself.

Maybe she hadn't changed. Maybe this was the true, treacherous Natasha finally emerging from an innocent looking bud. Like one of those stinky flowers that eats flies.

I reluctantly decided that shooting one or both of us probably wasn't an empty threat.

Mac and I went out to the living room and were surprised to find Dan at the door. It was almost dark now, only faint remnants of a setting sun still lingering in red-gold streaks over the mountains. Behind us I could see that Natasha had the bedroom door cracked open. I couldn't see the shotgun, but I had no doubt it was there. A shotgun aimed at your back is something you just *feel*. Worse than a really bad itch.

Mac opened the front door, which Natasha had insisted on closing and locking after Jack and Marnie left. "Hey, it's kind of late for you to be out here. Is something wrong?" Mac asked Dan without giving him a chance to come inside.

"I talked to Deputy Cargill about your unpleasant visitor the other night. He says he'll be out to talk to you in the morning, but I wanted to get out here right away and warn you about the guy."

"The sheriff's department knows him?"

"Oh, yeah. I passed along the name and description you gave me, and Deputy Cargill said he was almost certain this is a guy the sheriff's department knows as Sam Larson. They've had a couple of minor run-ins with him at bar fights in Double Wells, but nothing to get them really interested until just a few days ago."

That was when information had come through official channels about an ex-con named Sam Wainwright

225

who was wanted in connection with a convenience store robbery and shooting pulled off by two men in Texas. One man was caught, one wasn't. The crime had occurred last spring, but only now had the caught guy, trying to wangle a plea bargain for himself, identified Wainwright as his partner in the crime and also said the man may have come to this area. There was a warrant out for Wainwright's arrest, but local law enforcement hadn't been able to locate the man they knew as Sam Larson since learning about the warrant.

"Do they consider him dangerous?" Mac asked.

Dan nodded. "Armed and dangerous. The other guy says it was Wainwright who shot the clerk in the head during the robbery. Which might or might not be true, of course. The guy might just be trying to bolster his own chance for a plea bargain."

"But it could be true," Mac said.

"Right. My thinking is that if your visitor in the barn was Wainwright and he didn't get what he came for, he'll likely be back. Armed and dangerous," he repeated.

If Larson/Wainwright knew how much of a stash was here in the house right now, he'd definitely be back. Although, as convinced as he apparently was that Dawson had money hidden here, he'd probably be back even if he didn't know a definite figure. Except, as of now, he'd have to go through Natasha and her shotgun to get to it. I figured he might well be up to the task.

Which wasn't of any particular help to us. Right now we had one psycho willing to shoot us for the money. Sam might shoot her, but then we'd be next in line. A proliferation of psychos.

We were still standing at the door, Dan on the outside, the two of us on the inside. I thought Dan must surely think it was peculiar that we were just standing there without inviting him in, but, unlike the Hawkins couple, Dan didn't push his way in. So, what now?

We outnumbered Natasha by three to one. We could also get our hands on guns. I was closest to the bucket of guns there by the door. They were still loaded. Dan had earlier objected to that, but Natasha had insisted. I could grab one— Yeah, right. And then what? Start looking for an instruction manual on how to operate it? The minimal instructions I'd watched Dan give Natasha about using a gun didn't exactly make me feel like a 21st century Annie Oakley sharpshooter. I didn't know if Mac was thinking about guns in the bucket.

"Look, Melanie and I both think you and Ivy and Dawson's stepdaughter all ought to get out of here and come into town. I don't think it's safe out here with this Wainwright guy on the loose."

Of course Dan didn't know that Natasha had just turned into a lethal threat herself. But maybe we could just casually walk out the door and leave Natasha behind? I took another cautious glance at the cracked-open door to the bedroom.

No. Natasha would gun us all down here and now, Dan included.

I think all this went through Mac's head too. Great minds think alike? Or maybe it's panicky minds think alike. Mine was certainly panicky, although Mac looked normal enough.

What he did, in a very calm way, was say, "Well, we appreciate your coming out to warn us, and we'll certainly keep an eye out for this Sam guy. But we'll be coming in sometime tomorrow anyway, to get ready for the wedding."

Dan tried for several minutes to persuade us to do it *now*, but finally, muttering something about his dad's stubbornness, he went back out to his SUV. We stood there until the red taillights of the SUV blinked out of sight at the top of the hill. I knew Mac was relieved that Dan was now safely out of Natasha's target zone.

So there we were, Mac, me, $974,861, and a shotgun-armed woman with a killer instinct.

The shotgun was in Natasha's hands when she shoved the bedroom door open and stood there looking at us. She'd managed to get to the door using just one crutch and carrying the gun, and she was now supporting herself by leaning against the doorframe, leaving her hands free to manage the gun. She apparently remembered how Dan had showed her to rack the shell into the barrel, because she now did it. With the gun pointed at us, the sound was ominous as the rattle of a snake.

Trying to sound casually confident, I said, "This isn't going to work, you know."

"You don't think so?" she challenged. "And what is it you think won't work?"

I didn't want to give her a bullet-point list, in case my thoughts made her alter her plan to take care of any loophole I pointed out. But I saw that she couldn't just sit here guarding the money indefinitely. Eventually she'd fall asleep and we'd overpower her. She couldn't load the money into her car and drive off with it, leaving us here. We could have the authorities after her as soon as we could get to town.

There were, of course, unpleasant solutions to those problems. She could take one or both of us hostage, with the demand, if she was stopped, that she be allowed free passage to some country unfriendly to U.S. extradition requests.

D.B. Cooper in a Subaru, and no dangerous skydive involved.

Or, less complicated, she could shoot both of us right now and take off with the money. Even with the hindrance of the cast on her leg, she could get a long way before Dan came out tomorrow to see why we never showed up in town.

"I want the money loaded into my car," Natasha said. Which sounded as if the may have the shoot-Ivy-and-Mac-plan in mind. "I want your cell phones and pickup keys too."

"Why should we help you?" Mac scoffed.

"Because I'm going to shoot Ivy unless you do."

Mac gave me a frustrated glance. "Well, okay, then," he muttered.

So Mac handed over his keys and cell phone and I added my cell phone. I wished I could say I had a key to the pickup stuffed in my bra, but, unlike some clever sleuths, I don't tend to use my bra as a carryall for everything from cash to gun.

"The cell phones don't work here anyway," I pointed out. "Why do you want them?"

"I'll ask the questions," Natasha snapped.

Hey, wasn't that a stereotyped line from any number of old movies? I thought about pointing that out to her but decided this probably wasn't the right time for a crime dialogue critique.

So we stuffed the money into plastic sacks again, set them on the bedroom floor, and then watched as she loaded a few personal items into a suitcase. She made us stand over by the cot while she did the packing with one hand, the gun in her other hand. An awkward system, but she managed. She didn't pack much.

She didn't need to pack much, of course. You can buy a lot of toothpaste and vitamins with $974,861.

And right at that moment, for no particular reason, something thunked into my mind like a bowling ball dropped

229

from a five-story height. Probably irrelevant at the moment, but you know how it is when you're not thinking about something and all of a sudden it just pops into your head? Anyway, there it was.

"I think I know where all that money came from."

Mac turned to look at me. I thought he figured this was just some kind of stalling tactic.

Natasha said, "It doesn't make any difference where it came from." She tried to sound indifferent, but I could see her reluctant interest.

"You remember that tuna box with Dawson's important papers in it?"

"There wasn't anything all that important."

"There were all those newspaper clippings, remember? Did you read any of them?"

"No. Why should I? I saw an oyster recipe and an old 'Far Side' cartoon, one with a couple of cows sitting in armchairs looking at a phone. Dawson was just weird."

Look who's talking. But what I said was, "Elle picked up the clippings while you were throwing them away. She's interested in crime stuff, and that's what most of them were about. I think she set them over on the bookcase—" I looked at Natasha warily. "Can I go look for them?"

Natasha hesitated, as if she figured I might have some sly trick in mind. Which I didn't, unfortunately. I was totally trick-less at the moment. I just stood there waiting until she finally nodded. "Don't try anything."

Like what? Hurl books at her? But she could hurl a shotgun blast at me. Guess which of us would go down first?

I rushed over to the bookcase and pawed among the books haphazardly stacked there. No clippings. I hurriedly checked the other shelves. "I guess she must have taken the clippings home with her."

"So what was in them that you think was so important?" Natasha asked.

"They were mostly about small-time burglary cases around Denver, but one was about an armored car heist there. One man was killed, but the other one got away with something like a million and a half. The serial numbers of the bills hadn't been recorded."

We all looked at the money on the bed. I mentally cobbled a timeline together. While Dawson is married to Lillian, he briefly turns into D.B. Cooper and skyjacks a plane. They separate shortly afterward and he disappears, but he can't spend the skyjacked money because the serial numbers on the bills might lead back to him. So he takes up a life of small-time crime in Denver, eventually working up to the armored-car heist, in which his buddy is killed and he's injured. No hunting accident injury in Alaska. He needs someplace to both hide out and recuperate, so he goes back to Lillian. He stays with her until he's well enough to leave, though he now has a limp. He gives her $10,000 of armored car money for her help, and disappears again. Why didn't he go to Alaska then? Who knows? But this time he gives up his criminal endeavors to live a hermit-ish life in Montana, keeping some of the armored car money in the freezer, dipping into the stash under the roses when he needs more.

This was Dawson's "other pension" that he'd mentioned to Dan to explain his occasional big purchases. Stolen money. Those clippings he'd saved with his important papers were a personal biography.

I laid it all out for my audience of Mac and Natasha.

"What about the skyjacking?" Natasha asked. "Were there clippings about the skyjacking in with those he saved?"

"I didn't see any." It occurred to me that you could eliminate the D.B. Cooper portion of my timeline, and the

231

result at the moment would still be the same. A trunkful of stolen money hidden under the roses.

She frowned, as if the lack of clippings about the skyjacking troubled her. But only momentarily. "If this isn't skyjacking money, then that money is still hidden somewhere else around here."

Mac tossed up his hands in frustration with Natasha's stubborn line of thinking. "Non sequitur," he muttered.

It took me a moment to dredge the meaning of that word to mind. I can't say it's one I use frequently. "That means 'it does not follow,'" I said. "Just because this isn't the skyjacking money doesn't mean the skyjacking money is still here, hidden somewhere else."

"I know what a non sequitur is," Natasha snapped. Which seemed to be her usual way of speaking since she'd jumped the line from D.B.Cooper researcher over to potential killer.

"You still think Dawson was D.B. Cooper?" I asked.

"Of course. My mother identified him." She paused, and another frown suggested she wasn't necessarily as sure of that as she had once been. "But whether he was D.B. Cooper or not doesn't matter now. I'm taking the money. And leaving."

"We're not stopping you." Mac sat down on my cot and folded his arms. I sat beside him and did the same. Maybe it wasn't the most noble of attitudes, but I had no intention of making some fatal sacrifice to try to save bags of money that surely had, one way or another, started out as stolen.

"No, but you are going to help me—"

Natasha swung around, apparently intending to aim the shotgun at us. But the turn, with only one crutch, unbalanced her. The crutch momentarily balanced upright,

232

then fell. She threw up the hand holding the gun to balance herself. The gun rose, arced overhead, then crashed like a falling bomb to the floor.

The *blam* rocked the bedroom.

Chapter 20

IVY

Small bedroom. Big shotgun. Very large boom.

The blast filled my ears and head. It vibrated my body and tingled my toes. It gonged inside me. I didn't think I'd ever hear again. Or even move. Maybe I was dead.

But after a few moments, my fingers wiggled. Toes too. I wrinkled my nose and blinked my eyes. Hey, not dead! I wasn't even hit by the blast. But Mac—? In panic I turned to where he'd been standing a moment earlier. He was still standing there. He reached over and hugged me. *Thank you, Lord!*

Natasha wasn't standing. But neither was she dead. She'd already been unbalanced on her one crutch, and the blast from the shotgun had knocked her off her feet. She just sat there on the floor blinking and looking a little dazed, the cast twisting her leg at an awkward angle.

Tattered scraps of plastic bags and shredded money drifted around us like a bizarre indoor storm. Bits and pieces littered the floor. The bed. The room. A smell of gunpowder saturated the air. BoBandy peeked warily around the door. My ears still gonged.

"What happened?" Natasha asked. She sounded hoarse. And bewildered.

"You shot the money," Mac said.

Yes, that was exactly what she'd done. Shot the money. I picked up a bundle of what had been twenties from the floor. Shredded. I dug a bundle of hundreds from the middle of the now-scattered pile. Not shredded, but holes pockmarked the bills. A couple of shotgun pellets fell out.

Natasha looked aghast. "I didn't mean to! I didn't do it on purpose!"

"You either pulled the trigger when you started to drop the gun, or it went off when it hit the floor," Mac said.

Right. If you can kill a pile of money with a shotgun blast, Natasha had surely done it.

Now I could see that some of the pellets had gone outside the pile of money too. Scattered holes pockmarked the blankets and pillows, the curtain and lampshade. Even a calendar on the nightstand had a hole in it. The hole punctured the date of our wedding. I'm not much of a believer in dark omens, but that hole in the calendar jolted me like an echo of the blast. As if the day were targeted for disaster. . .

"I really did it," Natasha finally said. She sounded not so much appalled as incredulous, like someone who's just discovered she could fly. "I shot the money."

We all just sat there looking at the shredded mess of money and plastic as if hypnotized by it, and suddenly, I couldn't help it, I giggled. $974,851, and Natasha had blasted all that money as if it were a game. Shoot the Big Bucks! See it on prime time! Destroy the most money and be the big winner! Although Natasha didn't exactly look like a winner as she surveyed the results of what she'd done.

I thought she might pick up the shotgun and blast us next, and I prudently snatched it up and set it behind me on the cot. She didn't protest; she just sat there. Finally she unexpectedly giggled too. "I shot the money," she repeated. She threw up her arms in pantomime of an explosion. "Boom!"

235

Then we were both laughing. Mac momentarily looked at us as if the shotgun had blasted not only the money but our mental marbles as well. But then he looked at us and the money again, and he started laughing too. BoBandy didn't laugh, but he danced around, scattering more shredded money and fluttering plastic.

Ever watched an old TV show with an out-of-sync laugh track and wondered what the laughing was all about? I finally managed, as I wiped my eyes, to say, "I guess it isn't really funny."

Natasha picked up a handful of shredded money and threw it at me. "Oh, yes it is!"

Which set us all off on another round of laughter. Finally we helped Natasha get to her feet and back on her crutches.

Now what? The money was still there. Some of it was probably still usable even in its present porous form. Many of the other bills, if they weren't totally shredded, might be redeemable if turned in to the government. The government did that, I'd heard about some burned money, as long as you had a piece big enough to be identifiable. The internet would no doubt tell you how to do it. And these were bills apparently not stigmatized by recorded serial numbers because Dawson had been spending this money. This was the "other pension" he'd told Dan he had.

An unrelated question popped into my head. I looked at Natasha. This seemed as good a time as any to ask it. "Did you push Dawson down the stairs?"

"*What?*"

I repeated the question.

"Why are you asking me that *now?*"

"Umm . . . I guess because I never asked it before."

"How could you think I'd do that? And *why?*"

236

"You're the only one who had anything to gain by his death." I paused and then amended that statement. "The only one who *thought* she had something to gain." Because she really didn't, not with that new will Dawson had written leaving the ranch to the boys' club. It also appeared there may never have been an old will.

"No, I did not push him! It happened before I got here, remember? I was as surprised as everyone else. And what does that have to do with *this?*" She swept a hand toward the shotgunned pile of money, then regarded me with an indignant expression. "Do you really think I'm the kind of person who'd push my stepfather down the stairs?"

Well, yes. "You've threatened to shoot us several times now," I reminded her.

"I'm over that." She scattered more money with the whack of a crutch. "I-I don't know what came over me. I guess I just saw all this money and . . . went a little crazy. That's not the real me."

I didn't know what to think of this sudden change of heart. Had the blast of the shotgun into the money really blasted her to her senses? Or was this just temporary, and in another minute she'd wrestle me for the shotgun and aim it at us again?

"What now?" I asked.

"I'm leaving."

"Leaving?"

"I'm going home."

"And taking the money?"

"No! I don't want the money. I want to get as far away from it as I can. As soon as I can." She eyed the money as if it might reach out and grab her with green tentacles. "It made me go . . . crazy. Unbalanced. Weird."

237

Okay, I could agree with that. She'd definitely gone weird on us. Although she now appeared to be a New and Improved Natasha, I wasn't sure she wasn't still a little weird. Maybe spelled p-s-y-c-h-o.

"I'm leaving," she repeated. "Help me get this suitcase out to the car."

"You can't just take off and drive to California with your leg in a cast," Mac protested.

"Yes, I can. It's awkward and uncomfortable, and I may not be able to drive very long or far without stopping to rest, but I can do it. I'll drive tonight until I get to somewhere with a motel." She took a deep breath. "I have to do it. Now. Before the money affects me again."

That sounded a little melodramatic, as if the money were some malicious entity broadcasting evil vibes that might morph her into Weird Woman again, but she gave the mangled pile another almost yearning look. "Don't let it get to you too," she warned.

"At least wait until morning," I said.

"No. I need to go now. Before I go weird and crazy again."

Well, maybe she was right. I certainly didn't want a rerun of a Weird and Crazy Natasha, and that yearning look at the money was not a good sign. Maybe it was sending out evil vibes. So we followed her out to her Subaru. Mac put her suitcase in the back seat. Natasha maneuvered herself and her cast into the driver's seat, and I set the crutches beside her on the passenger's seat.

"I'll call the mortuary and have Dawson's ashes sent down to San Diego. You can turn the money in to the authorities, or whatever you want to do with it. It's bad money. Very bad," she said. Unexpectedly she smiled. "I leave it to you to explain to the authorities why it's shredded

238

and full of holes. Maybe you could convince them there are such things as money termites?"

I figured we had to tell the truth, but we'd go as easy on Natasha as we could. I wondered if shooting money was a crime.

She started the engine, but then she rolled down the window. "You're good people. I'm glad I met you, and I'm sorry I made threats and all that." She paused and a little awkwardly added, "I wish I had your faith. Then maybe the money wouldn't have made me go . . . weird."

"Pick a church. Go to it. Find a Bible. Read it."

"Maybe I will," she said. Not exactly a life-changing conversion, but encouraging. "I hope you have a nice wedding and a great marriage."

"Thanks. Give your mother a hug for us."

We watched until the red taillights disappeared over the hill. *Look after her, will you, Lord? Work on her. She needs you.* We went back inside.

So now it was just us and a scattered pile of shredded, pockmarked money. I didn't attribute some evil power to the money, as Natasha apparently did, but I wanted to be rid of it.

"Let's load up the money and take it to the authorities," I said.

"Now?"

"Yes. Right now."

Mac nodded. "Good idea." He took a step toward the pickup but stopped short. "Although there is this one little problem." He looked up the empty road to the top of the hill.

"Problem?" I repeated. Then it came to me. I groaned. We'd had parallel moments of senior forgetfulness when we let Natasha drive off.

"She has the pickup keys."

239

"That's the problem," Mac agreed. "Do we want to try hiking to town tonight?"

Did we? It was a daunting prospect. How long would it take us? What shoes do you wear for a ten mile hike? Of course, ten miles wasn't anywhere near as long as a marathon, and people *ran* those. Oh, dear. I felt tired already. I plunked down in a chair.

Then I jumped up. When in doubt, think *food!* "We missed dinner. How about fixing something now? And we'll think about all this."

"Great idea."

So I whipped up an omelet with bits of bacon and onion and green peppers. Mac made toast and hot chocolate, and we had more cheesecake for dessert. There was a nice feeling of cozy togetherness even with the pile of shredded/pockmarked money in the other room and the prospect of the long after-dinner hike.

Once, with sudden inspiration, I asked, "Don't you keep a key hidden somewhere on the pickup in case you get locked out?"

"I guess I should," he muttered, which answered my question. "I will from now on."

We were almost finished eating when Mac suddenly had an inspiration of his own. "Hey, we don't have to walk to town. Dawson's ATV is down in the barn, remember? We can ride it!"

"Now?" I asked doubtfully.

"Yes, right now. Why not? It has headlights. It's not exactly luxury transportation. We'll get dusty and dirty. But it'll get us out of here."

Was he thinking about Sam the hired man showing up, ready to use something more efficient than bolt cutters to make a claim for the money?

240

"What about Koop and BoBandy?"

"We'll carry them with us."

"What about the money?"

"We'll wrap it up and tie it on."

I hesitated. One part of me really wanted to get away from the ranch. I'd felt uneasy here, especially since we'd found the money, but before that too. Now, while we were eating, I wasn't feeling *watched*, but I couldn't get rid of the feeling of having been watched earlier. But taking off in the dark on the ATV, loaded down with dog, cat, and an awesome amount of shredded/pockmarked money, had never made even a guest appearance on my bucket list of things to do.

But . . . why not? A different, more reckless part of me suddenly grabbed at the adventure of it.

"Let's do it!"

"Okay, you bundle up the money. Or we can just leave it here and let the authorities come get it. I'll go down to the barn and get the ATV."

I hesitated only momentarily. "I'm coming with you."

He tilted a silver-fox eyebrow at me. "Welded at the hip?"

Right! Plus the fact that I didn't think this was a good time to be separated. We needed to stick together.

We ate the last bites of omelet. I checked on Koop and found the shotgun blast had sent him into hiding upstairs. He had dug his way under the covers on Mac's bed, a hundred dollar bill mysteriously clinging to his stubby tail. I left him there for now. Maybe I could tuck him inside my jacket for the ride to town.

Mac grabbed the shotgun, and I located the powerful flashlight Sam had generously donated to us. Mac picked up

241

the ATV key where he'd hung it on the hook by the back door, and we headed for the barn. BoBandy ran ahead of us.

Just a few minutes now, and we'd be on our way, away from the ranch and rid of the money. With our wedding day almost here!

Chapter 21

IVY

We didn't really need the flashlight, however. The kind of moon that inspires wolves to howl and romance to bloom soared high in the sky, illuminating every blade of dry grass, silvering the leaves on the cottonwoods, turning even the brittle weeds into small works of art. *Nice work, Lord!*

Mac opened the barn door, and BoBandy immediately rushed in and started digging under the stack of hay bales at the back of the barn, the new kerchief Elle had given him flapping as dirt flew around him. Inside the barn we did need the flashlight, and I held it while Mac climbed on the ATV and turned the key.

Which then did what mechanical things all too frequently like to do in my presence. Gave a few sputters and growls. And then sank into sullen silence.

"What's wrong?" I asked.

"I don't know." Mac checked the fuel and said the tank was at least three-quarters full. He found the small battery in a compartment up front and cleaned the connections. He raised the seat to open the engine compartment, poked at some parts in there, then got a feed sack from the pile over by the stalls and used it to lie down on to look at more engine parts from underneath. He got a screwdriver and wrenches from the tack room and started tinkering with screws and wires. I didn't know what he was doing, although I did recognize a spark plug when he pulled it out and cleaned it. Mac did his own oil changes on the pickup, so he knows something about engines, and a man with a motorcycle tattoo on his arm should know something about ATV engines too, shouldn't he? Or maybe that was another *non sequitur*. Sometimes life seems full of them.

Mac kept tinkering. BoBandy abandoned the hole he'd dug, briefly investigated a couple of other spots, then went back outside. I took off a shoe and whacked some grit out of it, then checked my watch. We'd been here at the barn for fifteen or twenty minutes. Natasha wouldn't have gotten even as far as Wolf Junction yet. Then I realized Mac was now down on his hands and knees searching for something on the dirt floor.

"I dropped a washer. It has to be around here somewhere. Help me find it."

I got down on my knees beside him. I felt around for a minute, then saw the lost washer hiding in the dirt under the ATV. I handed it to him. Mac is a man of many talents, but *seeing* something isn't one of them. I do believe he, like a lot of men, could look for a full-size turkey on a refrigerator shelf and miss seeing it.

"Hey, great! That should do it. Thanks."

He put the tiny washer around a tiny screw and fastened them into the engine, and I have to admit that even though I could find the washer I wouldn't have known what to do with it. Teamwork! The family that finds lost washers together stays together. Mac put everything back together and got back on the ATV, and this time when he turned the key, the engine roared to life.

"You did it!"

"Don't look so amazed," he grumbled. "I'll drive outside and then you can get on behind me and ride up to the house."

But when I started toward the big, vehicle-sized door to open it, I realized BoBandy was now looking toward the house with a stiff-legged stance. Why the interest? I stepped up beside him while Mac was getting the ATV turned around. I couldn't see anything moving around the house, but had that lump of shadow out there in the trees beyond the pump house always been there?

Could handyman/burglar Sam have sneaked up on us? Had he been watching as we counted the money? Was that shadowy shape his pickup?

I turned and held up a hand to stop Mac. It seemed a time to whisper, but you can't whisper and be heard over the rumble of an ATV. I raised my voice. "I think there may be somebody up at the house."

He did something to the ATV that dropped the noise level. "We haven't heard or seen any vehicle come down the hill."

"Someone could have come in the back way with lights off. Actually, I kind of felt as if we were being watched earlier, when we were counting the money."

"You didn't say anything," Mac said. I noted he didn't discredit my *feeling* of being watched; he was just mildly reproachful about my not mentioning it.

"I guess I should have. I'm wondering now if Sam came back. I've wondered if he knows something about a connection between Dawson and D.B. Cooper."

"I've wondered if he knows about Dawson and an armored car heist."

Yeah. That too.

"We'd better see if something's going on at the house," Mac said.

I wasn't sure I wanted to roar up to the house on the ATV and be met with a blaze of gunfire, which seemed all too possible if Sam was there in the bedroom grabbing money, so I was relieved when Mac had a different approach in mind.

He left the flashlight turned on in the barn so that if anyone was watching they'd think we were still there. Mac picked up the shotgun, and I grabbed BoBandy by the bandanna tied around his neck to keep him from racing on ahead. We slipped out the edge of the door, trying to make our exit as inconspicuous as possible. I often feel as if I've aged into invisibility, which can be a little dismaying, but invisibility can also be an asset at times. I was certainly willing to embrace invisibility at the moment.

I pointed out to Mac that odd lump of shadow, and we crept toward the shelter of the pump house to get a better look at it, BoBandy straining against my hold on his bandanna all the way. We'd left the lights on in the house, and light from the windows now made oblong shapes on the ground.

The shadow took on more definite shape as we edged closer, but it wasn't the pickup I'd expected. It was an ATV similar to the one on which we were planning to make our getaway. Did Sam also have an ATV? This one had a big plastic box fastened to the carrying rack on the back. Hey, we could rig up something like that to carry BoBandy to town in. Although Sam probably had different plans for his box. Like filling it with money.

We crouched at the pump house for several minutes, then sneaked to a bush closer to the house. I hoped my invisibility was working and covering both of us. BoBandy growled. I put a hand around his muzzle so he wouldn't start barking. We couldn't get a good view into the dining room because of the closed curtains, but if Sam was out here before

I'd pulled the curtains he'd have had a clear view of us in there counting the money.

A couple of bats zinged by. A frog croaked surprisingly close. My foot started to cramp, apparently aiming for an ancient Chinese foot-binding shape. I stretched my leg and wiggled my toes. BoBandy whined. I blinked, my eyes watering from peering so intently at the house. Was that something moving on the other side of the curtains?

"Do you see someone in there?" I whispered.

"I think so."

"Are we going to try to sneak up on him?"

Sneaking up on Sam, no doubt armed with more firepower and gun expertise than we had, did not strike me as a really good plan, so I was relieved when Mac said, "I think we'll wait and see what he does."

I was also still ambivalent about risking our lives to protect stolen money. And if Sam, who'd shot a man in Texas, was now after the money, it also seemed likely he'd pushed Dawson down the stairs. A slight scraping noise from the back porch. The back door opening? BoBandy growled again. He wiggled frantically to escape my restraint. I got a better hold on the kerchief around his neck.

One moment I had a tight grip on him – and the next all I was holding was a dog-less bandanna.

BoBandy raced for the house, barking wildly. I couldn't see anything on the back porch because of the overhanging roof, just BoBandy standing at the bottom of the porch steps in the moonlight. But he was apparently ambivalent about whoever was on the porch, because his tail wagged even as he barked.

"Shut up, you stupid mutt."

I was startled. Not Sam. A *female* voice

247

"Are they down at the barn?" A second voice, this one male.

"There's still a light there."

Hey, I knew those voices. Marnie and Jack. BoBandy must recognize their voices or scents too, which explained the barking/wagging combination. He liked Jack and his doggy treats. Then BoBandy suddenly went silent. Oh no . . . would they hurt him? No, no reason for that, I assured myself. Jack had probably just tossed him one of those doggy treats he always carried. I almost called out to them, but Mac silenced me with a touch of elbow in my ribs.

"Why would they go down to the barn?" Jack asked. "What are they doing down there?"

"I don't *know*." Marnie sounded on the edge of exasperation. "What difference does it make?"

"What are we going to do if they come back from the barn and find us here?"

"Don't worry about them. They're too old to give us any trouble."

"I wouldn't be too sure of that," Jack said. "I think they're a couple of pretty tough old birds."

I wasn't sure that was meant as a compliment, but I kind of liked being thought of as a tough old bird. That view of us did not impress Marnie, however.

"Jack, will you stop *fussing*. Maybe they went for a walk in the moonlight. Maybe they took the dog for a walk. Let's just get the money and go."

Jack and Marnie were stealing the money?

Hey, that wasn't what I expected of people who bought a horse for their grandchildren, and brought cheesecake. Although I had been a bit suspicious of them earlier . . .

"I can't figure out what they did to the money," Jack said. "It looks like they tried to destroy it. Some of it's probably worthless now."

"Don't *worry* about it." Marnie really sounded exasperated now. "We'll sort it out later."

"What about the dog?" Jack asked.

"I don't care. Just get rid of him."

"I'll put him in the basement."

I heard the basement door open, a protesting yelp from BoBandy as he was apparently shoved down the steps, some consoling murmurs from Jack, and then a thud as the door closed. At least they didn't have in mind hurting BoBandy. At least Jack didn't. Marnie I wasn't so sure about.

"What are we going to do?" I whispered.

"We can try to stop them," Mac whispered back, though he didn't seem in any rush to jump up and do so.

And if we tried to stop them, were we willing to shoot them for stealing stolen money? Also important, were they willing to shoot *us* to steal stolen money? *Stealing stolen money* had kind of a catchy rhythm to it, but I figured the answer to my second question was a definite *yes*. They'd surely shoot us if we protested their making off with the money.

But maybe they didn't even have a gun. Maybe this was just a spur-of-the-moment thing.

Or maybe it was all planned out, and they both had guns. . .

But maybe they weren't really *stealing* the money. Maybe. . . I floundered looking for some other explanation. All I could come up with was that they didn't know for sure what had become of us, so they were taking the money somewhere for safekeeping.

Yeah, right. And if I believed that, I was probably an easy target for a con man selling a miracle elixir to turn your dandruff into gold dust. With a money-back guarantee.

Upright, honest citizens do not sneak up on a house, prowl around peering through windows, and then decide to grab whatever they've clandestinely spotted inside.

How come they'd sneaked up on the house and us to begin with?

Because they weren't stupid or blind. They'd earlier seen the hundred-dollar bill draped over my foot and the bills slipping out of that blanket-covered lump in the corner. Nice honest people, of course, would just ignore that as a none-of-their-business situation. Nice but nosy neighbors might ask about it and suggest we take better care of our money. But Jack and Marnie hadn't done either. They'd left and returned by a back way under cover of darkness, with skullduggery in mind.

Had they already suspected Dawson had a hidden stash of cash even before seeing it there on the dining room table? Did they know about his D.B. Cooper connection and suspect he had that skyjacking money? Had they wanted to buy the ranch as a way to acquire the stash, but they were willing to take a darker route and steal it if they had to?

"If they come back up here, don't think it's going to be as easy as pushing Dawson down the stairs was," Jack warned.

Marnie muttered something I couldn't hear. Or maybe I was just too shocked to hear any more. Because there it was as a cold, hard fact. *Marnie had pushed Dawson down the stairs.* Because they'd known about this money long before seeing us counting it on the dining room table but just didn't know where it was?

250

"I don't like this," Jack muttered. "They could come back and—"

"Oh, c'mon. Surely you're not afraid of one little old lady and—"

"No, I'm not afraid of them," Jack snapped. "Let's just get out of here before they come back. I don't want —"

Whatever Jack didn't want to do was lost in their return to the interior of the house. But it obviously wasn't that he didn't want to steal the money. He was ready to do that.

I nudged Mac. "Did you hear that? Marnie pushed Dawson down the stairs!"

Which changed the situation. I still had mixed feelings about the possible life-or-death risks involved in stopping someone from stealing stolen money, but we couldn't let people who'd *killed* someone just walk away. Still, I had to admit I wasn't too keen on jumping out waving my empty bandanna and righteously shouting, "Halt!"

Mac had the shotgun, of course. But could he shoot faster than the two of them could?

"What are we going to do?" I whispered.

"We can wait until they come outside with the money. I'll step up with the shotgun and confront—"

"I have another idea."

"Which is?"

"We sneak over to their ATV and just ride off on it. They'll be stuck here with no way to get away."

"Jack knows Dawson had an ATV. They can go down and get it. But hey, I've got the key to Dawson's ATV here in my pocket!"

"So they'll be stuck here without any transportation. All they can do is walk over to their own ranch. But on the

ATV we'll beat them there and use their land line to call the sheriff."

Mac didn't say anything for a long minute, no doubt looking for holes in my scheme. Apparently he saw some because he said, "I don't think—"

I saw some too. Taking their ATV and running off in the dark wasn't exactly a *heroic* plan. And maybe we couldn't get their ATV started. Jack may have stuck the key in his pocket, same as Mac had done. Even if the ignition key was there, they'd surely hear the sound of the engine when Mac started it and come running. Probably shooting as they came. Even if we got away, we didn't know the off-road route to their place and might find ourselves wandering lost on miles of Montana rangeland.

Mac interrupted my worrisome thoughts. "But it just might work. Let's do it!"

He grabbed my hand and we crept toward the ATV. BoBandy started barking from the basement. I stumbled over something on the ground. My foot squashed down on it. Another egg. But no rotten scent arose. I'd just stepped on a good egg. Okay! Things were looking up.

I don't remember Nancy Drew or Jessica Fletcher ever having to cope with eggs in any form. Their sleuthing always seems to involve more dignified situations than mine does.

I paused to wipe my foot in the dirt, but Mac yanked me along. "C'mon. Do that later."

The back door slammed just as we reached the ATV. Mac threw one leg over the seat, and I climbed on behind him. I looked back toward the house. Jack came down the steps fairly cautiously, his speed impeded by the big, blanket-wrapped bundle of money he carried. Marnie was behind

252

him, gun in her hand glinting in the moonlight. They hadn't spotted us yet.

Hurry, Mac, hurry!

Mac finally found the key in the ignition and turned it. The engine roared to life. A second later, we jolted backward and my chest slammed against his back.

"I don't know the gears on this thing!" Mac said frantically.

"Hey, they're stealing our 4-wheeler!" Marnie yelled. She sounded indignant, as if we were the only ones breaking the law here.

The blast of her gun boomed in the night. I actually saw the flame-like explosion flash out of the barrel, and I could swear a bullet whizzed by, just inches from my ear. But I'm not sure you can feel or hear a bullet, so maybe that was just my scared imagination.

Mac found the right gear. We jolted forward. A tree loomed in our way. Mac found another gear, and we arced backward.

"Hold on!" he said.

I wasn't sure what I was supposed to hold onto, but I wrapped my arms around Mac's waist and we plowed ahead.

Another blast from the gun . . . and a furrow ripped through Mac's hair.

Chapter 22

IVY

He grabbed his head with one hand. The ATV skittered to a halt.

"Are you hit?" I frantically ran my hands over his head. "Are you hurt?"

"No, I don't think so. But it feels funny, kind of hot—"

Marnie had come within a fraction of an inch of shooting him in the head! A few inches lower and she might have taken out both of us with a single shot ripping through my back and on into him. Her next shot—

I didn't know whether to yell *Go!* or *Stop!*

Without any help from me, Mac chose *go*. We bounced over . . . what? What was back here anyway? Rocks? Old lumber? We came up hard against something, and Mac had to find reverse gear again.

But it was too late. Jack wasn't a big man, but he hit us like a rodeo cowboy wrestling a steer to the ground, and we all tumbled off the ATV. Mac must have hit the ground first because I was in the middle with a body underneath me and another body squashing me down. We squirmed and wrestled on the ground, a jumbled tangle of arms and legs. Was this what it felt like to be on the bottom of one of those pileups in a football game?

"It's okay. I've got 'em covered."

Jack floundered off us and stood up. I felt squashed and out of breath, my foot tangled in something under the

254

ATV. But Mac . . . Mac was out cold! Or was it worse than unconscious? I gave a little cry and yanked my foot free and scrambled toward him. I could see the old chunk of concrete he'd hit his head on, and a dark ooze of blood filling the crease in his silvery hair. His eyes were closed, and I had the frantic feeling they might never open again.

"He needs a doctor!" I yelped.

Jack leaned over Mac. "Yeah, we'd better get him to a doctor—"

"Are you out of your *mind*?" Marnie snapped. "Just get the money picked up."

I could see now that Jack had dropped the blanket bundle when he jumped us, and scattered shreds and rolled bundles of money littered the ground.

"If he comes to, knock him out again. I'll be back as soon as I take care of her." Marnie prodded me with the toe of her boot.

I suppose Marnie's handgun was ordinary size, but from my position on the ground it looked big enough to launch missiles, and both her instructions to Jack to "knock him out again" and her intention to "take care" of me sounded like a game I didn't want to play. But Mac, lying there unresponsive, was all that mattered. "I'm not leaving Mac!"

"You're coming with me or I shoot him right now."

Hey, what was with these women? Had they watched the same TV crime show? First Natasha and now Marnie, knowing that the way to get to either Mac or me was to threaten the other one. Whatever, it was an effective ploy. Maybe he was already dead. My heart plummeted and a cannonball lumped in my stomach.

But maybe he wasn't dead! I couldn't let her shoot him. I stumbled to my feet.

255

"I'll be back in a few minutes," Marnie said to Jack. To me it was, "Okay, start walking."

"Where are you taking her?" Jack asked. He sounded alarmed. "What're you doing?"

"What has to be done."

"Wait a minute," Jack said. "You never said anything about doing anything like this! We were just going to get the money. You never said anything about doing more than that!"

I thought about remarking that she'd already done more, pushing Dawson down the stairs. But it didn't seem like a prudent time to tell them I'd heard that.

"We can't back out now," Marnie snapped.

"But we can't—"

"They heard you, you idiot. Haven't you got that through your thick head? You and your big mouth, they *heard*! And they'll nail us for it if we let them go."

Yeah, we'd heard. I don't like to lie about anything, but this seemed like an acceptable time to tell a small fib. "We didn't hear anything," I said. Except it came out in this strange squeaky voice, like one of Alvin's Chipmunks.

"Yeah. Right," Marnie muttered. I guess sounding like a chipmunk doesn't make a convincing fib. Then she started issuing commands. To Jack: "Get the money loaded up. Be ready to go as soon as I get back." To me: "Now. Get going." She jabbed the gun in my back.

She marched me toward the barn. What did she have in mind? If she intended to shoot me, why take me all the way down to the barn to do it?

What now? I had to do something so I could help Mac. Maybe I could trip her. Or I'd read about poking something deep into an assailant's eye—

I surreptitiously felt in a pocket for a poking thing. I found a breath mint. A breath mint has serious limitations as a poking tool.

I turned my head until I could peek at her marching behind me. The gun was aimed dead center at my back. So finally, all I could think was to use the only weapon that seemed available to me. Talk.

"It's too bad we didn't really get to know each other," I said conversationally. "Maybe you wouldn't feel it necessary to do . . . whatever it is you're thinking about doing."

Cavewoman grunt from Marnie.

"How'd you know about the money?" I asked. "Did Dawson tell you?"

Not even a grunt in response to that.

"This isn't the D.B. Cooper money, you know," I said.

That finally got a reaction out of her. "What's D.B. Cooper money?"

"You know. The guy who skyjacked a plane and got away with two hundred thousand dollars years ago. Dawson's stepdaughter said Dawson was actually D.B. Cooper."

"You're kidding. I saw some TV show about that a while back. They never found the guy or the money."

Would I be kidding at a time like this? I think not. But she sounded reluctantly curious, so I expanded as wordily as possible on what I knew about D.B. Cooper and Dawson, finally asking, "Didn't Dawson ever mention any of this to you?"

"No."

"But you knew he had some money stashed away?"

"Of course I knew. But shut up. Just shut up."

"You can't get away with this, you know," I said.

257

"We'll get away with it just fine. Don't you worry about that."

Worry? Well, yeah, I was getting rather worried here, but worry about Jack and Marnie not getting away with their plan was not at the top of my worry list.

But she didn't march me into the barn as I expected. We went right on by it. Then it finally dawned on me. Not a pleasant dawning. The old windmill and well underneath it.

It was a deceptively pleasant sight out there behind the barn. Moonlight silvered the blades of the windmill, and the sagebrush looked like something out of an old western movie. Maybe one with a romantic sub-plot. A slight breeze turned the windmill lazily and brought a sweet-tangy scent of the sagebrush. I could still hear BoBandy's muffled barking in the basement. But Mac . . . *what about Mac?*

"I'd really like to get back to Mac and see if he's okay."

I didn't hear her actually *say* anything, but I certainly heard the words in my mind: *Forget it. You've seen the last you're ever going to see of Mac.*

Marnie stopped a few feet from the windmill. "Now you're going to pull the cover off the well."

"I can't do that. It's too heavy. It took both Mac and me to get it off before."

She prodded me with the gun. "I'm sure you can do it if you try."

The prod was an incentive, of course, but she couldn't threaten to shoot Mac to make me do it, and I just stubbornly planted my feet and crossed my arms and turned to look at her. A shot blasted and dug into the dirt right beside me.

"Get the cover off the well or I start taking you apart piece by piece," she snapped. "What do you want to lose first, a hand or a foot?"

Was she a good enough shot to do that? Or would she miss and simply blast me mid-center? Whatever, Marnie obviously had a nasty Mafia level of imagination. I got down on my knees and pushed on the well cover. It didn't budge.

"I told you I couldn't move it," I said. Although I had to admit I wasn't trying too hard. Opening up a deep, watery grave for myself hardly seemed a prudent activity on which to exert full effort.

She watched me struggle for a few minutes, gave an exasperated grunt, and went around to the far side of the well covering. She set the gun down, well out of my reach, but not out of hers. "You push. I'll pull."

Marnie either had muscles that didn't show or a lot of determination. Probably both. In any case, with me pushing hardly enough to roll an egg across the floor, but Marnie apparently pulling like a champ on a tug-of-war team, the heavy well covering moved. Marnie edged backward to keep out of its way. She had to stop to rest once, then she was right back at the tugging.

The well was uncovered. I didn't want to look down, but I couldn't help it. I looked. And saw nothing but a black, bottomless hole.

She picked up the gun and stood up. She told me to do the same.

"You're going to shoot me and dump my body in the well?"

She circled the well cautiously until she was only an arm's length away from me. "No. It'll look like an accident."

"Like Dawson's fall looked like an accident?"

259

"Exactly." She smiled. "Find a system that works, go with it. You were just stumbling around out here—"

"Why would I be stumbling around out here in the dark?"

"Because old folks do dumb things like that."

"I wouldn't—" I started out indignantly. *Old* and *dumb* were not inextricably linked. Although, on second thought, to anyone who knew me, my wandering around outside in the dark probably wouldn't sound unreasonable.

"Someone stupidly left the well uncovered, and you fell in. You'll be dead down there before anyone finds you. No gunshot wound to make anyone suspicious. Just an accidental fall." In spite of being winded from pulling on the well cover, she sounded smugly confident about her plan.

What about Mac? I didn't want to ask, but she told me anyway.

"And poor Mac. He's so clumsy too. He was probably out looking for you, but he stumbled and fell and hit his head on that old chunk of concrete." She gave a theatrical sigh. "So sad. Kind of a star-crossed lovers thing. Two old folks planning to get married and spend their last years together, but fate intervened just before their wedding day. So instead of getting married, they're being buried together. It'll probably go viral on the internet." She ended the melodramatic scenario with a sharp command. "Now, stand up."

Stand up so she could push me in? No way.

I stayed sprawled on the ground. Not exactly an impressive response, lying there like an old Raggedy Ann doll. Not the stuff of your average action movie. But nothing said I had to make this dramatic . . . or easy . . . for her.

She pushed me with the toe of a boot. Pushing a limp, sprawled-out LOL is about as effective as pushing

260

toothpaste back in the tube. But she was determined. She set the gun down, got hold of my feet, and dragged them toward the edge of the well.

I abandoned limp resistance, yanked one foot free and kicked. Got her in the shin, but all she did was grunt. She grabbed my foot again.

Hey, she was going to make this work—

Because there I was, Marnie puffing and my body still sprawled on the ground, but my feet dangling over the edge of the well.

I dug my fingers into the hard dirt. She stomped on my hand. Hey, no fair! And then she got hold of my hair—

I was going over! I flailed frantically with my hands and grabbed the only thing I could reach. A leg. She kicked, but I held on—

And then we both went over, emptiness opening beneath us.

Chapter 23

IVY

We banged and bumped against the ragged wall as we tumbled down the well, bouncing around like popcorn in a microwave bag. Bits of the crumbling wall tumbled with us. Hitting the water was like slamming into a solid wall. Dark, cold, bottomless. Terror! Flailing, grabbing at the crumbly walls, sinking—

Well, no.

Marnie floundered too. A flailing hand hit me on the hip. A splashing foot kicked me on the ankle. "Help me! Help me, I can't swim!"

"Then put your feet down," I said. Which was what I'd done after my own initial burst of panic, when I realized what I'd hit below the wall of water was actually the bottom of the well. "The water's not more than a couple feet deep."

She put her feet down and stood up. I figured she'd be at least a little embarrassed by her frantic plea for help from the woman she was trying to kill, maybe even say thanks, but she just snapped, "Don't touch me." I couldn't see her, but water sloshed around my legs as she apparently stumbled as far away from me as she could get.

I certainly hadn't intended to give her a BFF hug, but not touching her at all was rather difficult in such close quarters. As wells go, I thought this hand-dug one was probably fairly roomy, but I doubt any well offers privacy areas. Now I also knew what that old saying, "dark as the bottom of a well" meant. Above us, a square of lighter darkness showed the underside of the windmill, like some grotesque, bladed monster looming over us. A few stars glimmered around the edges, but the moon was somewhere beyond the square of night above the well.

I didn't want to think about Mac. Mac lying up there injured, with Jack standing over him ready to make him dead if he wasn't already. My heart raced and ached, and tears felt like explosions gathering to detonate in my head. *Oh, Mac...*

I clamped down on the panic. *You can't help him if you're a big quivering bundle of panic.* Calm down. Figure some way to get out of here and help him. *Will you help me, Lord?* I looked up again. I've never been particularly claustrophobic. I was in a stalled elevator once, with a crowd of people, and I didn't panic. But down here, the monster overhead seemed to be moving closer, trapping me in a deadly prison, bearing down with fiendish blades. The walls closed in—

I stomped my feet. I don't know why that would help, but it was all I could think to do and it did help. The circular-bladed monster went back to being simply an old windmill, not some fiendish killer. At least temporarily. Actually the killer was right down here with me. Not a reassuring thought.

"Are you claustrophobic?" I asked.

"Just keep away from me."

Sure. Fine by me.

The water wasn't icy, but it was cold enough to make me shiver. What did you get in cold water? Hypo-something. Hypothermia. We should probably be clinging together for warmth, but that was about as appealing as cozying up to a snake.

I had no idea if the well had never been any deeper than it was now, or if it had caved in over the years, but the bottom felt solid. Kind of gritty. I checked myself for damages, running my hands over arms and legs and backside. I had scratches and bruises, an iffy twinge in my knee and a rip in my jeans, but I seemed basically okay. At least as okay

263

as a LOL can be after tumbling down a well. How deep had we earlier decided the well was – fifteen feet? Twenty? A fair distance to fall, but I can remember kids from long ago cannonballing into pond water from higher than that.

"Are you hurt?" I asked.

"Of course I'm hurt. You dragged me into this stupid well."

Well, *pardon me! You were trying to kill me, you know.*

I ran my hands up and down the wall of the well. The well had apparently been dry down to this level for a long time. Shallow, as wells go, but we were still way down deep when it came to getting out. I couldn't see Marnie and, here in the dark, I couldn't even see my own hands. Invisible. Not an unfamiliar feeling, although this one was more noticeable than most times I've felt that way. But not invisible to the Lord, I reminded myself firmly. Never invisible to the Lord! I recalled comforting words I'd read many times. *Never will I leave you; never will I forsake you.*

"The Lord sees us down here," I said. "Both of us."

She muttered something that sounded like, "Big deal."

"So what are we going to do?" I asked.

"I don't have to do anything. When I don't come back, Jack will come looking for me."

Superior confidence in that statement. Also the unspoken message: *this does not include you.* I shivered again. Maybe from the cold water covering my legs. Maybe from the wet clothes covering my entire body. Maybe from a reminder how this could end. Probably *would* end. I tried to swallow a windmill-sized knot in my throat.

"Sorry about your wedding and all that," Marnie added with all the sincerity of a politician apologizing when he's caught in some sleazy situation.

264

"How will Jack know to look for you in the well? Did you tell him that's how you were going to get rid of me?"

"No. He's squeamish about . . . things. But he'll figure out where we are."

"You don't get squeamish?"

"I can do whatever has to be done." She sounded proud of that ability. I had the unpleasant feeling she was a person who could un-squeamishly get rid of an unwanted litter of kittens or puppies.

"Like not being squeamish about pushing Dawson down the stairs?" I suggested.

"I didn't actually *intend* to do that. It was just a *little* shove. Who knew the old fool would go barreling down the stairs like a can of Dr. Pepper? But half the money was rightfully mine. The crooked old shyster deserved exactly what he got."

"Why is half the money yours? Who *are* you?"

"My husband was Arlie Monroe."

"I should know who Arlie Monroe is?"

"You must, if you knew about the money."

"We were looking for D.B. Cooper money."

"I already told you. All I know about D.B. Cooper is what I saw on that TV show. I can't imagine old Dawson jumping out of a plane in the dark."

"He wasn't all that old back then."

"But I know where his money really came from. And it wasn't any hijacked airplane."

By now, I also had a pretty good idea where the money came from. I asked anyway. "Where?"

"Why should I tell you?"

"Why not? We may both wind up dead down here."

"Not me," she retorted.

265

Trapped in a well with a killer woman was another item that had never been on my before-I-kick-the-bucket list. Too bad we didn't have a phone. We could take a selfie together and leave it for posterity. But maybe—

"Hey, do you have a cell phone with you?"

"Yes!" She sounded excited until she remembered that cell phones didn't work at the ranch. Maybe not at the bottom of a well anywhere. "What difference does it make? It won't work anyway."

But she fumbled in a pocket and dragged one out. I couldn't see it, but I could hear water dripping from it. I've heard of phones working after they were submerged.

But not this one. No light, no sound, nothing. Maybe it would work again after drying out, but right now it was about as useful as those rotten eggs that zip to the surface.

She shoved the phone back in her pocket. "It doesn't matter. Jack will come get me," she insisted.

Okay, call me self-centered, but where did that leave me? And Mac? He could already be dead . . .

No, no, no! *Lord, please, take care of Mac! Don't let him be dead.*

"Jack will be here. Any minute now. We're soulmates. Together forever."

Hmm. I believe she'd called him an idiot with a thick head a little earlier this evening. Did that make for a good soulmate relationship? Or maybe even soulmates had time-outs.

"Jack isn't going to let that pile of money get away from him," Marnie added confidently.

I figured that much was true, but I pointed out a small detail to her. "But he doesn't need you to get the money now."

I thought maybe that brought a frown, but since you can't hear a frown I couldn't be sure. Again she insisted, "He'll come get me."

"There isn't as much money now as there once was," I also pointed out. "Dawson spent some of it on the pickup and the ATV and the snowmobile. The ranch too."

"He got the ranch cheap. We checked the records in the County Clerk's office. There's still plenty left."

"And some of the money was destroyed in the shotgun blast," I said. "I guess you noticed that."

"That's what happened to it, a *shotgun blast*? That's why it's all torn and shredded? What were you people *doing*? Why were you *shooting* at it?"

"Natasha shot it. It was kind of an accident."

"I knew she was an idiot."

"Okay, to get back to who *you* are. Jack isn't your husband?"

"Of course he's my husband. My first husband, Arlie, met Dawson at some construction job they were both on. Arlie found out Dawson was picking up extra money doing burglaries on weekends. Dawson was kind of a mentor for Arlie and helped him get into it too." She spoke of this as if burglary was a respectable second job, like yard work or restoring old cars in the garage in your spare time; Arlie was a burglary intern. "And then they started planning this really big deal together."

"The armored car robbery in Denver."

"Arlie worked for the armored car company for a while. He knew a lot about how they did things."

"You aren't from Georgia, are you?"

She laughed. A peculiar, madhouse kind of sound in the bottom of a well. "I've never been anywhere near

Georgia. I told everyone here we were from Georgia because I didn't want anyone to connect us with Denver in any way."

"And you don't even have any granddaughters."

"Of course I have granddaughters, wonderful granddaughters." She sounded indignant that I'd accuse her of making up granddaughters. "Arlie and I had a son and they're his daughters."

"Does your son know about the armored car heist and that you're up here trying to get the money?"

"Of course he knew about the heist. But he was killed in a motorcycle accident before I ever married Jack."

"That's too bad."

"Yeah, it is." She momentarily sounded breath-catchy with memory of the loss of her son, but she quickly moved on. "Lexi and Jana will love having Secretariat to ride when they come to visit."

"You're planning to stay on here, then?"

"Of course. Why would we leave? No one is going to know about the money, and we like it on the ranch. Maybe we'll even offer that old lady enough to buy it."

"You make really good cheesecake. Do your granddaughters like it?"

"They're mostly chocolate-chip cookie and brownie girls, but I might try cheesecake on them."

This was probably as irrelevant a discussion as has ever been held at the bottom of a well. No deep, philosophical discussions of life and death here. But I wanted to keep her distracted and talking. Better than giving her a chance to decide she may as well drown me right now. I may be a "tough old bird," but Marnie is younger, bigger, and meaner than I am. Maybe we could start exchanging recipes.

"Your granddaughters are in Georgia?"

268

"No, they live in Denver. And now I'll have enough money to see they both get good college educations. Maybe, with enough money to offer their mother, I can even get her to give us custody."

Great. Killer Woman as conscientious grandma, baking cookies and paying for college educations. "So then, after Dawson and your husband ran their after-hours burglary business together, they pulled the armored car holdup and Arlie got killed?"

"And Dawson just took off with all the money, including the half that should have been mine. Never contacted me, never gave me a dollar. I had no idea where he'd gone."

"That was a lot of years ago."

"Right. I got married again. Big jerk. Got divorced. Then I met Jack a few years ago. My soulmate. I kind of hinted to him before we were married that I had some big money available, if I could get to it. After we got married I told him the whole story, and he was gung-ho for finding Dawson and collecting what I had coming."

He apparently hadn't figured on killing anyone to do it, but I doubted that meant he'd insist on rescuing me along with Marnie.

"So how'd you find Dawson after all these years?"

Another laugh that gave me the creeps. I figured it was the laugh I'd hear after Jack rescued her and they left me stranded down here. "The good old fashioned way," she said. "I hired a private investigator. He was kind of sleazy and charged a bundle, but Jack had the money to do it."

"So after the private investigator located Dawson here in Montana, you moseyed up this way and rented the Rocking R. Dawson never recognized you?"

269

"After all these years? And with a different name? No way. Dawson had no idea we were anything but the dumb new neighbors. I wouldn't have recognized him, either, with that beard and grungy old overalls. He was a pretty sharp looking guy way back then."

"So you decided to get rid of him, and then you'd find the money and grab it. All of it."

"No. I told you. I didn't really mean to kill him. But I told him that day who I was and I wanted my half of the money, and he said he had no idea what I was talking about. Just blew me off completely."

"Could you have been wrong, and he wasn't really the person who pulled the armored car job with your Arlie?"

"He was the right guy. I remember from way back then that he had a big blotchy birthmark on the side of his neck, and he still had it."

"So you pushed him down the stairs."

"I told you. I didn't actually *push* him. I mean, why would I kill him when we didn't even know where the money was yet? He was carrying something down to the basement, pretending he didn't know anything about the armored car robbery, totally ignoring me, and I just gave him a little . . . *tap* on the shoulder, because I was so frustrated and mad. I mean, half the money was *mine*. Arlie died getting it. The ethical thing to do would be to give it to me."

Marnie is complaining about Dawson's ethics while she's planning to kill me? I was pondering that when I heard something. Sound didn't travel clearly to the bottom of the well, but it was definitely an engine sound. Someone coming down the hill? Rescuers! But after an initial roar the sound faded away. I looked at Marnie. Well, I looked at where I thought Marnie was, across from me in the dark well. I was

270

getting cold and tired from standing, but if I sat down hypothermia might set in sooner.

"Did you hear that?" I asked.

"Jack may be looking to see if I took you down to the creek." She paused. "Maybe I should have. I could have drowned you there, and it would still look like an accident. And I wouldn't be here in this stupid well now."

Discussing alternatives for my demise, even if it was too late to carry them out, didn't strike me as an enlightening subject for discussion. I went back to Dawson. "Dawson had a limp. Did he get shot in the armored car holdup?"

"I think so, though I never saw him after the holdup until we came up here. He'd be alive now if he hadn't been so greedy." Righteous Killer Woman.

"But you're planning to kill *me* now, on purpose," I pointed out.

I thought maybe she shrugged, but in the darkness I couldn't see, of course.

Well, we'd had quite a conversation after all. Now I knew all about both Dawson's death and the money. Case solved. Although no one but me might ever know. A depressing thought. I decided I had to sit down if only for a minute or two.

I sat. I guess I sloshed water because Marnie, sounding alarmed, said, "What are you doing?"

"Sitting down."

Apparently she decided that was a good idea because a slosh of water washed my way as she also sat.

"Why'd you decide to come over tonight?" I asked.

"We knew you'd found the money. Hundred dollar bill draped over your foot. More hundred dollar bills falling out from under that blanket in the corner of the dining room. How much more obvious could it be?"

271

"You probably didn't know it, but Dawson made out a will leaving the ranch to a boys' club in Double Wells. They'll get it now."

"How nice. Maybe they'll put up a plaque in his honor."

"Actually, the attorney said Dawson was planning to donate the ranch to the boys' club before he took off for Alaska, but since he's dead they'll get it through the will. Was he moving to Alaska because of you and Jack?"

"Like he'd figured out who I was?" She considered that for a moment. "I don't think so, but I don't know. Doesn't matter anyway. He's dead, and I couldn't care less what happens to this stupid ranch. We have the money."

"But you don't actually have the money," I pointed out. "You're stuck here in this well. Maybe you'll never get out. What good will the money do you then?"

"Jack will come get me." She paused, then suddenly stood up. Actually, from the big splash she made, it sounded as if she jumped up. "Unless. . ." An uneasiness infiltrated her voice.

"Unless what?"

"Nothing. He'll be here any minute now."

I shifted restlessly on the gritty bottom of the well. How long did it take to get hypothermia? I'd read about hypothermia not long ago. I'd looked it up after reading speculation that D.B. Cooper could have died of hypothermia even if he survived the skydive. I ran over the symptoms. Did I have them?

Shivering? Yep. Lots of shivering.

Confusion? Check.

Fatigue? Another check.

Lack of coordination? Yes, but that symptom wasn't necessarily reliable, since I've never been noted for my coordination. My grand-niece Sandy is an awesome gymnast, but we apparently don't share any great-coordination genes. Actually, there isn't much opportunity for checking coordination at the bottom of a well. But I did try touching my finger to my nose and poked myself in the eye instead.

"How do you feel?" I asked Marnie.

"I'm stuck in the bottom of a well. I'm cold and wet. How do you think I feel?" She plopped back into the water and didn't wait for an answer. "Now just *shut up*, okay?"

Okay. Fine by me. I'd rather talk to the Lord anyway. I straightened, trying to make myself sit tall in the water. Trying to make myself taller had never worked before and didn't now. But I could talk to the Lord.

I know this must be part of your plans, Lord, but it's kind of hard to figure out, you know? I have to admit it's scary too.

I waited. I guess I was hoping for a big voice booming reassurances. Maybe a nice, "I've got your back, Ivy."

No booming voice. So I just continued talking in the way that's so nice because you don't have to say words out loud to the Lord.

But I'll trust that you do have a plan, Lord. I've always had faith that you'll provide, and you always have. You'll never leave us, never abandon us. Just because I don't know what the plan is doesn't mean there isn't a plan, right? Want to share your plan with me, Lord?

Silence, except for Marnie sloshing the water. What was she *doing*? Practicing a backstroke? Doing toe exercises?

I hope it's a plan for getting me out of here. Mac and I have this wedding planned, you know. A pastor and a wedding dress, the works! And a buffalo barbecue too. I love him—but you know that too, don't you? I'd really like to have some time married to him before it's time to move on. I think he'd like that too. But maybe it's already too late for that. Maybe he's already moved on.

273

That made a big hitch in my breathing. I saw Mac lying there in the moonlight, eyes closed, blood filling the crease in his hair. I felt tears trickle down my cheeks and dribble into the water. We'd had such wonderful plans. Getting married, wandering the country in our new motorhome, looking for the perfect place to settle down together...

Thanks for the time Mac and I've had together, Lord. Thanks for bringing him into my life. I appreciate that. Would you take care of my niece DeeAnn and her husband, please, and Sandy too? Oh, and my friend Magnolia and her husband Geoff. And Abilene and her husband out in Colorado too. And Mac's family. So many wonderful people you've brought into my life. Thank you! I'm sorry I'm so scared.

Marnie did something that splashed water all over my face. I resisted an urge to splat my palm against the water and blast her good.

Well, maybe the next time I talk to you it will be in person. I'm looking forward to that. Thank you, too, that Mac found you before it was too late.

I took comfort in the fact that if I never saw Mac again on this earth, we'd meet again on the other side.

I love him, Lord.

Still no big voice booming out of the darkness, but somewhere in the corner of my mind, a small sign appeared. *Trust me*, it said.

That you, Lord?

The sign stayed the same. Small, even insignificant looking. But the words were there: *Trust me.*

Okay, good enough for me. My back was hurting from keeping it so straight, but I found I could ease the discomfort a bit by scooching down and tilting my head back enough to keep my mouth and nose out of the water. I didn't exactly feel *serene* about this situation or what might be coming. I was still scared. There was still a knot in my stomach. I hadn't anything better to do so I tried to identify what kind of knot it was. I used to make fishing flies for my husband Harley, and there was a lot of knot tying doing that. A Davy knot. Clinch knot. Turle knot. Uni knot.

No, this wasn't any of those fancy knots, I decided. This was a plain ol' square knot.

Mentally I worked on untying it. There's not a whole lot else to do in the bottom of a well.

Chapter 24

IVY

I don't think I slept. Who can sleep at the bottom of a well with her chin slumped in cold water and Killer Woman over there probably thinking murderous thoughts? But perhaps I did doze a bit. When I looked up once I could see that the stars had changed position in the gaps around the windmill, some disappearing, new ones moving in. Gurgly noises from Marnie suggested she was sleeping at the moment. The next time I woke and stumbled to my feet, the water felt even colder. My circulation felt stalled, my toes numb. And Mac— was Mac still lying up there, injured and unconscious? *Dead?*

The pain of loss at that possibility staggered me. Sorrow that we'd never made it to our wedding day, regret that we weren't together in our last hours. *Oh, Mac. . .*

Then a blinding light shone down from the rim of the well.

A wave of cold water hit me as Marnie staggered to her feet. "Jack!" she cried.

The light moved around to the other side of the well. Then a voice. "Ivy, are you okay down there?"

Mac!

"Are *you* okay?" I called. "I was afraid—"

"Where's Jack?" Marnie yelled. The light moved, targeting Marnie, with scratched cheeks and hair stringing around her shoulders. The wet witch look. I should probably be grateful I couldn't see myself in a mirror. "What did you do with Jack?"

"I don't know where Jack is. He's gone." At the moment Mac did not sound particularly concerned about

Jack's whereabouts. "I need to find a rope or something to—"

"What about the money?" Marnie demanded. "Where's the money?"

"I don't know." His answer came back in a sharp you're-thinking-about-money-at-a-time-like-this? tone. "I'll be back in a minute."

The light left the top of the well, though it lingered in my eyes, temporarily blinding me, but I felt a wild burst of joy. Mac wasn't dead. He was here!

How could we manage this? He couldn't haul us up together, and no way would he haul Marnie up first. Could she hold me under water and somehow pretend to be me so he'd pull her up, like Jacob pulling the goatskin trick on his father in the Bible?

We should have a code for times such as this. *I'll jerk the rope three times as a signal so you'll know it's me.* But tumbling into a well isn't an eventuality you tend to plan for.

I reached under the water and pulled off a shoe. If I had to, I'd whack Marnie with it. I tried not to speculate about how effective a weapon my old tennie would be.

"I wasn't really going to kill you," Marnie said in a conciliatory tone, as if, with rescue in sight, she'd suddenly decided it might be wise to mend some fences here.

"You could have fooled me," I muttered.

Suddenly Mac's hand holding Marnie's gun appeared in the glare of the light overhead.

"See that?" he yelled. "I'm going to bring Ivy up first. One false move from you, Marnie, and it'll be like shooting fish in a barrel. And you'll be the fish."

In spite of the harsh threat, I couldn't see Mac cold-bloodedly shooting Marnie in the well. But she was no doubt

277

capable of such a move and apparently figured if she could do it, he could too.

"I'm not doing anything! See?" With the light still on her, Marnie scrunched her back against the wall and held up her hands.

"I'm going to let the rope down. Ivy, you tie it around yourself, and I'll haul you up." Could he do that? I've always been on the scrawny side, which would be a nice asset right now, but I'd put on a few pounds lately.

The rope, apparently the old one that had been hanging on the wall in the tack room, slithered down the side of the well. Mac held the light on me so I could see to tie it. I wasn't sure about the proper technique for tying a rope around oneself at the bottom of a well, but I dragged it down between my legs, back up to my shoulder, and tied it off, kind of a bare-bones sling arrangement. Blessedly it was a good long rope. I was glad I knew a little about knot tying.

"I'm ready!" I called.

"I have to put the light down so I can pull with both hands. Hold on!"

The bright light disappeared, though a glow still showed over the edge. The rope tightened around me, and I instantly felt I was about to be split into two semi-equal parts. The sling I'd made was obviously not an approved rescue arrangement, but I just gritted my teeth and held on tight to the section of rope across my chest.

My feet rose off the bottom of the well. An inch. Two. Three! We were up to maybe eight inches when I plopped back to the water. Which I hadn't actually gotten out of yet.

"Are you okay?" Mac yelled.

"Are you?" I yelled back.

"I can't lift you any farther. I'll have to get the ATV."

278

Mac's shadow flickered above us as he tied the rope to a leg of the windmill so it wouldn't fall into the well. After a minute, the ATV in the barn roared. Another minute and I heard it coming closer to the well. A welcome glimmer of light.

"I'm going to tie the rope to the trailer hitch on the ATV," Mac called. "But I need something to put between the rope and the edge of the well so it won't wear in two."

"How about those old feedsacks in the barn?"

"Yes!"

More silence. More darkness.

"You will rescue me too, won't you, after you're safe?" Marnie asked me. Very courteous now. Bottom-of-the-well etiquette.

I thought about saying, "You gotta be kidding, lady." Or maybe, "Give me one good reason we should rescue you." Actually I didn't say anything, although I did sigh to myself that yes, we'd rescue her. But we didn't have to be jolly about it, did we?

Mac set the flashlight back from the edge of the well, his silhouette large as he moved around arranging the feed sacks to protect the rope.

"Okay, here we go," he yelled.

The rope tightened and I grabbed hold of it. Slowly I moved upward. My feet cleared the surface of the water, and my body scraped and bumped along the rough side of the well. The rope felt as if I were straddling a piece of dental floss. It was an endless journey upward, but I remembered part of a verse from somewhere in the Psalms. *He lifted me out of the slimy pit, out of the mud and mire.* I couldn't remember what the slimy pit was in that Bible situation, but the well could definitely double as a slimy pit. And just when I thought I couldn't stand the rope cutting into me a moment longer, I

279

stopped moving. But I wasn't out of the well yet, so obviously we had a problem.

I looked up. It didn't take high-tech brainwork to figure out what the problem was. Mac couldn't just drag me out like an old mattress. I'd be crushed between the rope and the edge of the well. He ran back to where I dangled just below the edge. He leaned over, and I wasn't sure what I was seeing. His head looked peculiar, large and odd shaped. A little Frankenstein-ish. Or maybe it was my eyes and mind that had gone peculiar and Franenstein-ish.

"Okay, I'm going to lift on your arms. Maybe you can use your knees or feet to kind of help."

He pulled. I wiggled and dug my toes into the side of the well. Climbed and scraped my knuckles and skinned my knees and prayed. And finally . . . I was out! *Thank you, Lord!*

I collapsed on the ground, rope still tangled around my body, breathing hard. Marnie's gun was just a few feet from my nose, but I didn't reach for it. Killer Woman couldn't get to it now. She was down there and we were up here. At the moment, a most satisfactory arrangement.

Mac touched my shoulder. His hand felt warm and dry and wonderful. "Ivy, you okay?"

I was too winded to say anything. Mac let me rest a minute, then got me out of the makeshift harness and into a sitting and then standing position. I braced myself with one hand on a leg of the windmill, then let go and just wrapped both arms around Mac and leaned on him.

Another grateful thanks to the Lord.

"Don't forget I'm still down here!" Marnie yelled. Then, remembering her etiquette, she added, "Please."

I tilted back in Mac's arms to look at him. I'd lost both shoes so I was standing in wet socks now, soaking wet, shivering and cold, scratched and battered. But I was too glad to be out of the well to care about any of that. Even with a peculiar looking bundle on his head, Mac was every inch the knight-in-shining-armor hero. "I was afraid you were dead."

"No way." He grinned. "I have a wedding scheduled for Saturday."

"Why does your head look like that?"

"Like what?" Mac reached one hand up to feel the bulky lump. "I don't know. When I came to, Jack was wrapping something around my head. A bandage, I guess."

I peered closer. It would take a generous interpretation to call the wrapping on Mac's head a bandage. It was a dishtowel. Held in place with a generous application of duct tape. But it's the thought that counts, right?

"How do you feel?" I asked.

"I'm okay. Maybe a little, uh, sore and stiff." He wiggled his shoulders.

"Marnie told Jack to knock you out again if you came to, but he didn't?"

"He wrapped my head, then muttered something about being sorry he had to do this and tied plastic bags around my wrists and ankles. I guess I was kind of in and out of consciousness. By the time I was fully conscious he was gone. It took me a while to get loose from the plastic bags or I'd have been here sooner."

A piece of plastic bag still flopped around Mac's leg. I wondered why Jack hadn't used duct tape to tie him up. It would have held him a lot longer. And why he'd done what he could with a makeshift bandage. Not quite a good guy. But apparently not a killer. I appreciated that.

Then something else occurred to me. "Jack must not have looked for Marnie before he took off."

"Maybe he figured he might be next on her list of disposable people."

Good figuring.

"We need to get you to a doctor." I had no idea what kind of injuries might be under the dishtowel-and-duct-tape bandage. I didn't think the bullet that creased through Mac's hair had done any real damage, but hitting his head on the chunk of concrete hard enough to knock him out could be serious, even if he was determinedly ignoring it.

"What about Marnie?" Mac asked.

I shivered. The night air had gotten really cold, foretelling the coming of a Montana winter. One not-so-nice part of me wanted to leave Marnie sitting in the water at the bottom of the well until her own bottom went all wrinkly. A marginally nicer part of me granted we couldn't do that, but I also figured dragging her out of the well needn't be at the top of our to-do list.

Apparently Mac agreed. He rubbed my arms. "You're soaking wet. And shivering. First thing we need to do is get you to the house."

We rode the ATV up to the house and I changed into dry clothes and put on shoes. Mac let an ecstatic BoBandy out of the basement. We removed the "bandage" from Mac's head and, while I replaced it with real gauze and tape, I told him all that Marnie had told me down in the well. About her husband and Dawson robbing the armored car together, Marnie hunting Dawson down to collect her share, and then "accidentally" pushing him down the stairs when he balked about sharing. Mac's head wasn't so Frankenstein-ish now, although the new bandage I'd put on still looked way too much like a five-year-old's attempt at playing doctor. I couldn't tell how bad he was hurt because of all the blood matted in his hair. I didn't want to poke at it too much and have it start bleeding again. He kept saying he was fine and I was fussing too much.

"We'll ride into town and send someone out to rescue Marnie," he said.

That sounded reasonable enough. But my conscience, which can sometimes be as annoying as a two-ton mosquito, nipped at me.

"I think I'll go back and lower a flashlight into the well. It's kind of . . . spooky down there in the dark. It's cold too. I'll give her one of those old jackets out of the barn."

Maybe the two-ton mosquito nipped at Mac too. He didn't argue. "I'll take you down on the ATV."

BoBandy came with us and barked energetically while we lowered the flashlight and a jacket to Marnie. She said a polite thanks.

We got back on the ATV to ride away. The light shone up from the well like an opening into some other-world of zombies and monsters. I snidely figured Marnie should feel right at home in that company.

But what about hypothermia? Or drowning? Or maybe my scramble up the well had weakened it enough to cause a cave-in?

"Can we do this?" Mac asked.

"Do what?"

"Just leave her down there."

I gave a regretful sigh. "I guess not."

So we lowered the rope and used the ATV to pull Marnie out of the well. Good ol' Marnie. Without even a thanks, first thing she did was make a grab for her gun still lying on the ground. I snatched it first. She didn't thank me for that, either.

We made a little parade up to the house. Mac on the ATV, Marnie with her hands in the air following, BoBandy barking excitedly, me coming along behind with the gun. Trying to pretend I knew what I was doing.

At the house I used the gun to motion a glaring Marnie to Dawson's old chair in the living room. She sat, but the polite act was over now. She yelled threats and curses at us and scratched Mac on the hand and tried to kick me in the head before we got her ankles and wrists securely duct taped. She was wet, of course, and we wrapped a couple of blankets around her, though what I was inclined to do was stuff one in her mouth to shut off her tirade. I hoped she didn't use that kind of language around her granddaughters. By the time she gave more explicit instructions on what we could do to ourselves, I gave into the impulse and slapped a strip of duct tape across her mouth. That didn't completely shut her up, but she was reduced to angry *umphs* and grunts.

Mac and I went into the kitchen for a quick pow-wow to decide what to do next. We could just sit and wait for someone to come check on us, but that might not be until tomorrow evening. Mac needed a doctor before then. We could ride the ATV into town together, as we'd originally planned, but even as we discussed that I could see Mac getting ever more unsteady on his feet. Once he stumbled and would have crashed into the kitchen counter if I hadn't caught him. He admitted his head was "kind of hurting," which I figured meant it was actually pounding like an attack with a sledgehammer.

No way, with his head injury, should he be bouncing around all the way to town on a rough-riding ATV. But I didn't know anything about driving the ATV alone! I couldn't—

Yes, I said fiercely to myself, *I could.*

"I'll go," I said. "I'll send help and the law back as soon as I can."

"I don't want you out there alone on a dark road on an ATV you don't know anything about," Mac argued. "I

284

can—" But even as he argued, he staggered and had to grab the kitchen counter to keep himself upright.

"Just show me what to do."

So we went outside and he reluctantly gave me a five minute lesson on the basics of starting and stopping and handling the gears on the ATV. I finally managed to make a jerky circle around the yard, though it still seemed to me that the system of shifting gears with your toe needed some improvement. My toes were not all that dexterous. But it was not, after all, rocket science, I kept reminding myself.

"I don't like this," Mac said. He had a worried scowl, apparently not overly impressed with my ATV competence.

"I can do it," I assured him. And to myself, *Yes, you can do it. Just get going. Mac needs a doctor.*

We went back inside. I put on extra socks and a sweat shirt and the heaviest jacket I could find, some baggy old thing of Dawson's. I took the duct tape off Marnie's mouth, warning if she said anything it was going right back on. She glowered at me, but she didn't say anything. Mac settled in a chair across from her. Koop came down from upstairs to curl up in his lap. BoBandy settled down beside him. All very cozy and domestic looking . . . well, except for the shotgun in Mac's lap . . . but I didn't like the way Mac himself looked. Kind of . . . grayish. With a greenish undertone. I didn't want to leave him! But he needed medical attention and this was the only way I could get it for him. I kissed him on the cheek.

"Don't forget," I said. "We have a wedding scheduled for Saturday."

"I'll be there."

Then, like some pop-up warning on a computer, an evil-omen vision of that shotgun pellet targeting our wedding date on the calendar blasted into my head. Ominous possibilities followed.

285

The soulmate thing might kick in, and Jack would return to the house, this time with murderous intent.

Marnie might manage to get loose and grab a gun. Also with murderous intent.

Mac's head injury might be severe enough to—

I determinedly cut off the scary thoughts. I had a mission to accomplish here. I couldn't sabotage it with fear and worry. *Take care of him, Lord!*

Then I got on the ATV and rode off into the night.

Well, wobbled off into the night, because steering the ATV was a little tricky.

Chapter 25

IVY

I made it to the top of the hill in a low gear with no problems. I was congratulating myself on that success, but then I had to do the toe thing to change to a different gear, and using my already cold toes was like trying to thread a needle with boxing gloves on. But after some fumbling, I finally found a different gear and we shot off down the road like a demented rocket.

I finally remembered the brake levers. One for the front brake, the other for the back. Oh, yeah, and don't keep a death grip on the speed control at the same time—

It was a wild ride for several seconds, but I finally got hands and feet organized and from then on it was just dogged determination slogging on into town. A wind came up, blowing the trailing dust up to engulf me. Clouds moved in, obscuring the stars. All I could see was the ATV's headlights tunneling through the darkness. My ever-ready imagination populated that darkness with bears, mountain lions, and various other big-toothed creatures which might or might not exist in modern-day Montana.

Once a deer jumped out in front of the ATV. I dodged it but then wavered precariously on the edge of the road, getting stopped only inches before toppling headfirst into a ditch. The engine died, and I had several moments of panic until I got it started again and lurched back onto the road. I met no other vehicles, saw no lights. I thought about turning in at the Rocking R to use the phone there, but the thought of encountering Jack stopped me. Nothing except a lone yard light burned at Buffalo Man's ranch, and I just kept going.

My hands and feet felt numb and detached. Brain didn't feel particularly well attached, either.

But finally, as a faint hint of lighter sky showed in the east, I saw the scattered lights of town. I thankfully turned into Dan and Melanie's driveway. Our new motorhome stood in the field by the house, and another big motorhome stood in the driveway. It had the familiar mural of a magnolia on the back. My old friends Magnolia and Geoff were here!

All I need do was get off the ATV and wake someone. But now I couldn't seem to move. Everything had solidified into a cold, immovable lump.

Mac hadn't said anything about a horn on the ATV, and I couldn't find one. So I did the best substitute I could manage. I took in a good, deep breath and let out a banshee yell.

Hey, nothing like a banshee yell from an LOL to arouse some action!

Dogs barked. Coyotes echoed with yips. The motorhome door flew open. Big and little people streamed out of the house. A light went on across the road. Okay!

Chapter 26

IVY

We were in the room adjoining the ladies restroom at church. I was in the lovely old wedding gown, orchid colored shoes on my feet, bouquet of pink roses in my hands. Strains of organ music and a shuffle of feet drifted from the sanctuary.

Melanie and Magnolia, niece DeeAnn, grand-niece Sandy, and Elle, all stood there looking at me and smiling. Magnolia wore an elegant silvery-gray dress, her hair a magnificent match for my orchid shoes.

Was this really my wedding day? I felt a little out of touch with reality. I remembered people surrounding me after my banshee yell on the ATV. Helping me to the ground and then Dan swooping me up and carrying me inside. Dan calling Deputy Cargill, then he and Melanie immediately rushing out to the ranch. Dan and Melanie returning with Mac, along with Koop and BoBandy, then all of us rushing to the emergency room at the hospital in Double Wells. X-rays. Doctors. Waiting. Mac being wheeled to his hospital room with staples holding the gash on his head together. Everyone gathering around his hospital bed.

Dan and Melanie, Magnolia and Geoff, all urging postponing the wedding, but Mac, with surprising strength for a man with staples in his head, saying *no way*. We were getting married tomorrow as planned. Except that now it was today. I held his hand and nodded, worriedly hoping it was the right thing to do, knowing he might come right up out of the bed if I objected.

There was news from outside the hospital. Marnie was in custody, but Jack, along with his dog, pickup, and the money, had disappeared. Apparently after wrapping Mac's head in a dish towel, Jack had gone home, hastily packed and loaded up dog Otis, and then simply took off. Apparently there were a few loopholes in the soulmate, together-forever agreement.

So now I was still wondering. Was Dawson D.B. Cooper? Had he gotten on that plane and jumped out with $200,000? I don't know. I guess I never will. But he named his dog Cooper, didn't he?

So here we were on our wedding day. Mac's son Steve and daughter Tina couldn't make it to the wedding, although both had called with good wishes. The doctor hadn't been enthusiastic about releasing Mac and said get him back to the emergency room immediately if there were any problems. Mac insisted he was fine, and he did look great. Even his new bandage had a rather rakish slant. But I couldn't help worrying about him even though I was at the church in my wedding gown. Sandy had done my hair, making my usual casual style quite elegantly upswept.

But there were some little glitches. A side seam on the wedding gown had split a few minutes ago and required last-minute repairs. The shoes were the six-and-a-half size I'd asked Melanie to get, but they were big for the size and I'd had to stuff the toes. The shoes were a lovely shade of orchid, but they weren't the "something blue" I'd planned on.

But I had the other little requirements for a bride fulfilled. My wedding gown was "something old." My shoes were "something new." Diamond earrings from Magnolia were my "something borrowed."

Now grand-niece Sandy stepped up and kissed me on the cheek. "We love you, Auntie Ivy." She handed me a little package. "This is your something blue for the wedding. It's from Elle and me. We hope you like it." Sandy had a camera hanging from a strap around her neck. That was another glitch. The photographer had a rough encounter with a rodeo bull and wound up with a smashed knee, so Sandy, who wrote a teen column for the newspaper back home, was filling in for him. She took a picture now.

"We're going out to the sanctuary now," Magnolia said. "You put on your 'something blue' and I'll be waiting in the aisle for you."

"Oh, I forgot to tell you," Melanie said at the door, "be careful with the lock on the door here. One woman in here waiting to be baptized got locked in and thought it was a judgment on her sins and started confessing them all. At the top of her voice."

They filed out, and I opened Sandy's package. It was stretchy, pale blue lace centered with a lovely, dark blue rosette. It was a little unusual – I'd never seen a stretchy necklace before -- but I slipped it over my head, and it fit snugly around my neck, perfect with the old-fashioned dress.

Okay, time to do this. I took a deep breath, said a prayer for strength and thanks, and stepped out into the hallway. So far, so good. At least I hadn't locked myself in. Magnolia stepped up beside me, and we stood poised at the rear of the sanctuary for the organ to begin the ceremony.

Sandy, sitting in a rear pew, turned, gave me a thumbs-up sign and raised her camera again. There was a moment of silence, as we all anticipated the first strains of the organ, and in that moment Elle looked at me and gave a startled whisper. A whisper amazingly loud in the silence.

"Ivy, it isn't a necklace. It's a *garter*."

I stopped short, all the not-perfect elements of the wedding suddenly thundering down on me. My wedding dress was held together with Band-Aids. I had toilet tissue stuffed in my shoes. I was wearing a garter around my neck.

I didn't see any firearms, but I spotted a Weed Eater in the aisle beside a farmer-looking guy in overalls, as if he'd just taken a break from yard work.

And then, I couldn't believe it. Something went wrong with the organ. No wedding music ensued. The organ gave a squawk, a couple of wheezes . . . and died.

I groaned. The family was right. We should have postponed the wedding. Maybe we should never even have planned a wedding. Here we were, two old folks, surely beyond the age of marrying—

Then I saw Mac standing there at the altar, a smile on his face and love in his eyes. A concussion, a night in the hospital,and staples in his head hadn't stopped him from being here. A murder attempt on my life, a fall into a well, and a frantic ride on an ATV hadn't stopped me, either. But now here we stood, in silence, with this garter around my neck—

"Hum!" Magnolia yelled.

And hum everyone did. A church full of people, all together humming *Here Comes the Bride.* And from somewhere a harmonica chimed in.

Magnolia majestically marched me down the aisle, as dignified as if a ten-piece orchestra were providing the music. The man with the Weed Eater generously moved it out of the way. And then one orchid shoe fell off, and I stumbled. I felt another moment of panic.

But did a missing shoe matter? No! I kicked the other shoe off and kept going. The Lord had been with us all the way, bringing us safely through. I think I dragged Magnolia and ran the last few steps in my stocking feet.

And then there Mac and I were, standing together in front of the pastor, saying "I do" at the proper times, until finally I heard the words.

"I now pronounce you husband and wife."

And he kissed me. Our first husband-and-wife kiss.

Respectful silence from this hungry-for-buffalo crowd? No way. Someone yelled , "Whoo-ee!" from one side of the room, with an answering, "yee-haw!" from the other side, and, I don't know from where, someone added an enthusiastic, "Praise the Lord!" Then everyone was applauding, and the guy in overalls started up his Weed Eater.

And I was saying *thank you, Lord*, and gleefully thinking, *Hey, now I really can find out what Mac's blue tattoo is all about.*

The End

294

Watch for the next Mac 'n' Ivy mystery!

E-BOOKS BY LORENA McCOURTNEY:

THE IVY MALONE MYSTERIES
Invisible
In Plain Sight
On the Run
Stranded
Go, Ivy, Go!

THE JULESBURG MYSTERIES
Whirlpool
Riptide
Undertow

THE ANDI McCONNELL MYSTERIES
Your Chariot Awaits
Here Comes the Ride
For Whom the Limo Rolls

THE CATE KINKAID FILES MYSTERIES
Dying to Read
Dolled Up to Die
Death Takes a Ride

CHRISTIAN ROMANCES
Three Secrets (Novella)
Searching for Stardust
Yesterday Lost (Mystery/Romance)
Dear Silver
Betrayed   Canyon

The author is always delighted to hear from readers. Contact her through e-mail at:
lorenamcc@centurylink.net
or connect with her on Facebook at:
http://www.facebook.com/lorenamccourtney

Happy Reading!

CPSIA information can be obtained
at www.ICGtesting.com
Printed in the USA
BVHW032151020520
579080BV00001B/46